THE GANDY DANCER

A novel by
Jeff Andrews

Eiger Press
Virginia Beach, Virginia

ISBN-10: 0985722614
ISBN-13: 9780985722616

Library of Congress Control Number: 2012954213

Cover design by Adrijus Guscia www.rockingbookcovers.com

Wall texture courtesy of www.flickr.com/photos/profilerehab/

Front cover photograph courtesy of Scott Reynolds Nelson, as seen in his book, *Ain't Nothing but a Man: My Quest to Find the Real John Henry*. The back cover photograph is from the author's personal collection.

To Lauran Strait
A wonderful mentor, a gifted editor, and a dear friend.

DISCLAIMER

The Gandy Dancer is a work of fiction. All characters and situations portrayed herein are drawn solely from the author's imagination. Any resemblance to actual persons, either living or dead, is unintentional.

Jeff Andrews
November 2012

ACKNOWLEDGEMENTS

I wish to thank my friends in the Zoetrope writing community and the Hampton Roads Writers who gave so generously of their time and talents to provide me with the guidance, encouragement, and feedback necessary to bring this work to completion. I also wish to thank my dear wife, Mary Lou, for her love and support, her patience, and her invaluable editorial insights. Finally, a special thanks to Adrijus Guscia for his critical eye, professional expertise, and exceptional patience as he guided me through the process of cover design.

Chapter One

I stared at the plain maple casket suspended above the freshly dug grave. Mahogany might have been classier, but I was already short on cash and Grandma's estate wouldn't begin to cover what I'd already shelled out. Besides, I barely knew the old gal. It had been, what, thirty years since she'd come down on the Greyhound for a visit? Yeah, it had been my birthday. She brought me a cast iron train and some ratty old engineer's hat her old man had worn when he worked for the C&O. Whatever happened to that old train? When Erica was little she loved pushing it in figure eights between my feet and making whistle sounds while I sat at the kitchen table drinking my coffee. She was such a tomboy back then . . . . Whatever happened? I shook my head. Man, they grow up too fast.

Sleet stung my face as the mountains on the horizon disappeared behind a curtain of gray. If Grandma had only held on for one more month we could have buried her with a little sunshine and a few daffodils. Instead, I was freezing my butt off in a damned blizzard. Why hadn't I checked into cremation?

And how much had I paid for that two-bit country preacher? Too much, that was for sure. The old guy droned on and on—something about parting clouds, life ever after—I was too cold to follow. I stole a glance at my watch. "Eternity" was taking on a whole new meaning.

Speaking of old, the funeral director reminded me of someone . . . but who? As I studied his gaunt face it suddenly came to me—that guy in the painting, the one standing next to his plain-Jane wife holding the pitchfork. Yeah, that was it.

He looked like he'd been carved from a dried apple—and that assistant of his must have fallen from the same tree. Father and son? Had to be. How could anybody work in that racket, or grow up with an old man who did? Dead bodies, embalming fluid, sobbing relatives . . . how'd the younger guy ever get dates if the girls knew what his old man did? Maybe they thought making out in the back of a hearse was kinky.

The lady who managed the old folks' home huddled with one of her nurses beneath an awning that blocked the sleet but not the cold. They folded their hands like a pair of choir matrons. Last night at the viewing they'd nearly talked my ear off. To hear them tell it, Grandma was right up there with Mother Teresa.

Okay, so maybe I could have visited, or at least sent a card now and then, but, hey, I'd been busy—college, marriage, career, raising my kid, divorce . . . Well, maybe not doing such a hot job of raising Erica . . .

Yeah, I should have gone with the mahogany. It's bad enough I can't seem to live up to the expectations of the living, I guess now I'm even disappointing the dearly departed.

Off to one side, away from the other mourners, an ancient black lady sat bundled in a wheelchair. A woman behind her protected her with an umbrella.

Damn, that reminded me—Abe wanted that Black History Month piece on his desk in the morning for the weekend edition. I'd better do some research on the internet and throw something together after the game—if I even made it home in time for the game.

The old woman watched intently, nodding as the preacher spoke. Who was she, and why didn't she come closer to the graveside?

". . . to a joyful resurrection and the fulfillment of His eternal kingdom. Amen."

"Amen," the nursing home ladies echoed.

Mustering all the sympathy my money could buy, the preacher clasped my hand in both of his. "May the Lord comfort you in your loss, Mr. Corsini. I know how difficult this must be for you."

"Yeah, thanks, Padre," I said. "Nice job."

He gave me a curious, almost disapproving look and walked away. The others slowly turned and left as well, all except the younger undertaker. He smiled like it hurt. "Are there any final instructions, Mr. Corsini?"

I stared into his hound dog eyes. What was I supposed to say, "Man your shovels"? I guess I wasn't up on my graveside etiquette. I'd been too young to remember Dad's funeral and I had Mom cremated. Damn, where'd I put that urn? After Sandra left I'd cleared out a bunch of stuff. . . Jeez, not Goodwill—

"Mr. Corsini, you look troubled. Do you need more time?"

"Huh? Nah, do whatever you have to do." I shoved my hat on and walked away.

Chapter Two

A whistle pierced the clear mountain air. George Henry took one last bite of chicken and tossed the drumstick into a nearby snow bank.

"You gandy dancers, stow them lunch buckets and grab your bars. There's still a half-mile of track needs lining." Mr. Beckerman, the crew boss, stared at George Henry as he lit his cigar. He shook the match and tossed it aside. "Number forty-seven's rolling through here at midnight and she'll be pulling two dozen coal cars. I'll be damned if she's wrecking on my tracks."

His tracks? There weren't no blisters on that man's lily white fingers. George Henry hopped down from the flatcar on the siding where the work crew had taken their noon meal. He rubbed his own dark, calloused hands in the snow and then wiped them on the front of his threadbare canvas jacket.

Beckerman chewed his stogie as he sauntered toward the flatcar, stopping a few feet in front of George Henry. He craned his neck. "Boy, was you late again this morning?"

"We was at the shack 'fore dawn, Mr. Beckerman." George Henry jerked a thumb toward his brother, who stood beside the flatcar. "Me and Willie, we's always off the mountain 'fore sunup."

"I ain't paying you to sleep," Beckerman said, stabbing the air with his cigar. "Deadlines don't wait on no lazy ass nigras, and until Mr. Roosevelt brings an end to this here depression we'll have us plenty of white folks looking to take these jobs."

George Henry grabbed a six-foot long iron lining bar

from the flatcar. "I understands, Boss." He nodded. "We'll be on time—every day."

Beckerman spit. "You'd best see that you are if you figure on keeping this job. Now, you and your boys get back to work. Time's a wasting." He turned and walked away.

"And them white folks you's talking about," George Henry said under his breath, "they'll be asking three dollar and forty cent a day—a whole lot more'n you's paying us coloreds."

"Sh-h-h." Willie tugged on George Henry's sleeve. "One of these days, he'll be hearing you."

"Don't care if he do." George Henry shouldered the heavy iron bar and turned toward the men gathering a few yards away. "Get on along; there's tracks need moving."

The crew took their positions along one side of the tracks and shoved their lining bars into the crushed rock beneath the rail. One of the older gandy dancers started a chant. In unison, all the men leaned into their bars, grunting and rocking as they nudged the track into place.

* * *

"Fifty yards more, boys, then we're headed home." Beckerman pointed to the remaining section. "Every time them damned coalers roll through this turn full loaded they throw the track out of kilter, but you boys can be grateful for that—it keeps you drawing your pay."

"Yeah," George Henry muttered, "Colored man's pay. Ain't no white man lining track for two dollar a day."

"Hush," Willie whispered. "Don't you be starting no trouble."

"Been working this job ever since that depression done took hold and I still ain't got two nickels to rub together." George Henry pointed at Beckerman. "And that man thinks he's doing us a favor? I got a hankering to head on down to Richmond town and find me a real job—maybe work one of them Pullman cars."

"You two," Beckerman yelled. "Quit flapping your gums and move that rail. This here line reopens in seven hours, whether we're ready or not." He hitched his belt under his ample belly, adjusting the holstered .38 revolver on his hip.

"Seven hours?" Willie exclaimed. "Then somebody best be telling that fireball he's ahead of schedule . . ." He pointed to a plume of smoke billowing from behind a distant ridgeline. A moment later, the haunting wail of a train whistle echoed through the valley.

"God almighty! Where'd he come from?" Beckerman grabbed a red signal flag, waving it frantically as he stumbled toward the oncoming train. "Clear the tracks!"

George Henry flung his lining bar aside and scrambled up the snow-covered slope. The others followed.

"There she is, rounding Tuckerman's Curve," one of the crewmen hollered, grabbing George Henry's shoulder.

Gray smoke billowed from the stack, bending back like a squirrel's tail over the engine. With every turn of the drive wheels, clouds of steam shot from the pistons.

"One passenger car and two empty flats—must be an unscheduled run," Willie shouted above the rising cacophony.

"Lord," cried the old man who had led the chants, "when they hits that bad track, they's done for."

"Look yonder." Willie pointed. "They sees the boss. They's stopping . . ."

Beckerman anxiously jumped up and down beside the spur switches, waving his flag. A metallic screech rose from the rails as the drive wheels locked, then spun backward, slowly at first, finally picking up speed.

"He's goosed her into reverse," George Henry yelled, "but they ain't going to make it. She's too fast and them rails is too far out of gauge—no way she'll hold." He clung to a sapling on the embankment and stared as the train skidded into the stretch of bad track below. Nothing they could do. The sections already worked were tight, but that unfinished track . . . .

The locomotive plowed nose first between the unaligned rails like a charging elephant dropped in its tracks by a hunter's bullet. Crossties flew through clouds of steam and cinder. Iron clanged against iron as couplings jammed together, then tore apart. George Henry's heart raced as cars tumbled end over end, throwing snow, coal, and splintered boards into the gully below. The deep, mournful groan of twisting metal rose from the smoke-filled woods, followed by an eerie silence broken only by the hiss of steam escaping the ruptured boiler.

He stared at his brother. Lord almighty, had hell just opened its gates? What about passengers—and the crew?

A cry arose from within the tangled iron.

"Get a move on," George Henry yelled. "There's folks dying down yonder." He waved for the others to follow as he scooted down the steep slope and picked his way across the uprooted tracks. Halting at the edge of the drop-off, he studied the wreckage, then called again to his crew, "Give a hand. There's work needs doing."

The passenger car lay on its side with its windows shattered. One of the flatcars had knifed straight through it. Farther down the slope, the engine sat upright, its cowcatcher aiming downhill. George Henry scrambled up the engine's ladder and into the cab. No sign of the engineer or fireman. Inside the firebox, the glow of coals danced against blackened iron.

"Crew must a got throwed," George Henry called out to a cluster of workers scrambling down the slope. "Check them woods down yonder."

"George Henry, over here." Willie motioned as he knelt atop the passenger car, peering through a broken window. "There's folks in here. Some's still alive." He removed a shard of glass, then wiggled through the opening.

George Henry jumped from the engine and ran uphill to the passenger car. He squeezed through a broken door. Inside, some seats had wrenched free from the floor, but most held fast. Scrambling across shattered windows on what had been the side of the car, he hurried to where his brother knelt.

"Lord almighty, all that blood. This one's dead for sure." Willie gagged and turned away from a bearded man in coveralls whose eyes were locked in a vacant stare. A gore-covered wooden shaft protruded from his chest.

George Henry crawled beside a man who wore the distinct pinstriped denim of a railroad engineer. "Over here, this one's got some life." He pulled the man's bandanna from his pocket and pressed it against a dark stream of blood spurting from his arm. "You lay still, mister. Everything's going to be fine. We'll get you proper doctoring, just you be calm."

"Good God Almighty . . ." Beckerman crawled into the car. "Anybody alive?"

"Three in here, Boss, and two more that's dead. All of 'em look to be railroad men. They must have been moving a crew. We ain't found the engineer or fireman from the locomotive yet." George Henry tied off a tourniquet and moved to his next patient.

"I'd sure like to know what moron sent this train out." Beckerman rubbed his stubbled chin. "They had to been running a spare crew down to Roanoke. Thank God they wasn't hauling passengers. We have to get these men to the hospital in Clifton Forge." He pointed at George Henry. "Boy, you gather your crew and make up some stretchers."

George Henry shook his head. "They's busted up something awful, Mr. Beckerman. They won't make it being carried all that way."

"Boy, don't you argue with me. They need doctoring, and fast."

"I ain't arguing, Mr. Beckerman, but if we carries them back to town, some's gonna die."

With a sigh, Beckerman took in the carnage. "I suppose you got a better idea?"

Wiping his bloody hands on the front of his jacket, George Henry nodded. "Say you was to take a couple of the boys, have them run you to town on the handcar, that yard boss might could send out an engine with a boxcar to haul the injured back."

Beckerman appeared to consider the proposition for a moment, then scowled. "You patch them best you can, then get them up there alongside the tracks. It'll be two hours before I'll get back with that boxcar." He reached the door, then turned, wagging his finger. "And you get this straight, boy, don't you get uppity just because you tied a few bandages. That don't hold no water with me. If you want to keep this job, that mouth of yours had best stay shut."

Chapter Three

"Not exactly Pulitzer material."

I jumped, spilling coffee all over the sports page spread across my desk. Where'd he come from?

Abe Foreman stood in the doorway to my office clutching a half-eaten sandwich in one hand and a manila folder in the other. His sleeves were rolled below his elbows and his tie was loosened. Mustard clung to the corner of his mouth. "What made you think I'd buy this crap?" He raised an eyebrow. "Where's your head, Corsini? Are you on the sauce or something?" He tossed the folder toward my in-basket. It missed, slid across the desk, and landed in my lap.

"I'm holding space," Abe said. "I want it back by three—and this time, it better be good." He shot me one of his patented "I mean business" glares, then took a bite of his sandwich and stomped away.

What was his beef? I opened the folder. Strike-throughs and wiseass scribblings, all in Abe's trademark green ink, covered my manuscript.

"Crap? Hell yeah, you take me off Metro and assign me these fluff pieces—what'd ya expect?" I dropped the story into the wastebasket. And it wasn't booze affecting my writing; if Abe ever tossed a decent story my way, I'd show him some real reporting—page one, above the fold—like in the old days.

Abe entered his glass-enclosed corner office across the newsroom and settled into his high-backed leather chair. He punched some numbers into his cell phone and propped his feet on the windowsill. Soon, he was stabbing the air with a pencil, embroiled in some animated conversation. I had to laugh. It was just like him, dumping his high and mighty editorial insights on some other poor slob.

Ann pounded away at her keyboard in the next office. Why hadn't he assigned her that piece? No big deal, I'd slap a fix on it and get it to him after lunch. I smoothed the dampened sports page and raised the half-pounder with cheese to my mouth. Lose the bulge, Doc warned. Diet and exercise—yeah, maybe next week. I took a bite.

My telephone rang.

I wiped my chin and grabbed the receiver. "Richmond Journal News. Corsini."

The line went dead.

Moments later, a funny little man entered the newsroom and stopped in front of Ann's door. He wiped his nose with the back of his hand. The earflaps on his blaze orange cap fastened under his double chin. Water trickled from his yellow poncho. "Hey, lady, you got a guy named Corsini around here?"

"Mitch Corsini?" Ann said.

"Yeah, that's the one. Where's he at?"

"Next door."

He glanced my way and hitched his trousers. His wet rubber soles squeaked across the tile floor. Corduroy-wrapped thighs whooshed with every step. I bit my lip. What could that rube have, some bleeding-heart tale about his runaway dog? Maybe a hot scoop on neighbors who forgot to pull down their shades?

He centered in my doorway, clasped his hands behind him, and rocked up on his toes. "You Mitch Corsini?"

"One and the same," I said. "What can I do for you?" I propped a yellow legal pad on my knee and pulled a pen from my pocket.

"You sure you're Mitch Corsini? I heard he was some hotshot reporter."

"Yeah, that's me. How can I help you?"

"For real, you're the Mitch Corsini?" His grin exposed a gap in tobacco-stained teeth.

"Yeah, for real." Was the guy deaf?

"Good. Then consider yourself served, hotshot." The sonofabitch dropped some papers on my desk and hurried off toward the exit.

"What the . . . ?" I grabbed the packet of papers and jumped to my feet. "Hey you, get back here!"

The little jerk smiled and nodded to Ann as he strutted out the door.

"Dammit." I slammed the papers on my desk. Okay, chill. I took a deep breath and unclenched my fists. Maintain control. I pried out the staple and opened the papers. So, what's this, another demand from my 'ex'? What's the little darling want this time? Hell, it had been hard enough keeping her satisfied when we were married. Since the divorce she'd become insatiable. I lowered my glasses and began to read.

"Whoa! What the . . . ?" I threw down the subpoena as if it had burst into flames.

"Who was your little friend?" Ann appeared in my doorway, her short red dress clinging to her dark, slender legs. A yellow #2 pencil protruded from her tightly cropped Afro. She pointed to the subpoena. "Trouble with the wife again?"

"It's *ex-wife*, and no . . . this is a frigging paternity suit."

"Paternity? But you've been divorced from that woman for what, five years?" A smile slowly crossed her face. She wagged her finger. "You . . . you devil. Getting all high and mighty, complaining about her raking you over the coals, and all the while you've been stoking that fire. You're a player, Mitch, I'll give you that."

"No, it's not Sandra." I waved at the documents. "This is some bimbo I've never heard of."

"Really?" She snatched the papers from my desk. "This I've got to see." Ann scowled as she read. "Okay, you're saying you don't know this Bridget Allen?" She poked the paper with a manicured fingernail. "'Cause according to this, you knew her just a little too well."

"Knock it off, Ann. This isn't funny. Sandra *is* after me. She wants more money for Erica's college. And that SOB," I said, pointing to Abe's office, "is all over me about some

13

stupid Black History Month piece—"

"Excuse me?" She raised her eyebrow and frowned.

"You know what I mean." I shrugged. "Besides, aren't those stories more up your alley?"

"Like I'm the only one who can write an African-American article? Here's a news flash: this girl has her B.A. in Journalism and a Master's in English. I cover real news."

"Thanks a bunch, friend." I pushed away from the desk.

Ann smiled and picked up the subpoena again. "It appears that the only thing you're missing is a citation for beating your dog."

"Cut it out," I said. "This is serious."

"So, what're you going to do?" She planted herself on the corner of my desk.

"Hell, I don't know. I can't afford another lawsuit. I'm already dead broke—and I don't have a clue who that woman is." I pointed to the subpoena. "But I'll tell you this, I never slept with her."

Ann gave me one of her who-do-you-think-you're-kidding looks and adjusted her glasses. "Says here the baby's about a year old." She tapped the paper. "Do the math. Who were you fooling with say twenty, twenty-one months ago?"

"You mean that I remember?" I locked my fingers behind my neck. Hell, my social life wasn't exactly the stuff of legends—I think I'd remember making a baby.

"I know this guy in the detective bureau." She lowered her voice as she squeezed my shoulder. "I'll see what he can find out about your little friend."

"A cop?" I said. "Sure, why not."

"And give me that stupid file," she said.

"You mean this?" I pulled the folder from the trashcan.

She snatched the story from my grasp. "I'll square it with Abe. Whatever was he thinking?"

"What do you mean?"

"African-American history from the sensitive Redneck's perspective?" She laughed. "Yeah, that'll sure sell some papers."

* * *

14

Tuesday 11:58 PM

Erica smiled from her photo in the brass frame on the dresser across the room. Diamonds of light danced in the amber liquid as I lifted my tumbler from the nightstand. She'd been about seven when that was taken. Even then she was beautiful. After her mother and I divorced, she'd kept writing and calling, but what'd it get her? Unreturned voicemail messages, her mother hollering about some stupid missed support payments, and an old man more interested in the Shockoe Bottom bars than in visits with his kid.

Hell, who could blame her for giving up? And that subpoena claiming I'd fathered some other kid—she'd go nuclear if she ever found out about that. I took a drink.

A box with Grandma's belongings sat beside me on the bed. I removed a packet of yellowed letters wrapped in a blue ribbon and set them aside. I sipped my whiskey as I retrieved a worn Bible from the box. The crumbling remains of a red flower, perhaps a rose, were pressed between its pages. Old black-and-white photos lay beneath the Bible, their edges cracked and brown with age. One showed nurses on the steps of a large stone building. Another was of a man dressed like an engineer in front of an old locomotive. Could that have been my great-grandfather? A few photos depicted Black laborers posing with their shovels and picks alongside railroad tracks. I tossed the Bible and photos next to the letters. Maybe I could wrap all of them up and send them to Erica. Would she find them interesting? Hell, would she even care?

I turned the box upside down. Something rolled up inside a woman's handkerchief fell into my lap. I unfolded the frail cloth to reveal a small wooden pendant on a rawhide cord. On one side someone had carved a five pointed star. The seven stars of the Big Dipper were burned into the other side. Grandma sure didn't have much to show for her ninety-two years. I stuffed everything back in the box and picked up my drink.

Would Erica have gone with me to the funeral? Hell, would she have even taken my call? After I'd stood her up for the bizillionth time—some school recital or something—she stuck it to me by dropping "Corsini" and taking the last name of that creep her mother had married.

Could I ever mend those fences? God, how could I have been such a jerk? Where to start—a phone call? No, maybe a letter—she can't hang up on a letter. My hand trembled as I raised the glass, trying to imagine the words that could possibly lessen the pain she'd suffered through all those years of fatherly neglect.

The ring of the telephone shattered my solitude. I flinched, splashing whiskey all over my shirt. It rang again.

I grabbed the receiver. "Yeah?"

"DNA," Ann said.

"Huh? Ann . . . ?"

"Yes. Now listen, if the kid isn't yours, a DNA test will prove it."

"Hell, I knew that," I said. "What kind of moron do you take me for?"

"And I spoke to my friend, Detective Rutino. He did some checking on your mystery woman, your Ms. Allen. He can meet with you tomorrow. Is one o'clock okay?"

"One? Yeah, I guess so." I ran my hand through my hair. "Meet with a cop to discuss my love life? Sure, what was wrong with that?" I laughed.

"Glad you find it funny, Mitch. Now copy this number. It's a lab that does the testing. No needles, just a swab around the inside of your cheek. Even a stud like you should be able to handle it."

Chapter Four

Doctor West burst into the small classroom on the first floor of the railroad hospital. He clapped his hands sharply. "Ladies, give me your attention please. There's been an accident."

A murmur rose from the student nurses.

The doctor waved his hand, silencing the group. "A crew train jumped the tracks a half mile beyond Tuckerman's Curve. They're bringing in the injured now. I need all of you over in the emergency room right away. Hurry." He rushed out the door.

Crew train? Rebecca Marshall stiffened. Papa had left early that morning to bring an engine up from Roanoke.

"Four months of nursing school," Irene said, "and finally, we get to do something besides bedpans." She slammed her textbook closed as she stood.

Rebecca grabbed Irene's sleeve. "Did Doctor West say it was a crew train?"

"Yes, I think so. Now come on," Irene said. "Today we get to be real nurses."

Rebecca bit her lip as she brushed a strand of blonde hair behind her ear. She was a nurse and there was work to be done. She must put her fears behind her and remain strong. Please, Lord, not Papa . . . She smoothed her starched white apron and marched into the emergency room.

"This one's gone. Set him there." Doctor West directed the stretcher-bearers to an area behind a curtain and then turned to the next patient. "Compound fracture left tibia, possible arterial bleeding—don't loosen that tourniquet—I'll stitch him in a minute. Put him here. " He glanced at

Rebecca. "Nurse, cut away that trouser leg."

The men set the stretcher on an examining table in front of Rebecca. She pulled aside the thin blanket and gasped. Blood soaked the bandanna around Papa's arm and stained his trousers where a jagged bone protruded. Someone had splinted him from crotch to ankle, and done a passable job of slowing his blood loss. Still, his normally ruddy face appeared sallow and drawn. He squeezed his eyes tight, as if to block visions of the horrific crash. Wheezes interrupted his shallow breathing.

"Are you just going to stand there? This man needs help." Doctor West wiped his bloodied hands on his smock.

Rebecca lifted a bandage on the patient's bruised face. "Sir, he's my papa . . ."

Doctor West glanced at the man on the stretcher and then turned to Rebecca. "Clarence? Yes, now I see. Well, he appears stable for the moment. Someone with considerable skills has patched him up. The bleeding looks to be under control. I need to check on the others. I'll attend to him in a moment. Are you all right staying here?"

She nodded.

"Good. Clean him up as best you can. I'll be back in a few minutes."

Rebecca took a deep breath. She couldn't let Papa see her fear. He'd always been her strength. Now it was her turn.

"Papa? Papa, you've been hurt, but everything will be fine now." So much blood . . . how could he ever survive? She wiped away her tears. "You're in the hospital, and I'm here to take care of you." She stroked his forehead, clearing matted gray hair from his eyes.

Dear God, don't let him die . . .

* * *

Doctor West tied off the last of the sutures.

"Dead?" Rebecca asked.

"Yes, most likely," the doctor replied. "If that fellow hadn't fixed him up as good as he had out at the crash site, your father would be a goner for sure."

18

"Then I must find this kind soul and thank him." Rebecca dabbed a damp cloth on her father's stubbled cheek, wiping away dirt and soot. "Who is he? What's his name?"

"Just one of the colored boys," Doctor West said. "A gandy dancer from the track crew." He peeled off his gloves. "Your father's a tough old coot, but he'll need rest. If he mends as I expect, you might get him home in a few weeks, but he'll be off that leg for several months." He glanced at Rebecca. "Can you cook?"

She set her hands on her hips. "Most certainly."

"Meats and greens to get his iron up, and broths—lots of chicken soup—but no liquor, you hear?"

She scowled. "Doctor West, Papa is a Temperance man."

The doctor's lips twitched and then he smiled. "When he comes to, you tell old Clarence that I specifically forbid any nocturnal visits to the Johnson brothers' out there on Dry Creek. He'll know what I mean."

"Well, I surely don't."

Doctor West chuckled. "It's just as well, child. Now, will you be assisting with the others, or do you need more time with your father?"

Rebecca tucked the blanket under her father's chin. "I am almost a nurse and there are other patients that need me. Besides, there's nothing more I can do here." She kissed her father's brow. "Rest easy, Papa. I'll be back to check on you later."

* * *

Rebecca pulled her cloak around her, quickening her pace as she descended the steep hill in front of the hospital. The streets appeared deserted. At that hour, most railroading men would be hard asleep, knowing the dawn would bring another long day.

South of town, moonlight danced across the rail yards filled with engines, boxcars, flatcars, and Pullmans. Even now, night crews in their switch engines shuffled cars around the labyrinth of track, coupling trains that, come morning, would carry coal and freight to the entire eastern seaboard.

"Evening, Rebecca."

She turned with a start.

"Didn't mean to startle you none." A lanky young man in a red wool jacket touched a gloved hand to his hat. "I heard about your pa. I'm mighty sorry."

"Chester Johnson, it's past midnight. Whatever brings you out at this hour?"

He shoved something into his coat pocket, closing the flap over what appeared to be the neck of a bottle. "Just dropping off vittles for a friend. Can I walk you home?"

"Well, it is late," she said, looking him up and down, "and the night is dark. I suppose a lady would feel safer with an escort—if he behaves like a gentleman."

"Shoot, Rebecca, you know I'm a gentleman." He extended his arm. They followed the street as it wound up the hill and away from the rail yards.

"Your pa, he hurt bad?"

"A broken leg, and he's lost considerable blood, but Doctor West says he should mend. A colored boy on one of the track crews did a nice job applying bandages and a tourniquet out at the wreckage."

"A nigra, huh? What would any of them know about doctoring?"

"Enough, I reckon. Doctor West says the man saved Papa's life."

"Just the same, you'd best be cautious. I heard tell there's one out yonder beyond Rainbow Gap, and folks say she's one of them African witch doctors. She put a spell on a fella once and it liked to kill him, it did. All he done was cuss her some when she didn't move out of his way on the sidewalk."

"Maybe he should be more careful about who he cusses." Rebecca dropped his arm and looked away. An icy wind swirled leaves across her path. She pulled the collar of her coat close around her neck and walked faster.

"Hold on." Chester hurried to her side. "It was just a nigra. Ain't like he told off the preacher's wife or nothing."

"Thank you for walking me home, Chester. I will be fine from here." She reached in her purse, retrieving the key to the front door of the small Victorian home.

"Let me get that for you." He reached for the key.

Rebecca pushed his hand aside. "It is late and I have a busy day tomorrow. Thank you for your company." She climbed the steps. "Good night."

"Rebecca?"

She paused with the key in the lock.

He stood at the foot of the concrete steps, his hat in his hand. "I hear tell there's a social fixing to happen over in Covington Saturday next. They's having a band up from Roanoke. There'll be some right good dancing. You want to go?"

She stared at him a moment. "Thank you, but no. If I'm not busy with my studies I'll be tending to Papa." She turned the key and stepped inside.

* * *

"Gandy dancers, you say? Sure, check with Mr. Beckerman, yonder by the barn." The old switchman in the bib overalls pointed to a tall wooden building with tracks entering from all sides.

"At the roundhouse? Yes, thank you, sir." Rebecca started toward the large, multi-sided building.

"Hey, you's Clarence Marshall's little girl, ain't you?"

She paused and turned. "Yes, I'm Rebecca." To the east, a glow above the snow-covered mountains hinted at a dawn still more than an hour away.

"He doing okay? We heard he got busted up something awful."

"He is mending nicely, thank you."

"He know you's poking around the yards? This ain't no place for little girls. And them nigras," he said, waggling a finger toward the barn. "No respectable white girl got any business messing with them."

Rebecca shifted her books to her other hand and straightened her starched nurse's cap. She glanced at the switchman and smiled. "One of the colored men saved Papa's life. He splinted Papa's leg and stopped his bleeding. I intend to find this Good Samaritan and thank him."

"Just the same, you be careful. Don't be wandering down around their shacks." He pointed toward the east end of town. "And I wouldn't be talking to none of them here in the yards neither, 'cepting you got a white man there with you."

"Thank you for your concern. I will be cautious, I promise." She turned and walked between a set of tracks leading to the roundhouse. After several strides between widely spaced ties, she left the tracks for an easier walk along the gravel road. It hadn't been that long ago she'd walked the rails as well as any boy in town, but not today, not in her nurse's uniform, and not while Papa was laid up in the hospital.

* * *

"George Henry, that's the nigra you're looking for. They's over by Tuckerman's Curve, fixing that track where your daddy wrecked. We're hoping to get the big hook out there sometime tomorrow to pull that engine up. Stack's busted something awful from where she rolled, but she landed straight up, so I reckon she's fixable."

"George Henry, you say? All right, thank you, Mr. Beckerman. When will they be in? Can I catch him here tonight when the crew train returns?" Rebecca looked at the portly man standing before her. His bushy mustache wrapped the corners of his mouth. The stub of an unlit cigar hung from his lips.

"Crew ain't coming in until the job's done. I'm heading out this afternoon with the chow wagon. We're working through the night, tomorrow too, if need be."

"Perhaps I'll wait a day or so and then look for him at his home."

"I wouldn't recommend that, young lady."

"And why not?" Rebecca folded her arms across her chest.

"That boy's trouble, pure and simple, that's why—he's what you'd call uppity."

"Well, uppity or not, he saved Papa's life. Can I find him

east of town in the colored section?"

"Nah, they's yonder, around that horseshoe bend in the river. Him and his brother and his brother's woman, they all live somewhere up in one of them hollers." Beckerman rubbed his chin. "Ain't no fitting place for a white woman. If'n your daddy found out you was up there, he'd tan your hide for sure."

"Then it is imperative, Mr. Beckerman, that he not find out. Good day and good luck retrieving your locomotive."

Chapter Five

Dry leaves swirled against the storefronts as we strolled past fashionably renovated shops in Richmond's Fan district. Ann glanced at her watch. "We need to hurry if we're going to squeeze in lunch before our meeting with Detective Rutino."

"Hey," I said, "can you cover me today? I'm a little short." I wiped my sunglasses with my handkerchief.

"Dutch," Ann said, "let's see, isn't that where you buy your lunch and I buy mine?"

She had me. Just last week I'd bummed a twenty that I still hadn't repaid. "Come on, you know I'm good for it. Just until Friday?"

She gazed over the top of her sunglasses. "And you get paid when?" She looked away. "Never mind. I've been carrying you in the newsroom for the last two years, why should it be any different out here? You owe me." She jabbed me in the ribs with her elbow. "Cross over." Ann skipped between parked cars and dashed across the busy street. When a break came, I hurried after her.

"I'll make it up to you, honest. I know this guy—I can get you tickets. What would you like, some rap? How about Motown?"

She spun around in the middle of the sidewalk and stabbed me in the chest with her index finger. "Or how about 'Porgy and Bess'? Man, what's with you? You think you can dump that nonsense on me? I want NASCAR."

"Huh?"

"Listen, you'd like to get this sister on your good side, square the debt and all that, right?"

I nodded.

"Two tickets to the Sharpie 500."

"Sharpie? That's . . . that's Bristol Motor Speedway. Do you have any idea how much they'd cost? What have you been smoking?" I raised my hands in disgust and walked away. She had to be dreaming, and even if she wasn't, I didn't have that kind of pull. Nowadays, I'd be lucky to score a few Richmond Braves seats, Triple A, upper deck.

"Okay," she said, falling in step beside me, "maybe I was just a tiny bit greedy. The Rock & Roll 400's in town in September. I'll settle for that."

"When did you get into NASCAR?"

"Is there a problem?" She raised an eyebrow. "Am I messing with your paradigms?"

"I just never figured you for the stock car type."

"Because I'm black or because I'm a woman?"

Damn, no matter what I said, I'd be screwed. Why'd I always let her do that? I took a deep breath. "Look, I just figured that you being a sophisticated woman and all, you'd appreciate the cultural influences inherent in a musical concert."

"Not bad, Corsini." She smiled. "You almost had me for a minute there, but I'm not letting you off that easily. You're still a Neanderthal."

"Fine. How about one ticket—on a tramp steamer to South America, one way?"

Ann laughed and grabbed my arm. "How about Italian? I'm starving."

* * *

Wednesday 1:07 PM

The marble and smoked glass façade of the police headquarters glistened in the afternoon sun. I held the door for Ann as she entered.

"You sure this guy can help? What if he thinks I really fathered that kid?"

"Then he tells you where to go and you'll be no worse off than now. Come on." She pushed me onto the elevator.

26

We stepped off at the second floor and entered an open room filled with desks, some occupied. A tall, slender, dark-haired woman in civilian slacks and a tight blouse approached. Definitely hot. A pistol hung from her hip.

"May I help you?" The lady cop asked.

Damn, why couldn't she have been the one who pulled me over last weekend? I might have negotiated a dinner for two instead of a seventy-dollar fine. Jeez, had I paid that one yet?

"We're here to see Sal," Ann said. "He's expecting us." She nodded toward a glass-enclosed office.

"It appears you already know the way." The woman smiled and stepped aside.

"Nice meeting you, miss." I flashed a smile as we walked past.

Ann leaned through the open doorway and knocked. "Hi Sal. Are we early?"

"Ann, come on in." The beefy detective stood, a wide grin slicing through the shadow of his beard.

"Sal Rutino, Mitch Corsini." Ann stepped aside as I entered.

"Hey, good to meet another Pisano," the detective said, extending his hand. "Where you from?"

"Richmond," I said. "I'm local." I winced as he clamped down on my hand and pumped it like he was trying to detach my arm from my shoulder.

"No, I mean your family, a name like Corsini, it's got to be what, Sicilian?"

"Beats me." I shrugged, flexing my fingers and trying not to show the pain. Who was this guy, Mister Genealogy?

"Yeah, if you was from Sicily, you'd know it." He laughed. "Have a seat, both of you." He pointed to a pair of chairs beside his desk. "I've read your stuff, Corsini. You're pretty good."

I shot Ann a smug look. "Thanks."

"This is strictly off the record, right? If the chief finds out I'm moonlighting during working hours he'll have me on traffic duty."

"It's not moonlighting if you don't get paid," Ann said. She crossed her legs and smiled.

Rutino glanced at me and rolled his eyes. "So, on to the mother of your alleged child, one Miss Bridget Allen." He handed me a black and white photo that appeared to have been shot through a telephoto lens.

Even in the grainy, out of focus shot, she was a looker: blonde, long legs, the kind of woman I'd chase, if I were chasing. Still, her face didn't stir any memories. I passed the picture to Ann. "Background?"

"School teacher. Single. Thirty-two. One kid, but I guess you already knew that." Rutino folded his arms and smiled.

Wise guy. "Okay, so she's a real person with a real kid. That doesn't prove squat." I folded my arms and returned the smile.

"I spoke with her lawyer," Rutino said. "She claims you picked her up in a club down in Shockoe in April, maybe early May, about two years ago. She'd had too much to drink—coming off a bad relationship or something—"

"Yeah, aren't we all?" I grimaced.

"Claims you drove her home and slept with her."

"Sounds like you did a little more than sleep, Tiger." Ann nudged me with her foot.

"What, she's claiming I took advantage of her?" I snatched the picture and studied it again.

"Nah, no rape charges, nothing like that. As far as I can tell, they're agreeing that everything was consensual." Rutino came around and sat on the corner of his desk. "You understand, if that wasn't the case, you'd be in cuffs right now and getting a guided tour of our visitor's accommodations."

I rubbed my wrists and nodded.

"She's not crying rape, just paternity, and she has the kid to prove it."

"Prove it? Hell, I don't know that woman and I can guarantee you I never slept with her. She probably pulled my name out of the phone book, or got it off the byline on one of my stories." I walked to the window. A squad car pulled into the parking lot below. Two police officers opened the rear door and wrestled a handcuffed man into the building.

"Nah, you made it easier than that, slick." The detective tossed a photocopy on the desk. "You left her your business card."

Chapter Six

The crystal tumbler slipped from my hand, shattering on the kitchen floor. Shards of glass sparkled in the amber puddle. "Damn." I shook my head and reached for another glass, imagining Foreman's words.

"He's lost his edge. Corsini couldn't find a story if it landed in his lap." That's what he'd say.

"Big city editor—he thinks he knows it all." I rubbed my stubbled cheek. "Screw him."

The ring of the telephone broke the silence. It took forever for the answering machine to pick up. Was that Sandra's voice? Sounded urgent. Probably crying for more money again. "Screw her too."

I set my pen down and pushed the letter aside. The words weren't coming—not the right words anyway—and what I needed to say to Erica shouldn't be forced, or be the product of my current, somewhat inebriated state. She deserved better.

Westminster chimes echoed from the front hall. First the phone, then the doorbell, didn't those people know what time it was? I stepped over the broken glass, caught my balance, and staggered down the hallway.

"What's wrong with you?" I yelled as I yanked open the front door. "It's the middle of the night."

"It's eight-thirty," Ann said, pushing past me without so much as a glance. "Have you eaten yet?"

"Eaten?" I glanced at the mantle clock as I followed her to the kitchen.

"Whoa . . ." She stopped in the kitchen doorway. "What'd you do, run a demolition derby and invite all your drunken friends?" She snatched my empty tumbler. "You don't need any more of this rot gut." She pointed to a chair. "Sit."

My sleeve soaked up an earlier spill as I slumped into the chair and rested my elbows on the kitchen table. "Hey, how about pouring me a drink."

"I'm going to pour you into bed. But first, you're going to eat something."

"Just coffee."

She waved a slice of bread. "The only thing worse than a drunken, know-it-all reporter is a wide-awake, drunken, know-it-all reporter. You eat this sandwich and then it's bedtime—and then I'm going through this dump and I'm pouring every bottle I find down the toilet."

"You can't do that."

"Really? Watch me."

"You got no right to just march in here all high and mighty like and mess with my stuff." I pounded my fist on the table.

Ann pointed to the chair. "Sit."

"Come on, Ann, give me a break," I pleaded, "I'm going through some rough times."

Ann stepped around the broken glass and plopped a sandwich in front of me, then took a seat across the table.

I lifted a corner of the bread. "You gotta be kidding, right? Peanut butter? Can't a guy even score a decent ham and cheese?"

She leaned across the table and locked me in her gaze. "Damn it, Mitch. I looked up to you. I learned more just from watching you than I'd learned in all those years at journalism school." Ann took my hand. "This isn't like you. You're killing yourself one bottle at a time, and I won't let that happen."

I shrugged. "After Sandra left, stuff just sort of happened."

"Mitch, it's been five years. Don't you think it's time you changed course?"

"I'm working on it." I took a bite of the sandwich.

"Look," she said, "Abe's worried. Me too. We care . . ."

"I'm touched, truly, I am." I covered my heart with the sandwich.

"Wake up, Corsini. You're running out of chances." She grabbed the whiskey bottle as she stood, turned toward the sink, and emptied it down the drain.

"And I don't need your holier-than-thou crap," I shouted. "Get out!" I nailed her between the shoulder blades with my peanut butter sandwich.

* * *

Thursday 6:00 AM

A sudden blinding light invaded the warm, quiet darkness and a pounding, like the rhythmic thumping of a pile driver, filled my head. God, am I dead? I must be—and in hell. My hands found something soft. I grabbed it and pulled it over my head. Darkness returned.

"Get your lazy butt out of that bed, Corsini. You have one hour to get dressed and make it to the office."

I groaned.

"Come on, big boy, rise and shine." Ann yanked the blanket off my face. Sunlight suddenly streamed through open bedroom windows, filling the room.

"Will you close those damned blinds? Jeez, what the . . ." I became aware of another pain and sat up, rubbing my jaw. "It feels like I got kicked by a mule. What happened, did I fall down or something?"

"Or something." She punched the palm of her hand.

"You . . . you hit me?"

"You remember what I said about wide-awake drunks? The only thing worse is a violent wide-awake drunk."

"But—you hit me?"

"Self defense, your honor." She crossed her heart and held up her hand. "I had been assaulted with a PB&J." she picked up a steaming mug from the dresser. "Coffee?"

"You punched me because of a damned sandwich?" I swung my feet over the side of the bed and reached for the coffee, then grabbed my head as the room began a slow roll.

"Just for the record, after you slammed me with that sandwich I put you to bed, but you kept bouncing up like a pop tart on steroids. How was I to get any sleep with a sandwich-wielding maniac roaming the house?"

"You punched me . . . ?"

"Mitch, get over it."

She stood beside the bed holding the coffee mug. A football jersey covered her slender, nicely toned legs to mid-thigh. Damn, she looked hot. Wait, wasn't that my college jersey? "Whoa, you didn't . . . I mean, we didn't . . ." I stared at the bed.

Ann set the mug on the nightstand and walked into the bathroom. In a moment, the sound of running water came from the shower. "It'll be warm in a few seconds. Pull yourself together while I fix breakfast."

Steaming jets of water drilled into knotted muscles on the back of my neck. I braced against the shower wall and closed my eyes. I couldn't allow myself to doze; I'd fall, probably crack my skull—not that it didn't already feel busted. I needed to wake up.

Had I really slept with her? I turned into the stream and adjusted the water until an icy blast caught my face.

She'd have expectations and I didn't need my life any more complicated than it already was. What if people found out? Maybe she'd leave it be.

I shivered and turned the handle the other way. Steam again filled the glassed enclosure.

Damn, what if she was pregnant?

* * *

Thursday 6:45 AM

"Toast?" Ann held out a plate of charred bread slathered in grape jelly.

"Thanks." I tore the slice in half and poked one end in my egg. A yellow puddle spread across the plate, enveloping two bacon strips. I sopped up the yolk and took a bite.

"You're beginning to look like a member of the human race again," Ann said. "Welcome back." She slid two eggs from the skillet onto her plate and took a seat.

"The shower helped." I glanced across the table. "Listen, about last night—"

"Forget it, honey. You weren't all that bad." She batted her eyelashes and struck a pose.

"No, seriously, I mean . . ." I shook my head. "I don't know what I mean. Why'd you come over last night, anyway?"

"Brought you this." She placed a thick cardboard envelope on the table.

"Micron Biolabs?" I shrugged.

"I figured you'd forget to call them, right?" She opened the envelope. "Run a swab around the inside of your cheek, put it in the pouch, drop it in the mail."

"What are you talking about?"

"DNA, dummy. Swab your cheek, mail it in. I was going to have you do it last night, but with all that alcohol in your system they would have linked you to the Jack Daniels family tree."

"Very funny. So this will prove that I'm not that kid's father?"

"Or prove you are," she said. "It may also match you up with any of the thousands of other fatherless children out there who are looking for their baby-daddy."

"Yeah, right." I rubbed the swab inside my mouth, then placed it in the envelope. "This better work."

"Be careful what you wish for."

I stared into my coffee mug. "Look, don't take this wrong, but I figure I got a right to know."

"Know what?"

"About last night . . . you're on the pill or something, right?"

She laughed. "You ever hear of rhythm and blues?"

What the hell was she talking about? I shook my head.

She waved, as though in time to some silent melody. "If this sister doesn't have the rhythm, you're in for one bad case of the blues."

"Are you kidding? Didn't you ever hear of the pill?" I

slammed my coffee mug on the table. Another baby? Hell, I sure didn't need that. I drove my knuckles into my temples. When would that damn pounding stop?

The front doorbell chimed, followed by an insistent knock. I glanced at my watch. "My friends aren't up this early. Who knew you were here?"

She raised an eyebrow and shrugged. "Eat your eggs. Whoever that is, I'll get rid of them." Ann slipped the DNA kit in her purse and headed down the hallway. The front door opened. Indistinct voices exchanged words. She said she'd handle it. I sopped egg yolk with my toast and tried to ignore the commotion.

"Where is he?" Urgent footsteps followed the angry voice and then Sandra burst into the kitchen. She came to a stop and pointed an accusing finger at me. "Why didn't you return my call?"

I glanced past her to Ann, who was standing behind her in the doorway. Ann raised both hands, as if to say it wasn't her fault that she let this lunatic woman into my house so she could yell at me from across my own breakfast table.

"Ann, Sandra." I motioned with the toast. "Ann's a business acquaintance. We work together."

Sandra shot a disapproving glance behind her. "I'm not interested in your little playmates. Our daughter happens to be missing."

"What are you talking about?" I waved off Ann before she could respond and motioned for Sandra to sit.

Ignoring my invitation, she threw a large manila envelope on the table and folded her arms. "She took off for a long weekend backpacking with a friend. The police found their car, but no sign of Erica or Peter."

"Peter?" I dumped the envelope on the table. A faxed copy of a police report fell out, along with two photos. Erica's was new, must have been taken at college. Nice of Sandra to send me a copy. The other was of a young man . . . a studious, preppy looking black man. I shot Sandra a questioning glance and held out the picture.

"He . . . his father is a surgeon—a neurosurgeon—and a

state legislator." Her gaze darted nervously to Ann, then me.

So, it was supposed to make it okay if his old man was someone important? I shook my head. "Just the two of them? You let her go off alone with nature boy, here?"

"She's nineteen, Mitch—"

Ann stepped around Sandra and picked up the photo. "And he looks like a perfectly respectable young man." She tossed the picture in front of me. "You got a problem with that?"

Ex-wife, Ann, and a hangover? Why me, Lord? I bit my lip. "Where'd it happen? Where were they when they disappeared?"

Sandra sighed. The bitchy, assertive, in-your-face ex-wife seemed to melt. Suddenly, she appeared shaken, vulnerable— and very afraid. "Clifton Forge. They . . . they'd gone hiking in the mountains." Her eyes filled with tears.

"Come on, sit." I stood and motioned toward the vacant chair. Lost hikers? Probably wandered off the trail. The Forest Service would have them rounded up before lunch.

Sandra pulled a tissue from her purse and dabbed her eyes. "I called. I left messages. Didn't you check your machine? Where were you last night?"

I glanced at Ann and then picked up the police report. "Clifton Forge, huh? I was up that way just this week. My grandma grew up there. I don't think you ever met her. Anyway, it's too late for introductions, we buried her on Monday."

Sandra gasped. "Monday's when they disappeared."

"Hell, that was three days ago," I said. "Why'd you wait so long to tell me?"

She clinched her fists and stared at the ceiling.

* * *

Thursday 8:15 AM

"You look like hell. What'd you do, sleep in the gutter?" Abe motioned toward the chair beside his desk. "I don't expect personal problems to get in the way of good reporting—"

"It's my kid, damn it." What didn't he understand?

"And Monday it was your grandmother." Abe settled behind his desk. He waggled his pen. "That trip wasn't supposed to get in the way either, but I almost missed a deadline because of that Black History Month mess you slapped together."

"You got your article."

"Yeah, thanks to Ann." He scowled. "Damn it, Mitch, there was a time—you were the best reporter this paper ever had."

Another of Abe's temperance lectures? Drunks don't win Pulitzers, only sober, hard-working journalists win those— like I'd been seven years ago—when I snagged mine. If my head didn't stop pounding, I was going to puke all over his desk.

"Look, Abe, I know I've slipped up a few times lately—"

"You're kidding, right? Do you have any idea how many deadlines you've missed? For months I've been throwing filler at the white space where your articles were supposed to run."

"A day, maybe two. That's all I'm asking." I tugged at my collar. God, it was hot in there.

Abe leaned back and steepled his fingers, then tapped them pensively on his lip. "Okay, here's the deal." He pointed the steeple at me. "Take the time you need, you're on the clock. Whatever you find—human interest, crime, family drama, springtime in the mountains feel good crap—I really don't care—you write it up like your damn job depends on it. Am I clear?"

"Clear enough." I stood and reached for the door.

"And Mitch . . ." he lowered his voice. "Whatever it takes, you find that girl."

Chapter Seven

February 1936

Two long blasts of the locomotive's whistle announced the crew train's return to the Clifton Forge rail yards. Streetlights flickered and came on, bathing the darkening roads in pale cones of yellow light. George Henry casually leaned against the boxcar's open doorway, rocking with the motion of the train. "Four days working that wreck and she still ain't up the hill. I'm ready for some of your wife's home cooking." He patted his stomach.

"Warm cabin and a soft mattress," Willie said, "that's what I hanker for." He kicked a clump of straw." A boxcar ain't no place for living in the winter." Smoke from the engine curled through the open door.

An old man sat in the corner, a blanket wrapped around his narrow shoulders. "You won't be fussing none when the man hands out our bonus money," he said. "Two dollars a day, that's what he promised." He rubbed his thumb and forefinger together and smiled.

"Eight dollars extra," George Henry said. "Nigh on a full week's pay—and that engine's still setting there, waiting to pay us some more." George Henry patted his belt buckle. "But tonight I'm hankering for a rare T-bone steak and a bottle of store-bought whiskey." He hopped to the ground as the boxcar clanged to a halt. "Little brother, you got some money I can borrow until we gets that extra pay?"

Willie jumped from the car. "Just a dollar seventy-five from selling Lorinda Jane's eggs, but some of the boys is talking about a dice game, so I'll turn that into folding money real quick." He smiled and patted his pocket as they walked beside the tracks.

"Are you crazy?" George Henry replied. "She said she'd beat your skull, if'n you was to lose her money again."

"How's she gonna find out? I know you won't be telling." Willie laughed as he slapped George Henry on the back. "With hot dice and Willie Terrill's natural good luck, that egg basket's gonna be our pot of gold."

A single bulb hung over the doorway of the one-story clapboard crew shack. George Henry and Willie dropped their lining bars on a pallet and followed the other workers through the door. Inside, men huddled around wooden tables, some talking quietly, a few sleeping. One man idly shuffled a deck of cards.

"There be some hard times out there, George Henry," A tall, thin man said as he kicked a chair George Henry's way. "Set yourself down and take a load off."

George Henry spun the chair around and straddled the seat, his arms draped across the spindled back. "Yes sir, and we earned us some hard money for them hard times, Samuel. You can't argue none with that."

"Even with the big hook she wouldn't budge." Samuel lifted a blackened pot from the Franklin stove. "Coffee?"

George Henry held out a chipped enamel mug. "I heard Mr. Beckerman talking to one of the engineers. He says we has to back off a quarter mile and cut another track bed at an angle down to the wreck." He blew into his mug and took a sip. "Reckon they done gave up on pulling her up to the tracks, so we'll be laying fresh track down to her. More hard work, but it all pays." He smiled.

"Not so's I hear," Samuel said. He glanced around the room as if to ensure he wouldn't be overheard, and then leaned closer. "There's a white crew coming up from Scottsville. I hear tell they's the ones will be pulling those extra hours. Come day after tomorrow, we's back on straight pay."

"The devil, you say?" George Henry knocked over his chair as he stood. "Them's our tracks. We laid 'em, we lined 'em, and sure as hell we can replace 'em. To hell with them high-dollar white boys." He slammed his fist on the table.

The room grew silent. All eyes turned toward George Henry.

"Don't pay him no never mind, he's just tired. He don't mean nothing." Willie gave a dismissive wave to the gathered workers and tugged on George Henry's sleeve. "You gots to hush, 'fore you gets us both fired," he whispered. "I needs this job. I got a wife and a baby to feed."

George Henry froze. "You got a what?"

"Man, I was gonna tell you before, but then with the wreck and all, it just slipped my mind."

"Slipped your . . ." George Henry smacked the back of Willie's head. "Hey, everybody," he said, clapping his hands. "Listen up." He spun Willie around to face the gathering. "My little brother here has some news; he's gonna be a daddy. He and Lorinda Jane is fixing to have themselves a baby!"

Hoots and catcalls filled the small room.

"Must be talking next summer sometime—last I seen her, that gal was still skinny as a rail fence." Samuel pointed at Willie and laughed.

"Lorinda Jane says June, most likely. She ain't real sure," Willie said.

"She know what it is?" Samuel asked.

"Yeah, tell us, Willie," Another worker called out. "You gonna have a boy, ain't you?"

Willie shrugged. "I . . . I don't know about none of that. Lorinda Jane just said we was having us a baby."

"You tell her, go see Sister Millie Rose over to the Second AME Church." Samuel put his arm around Willie's shoulders. "She done called every child me and my Sally Mae ever had, all seven, and weren't nary a wrong guess in the bunch. She lays on the hands and reads scripture—the Lord does the rest."

"Sister Rose, you say?" Willie said. "My Lorinda Jane, she'll be pleased to learn that."

Clayton Jones, a large man with several teeth missing from his easy smile, stood in the back of the room and hollered, "Laying on them hands and reading scripture is fine and all, but I just wants to know one thing: when you done her, was your boots on or off?"

Willie glanced at George Henry and shrugged. "Off, I reckon, but—"

"But nothing," George Henry said, "there's nights when we's coming home from the yards and Willie here, he flat runs up that mountain, just to have him some time before I makes it home. When I sees that sparkle in his eyes, them's the nights I wander up that path real slow like."

"And them's the nights his boots is on, ain't they, boy?" Samuel slapped his knee and cackled.

"I'll wager his boots was on this time too, which means he's having himself a big strong baby boy." George Henry raised his coffee mug. "To Willie Terrill McConnell, Junior!"

"Hear, hear." Samuel drummed the table and laughed as cheers filled the room.

"Listen up." Willie patted his pocket. "I got the dice right here and I'm itching to get up a game. Who's going to be first to donate their overtime so's my boy can get himself born to a rich daddy?"

"I'll take a piece of that," a man in the back called out.

Count me in," hollered another.

George Henry pulled Willie aside. "There's clothes and medicines and schoolbooks to buy. Don't you be wasting my nephew's egg money on no crap game."

"Aw, what are you worried about, brother? I won't be losing nothing. When I get home tonight, my pockets will be spilling over with real money—folding money—just you wait."

"And Lorinda Jane will be planting her skillet on the side of your head if they ain't."

"You know she ain't that way," Willie said. "Besides, that egg money don't amount to nothing. But with a few lucky passes I'll have enough to buy her that crib in the window at Randal's Mercantile." Willie buttoned his coat. "Come on, we's setting up the game inside the roundhouse."

George Henry pushed open the door. "I been out on them rails four days straight and I'm plum tired. Reckon I'll stop by the hospital and look in on them that was injured, then see if Lorinda Jane can scare up some eggs and biscuits."

"What about your T-bone?"

"Maybe after payday."

"Don't you tell her I'm shooting dice."

"I'll make up something," George Henry called over his shoulder as he shoved his hands in his pockets and turned toward town. "But if them dice do treat you good, you'd best stuff the winnings in a cracker tin and hide 'em in the woodpile. Young'uns is cheap enough to make, but I hear tell the raising and rearing can leave a man poor as a possum."

* * *

"Yes, may I help you?" The nurse glanced up, her pen pausing over a folder in which she'd been writing. Wire baskets on the counter overflowed with files, clipboards, and papers. A brass desk lamp with a green shade cast a soft glow on the nursing station.

"Excuse me, ma'am," George Henry snatched his hat from his head, twisting it into a knot. "That engineer fella what got himself smashed up out there at Tuckerman's Curve, he doing okay?"

The nurse stood and removed her eyeglasses. She looked George Henry up and down. "Mr. Marshall, you mean? Are you an acquaintance?"

George Henry shook his head.

"Visiting hours are over. If he's not expecting you—"

"I didn't mean to cause no trouble, ma'am. He was busted up mighty bad when we brung him in. I just wanted to know if'n he was going to pull through." George Henry turned toward the door.

"Wait . . ." The nurse hurried around the counter. "Of course, you're that boy that stopped his bleeding and splinted his leg."

"Yes, ma'am. I mended him some, just enough to hold him till the doctors seen him."

"That was a whole lot more than simple mending. Mr.

Marshall owes you his life. If you don't mind my asking, where'd a colored man learn such things?"

George Henry shoved his hands in his pockets and lowered his head. Would there ever come a time when they would no longer be surprised at anything a black man might know? Up in Boston they had Negro doctors, Philadelphia too, he'd read about them in a magazine.

"My daddy, he done some doctoring in the army over in France during the Great War."

"Your father was a doctor?"

"No ma'am, a medic. Kept all his manuals after the war, though, and when I was old enough, he taught me everything the army taught him. Said a man needed to know how to care for his fellow man."

"Well, thank the good Lord he taught you well." She took him by the sleeve. "Come, Mr. Marshall wants to meet you."

"I reckon I shouldn't ma'am. I don't want to be waking him or nothing. I just wanted to know, was he going to live." George Henry pulled away from her grasp.

"Nonsense. I turned down his light not ten minutes ago. He's awake, and even if he isn't, he's been asking about you. If he was to find out you came by and I didn't wake him . . . well, I shudder to think of the words he'd be using. You wait here." The nurse stepped into a darkened room. A light flicked on, followed by hushed voices. A moment later, she returned to the doorway. "Come along. Mr. Marshall wishes to make your acquaintance."

The old man lay on his back, one leg wrapped from hip to toes in a white plaster cast and suspended above the bed by pulleys and weights. Gray, unkempt hair tussled about his ruddy face as though he'd just awakened, which, perhaps he had.

"Come here, boy. Let's have a look at this famous Negro doctor that saved my life." Mr. Marshall's eyes seemed to dance with excitement.

"I ain't no doctor, Mr. Marshall, I's just a railroad man who was doing my job, like yourself."

44

"That will be all, Miss Hadley." Mr. Marshall smiled at the nurse. "I'll call if I need you." He turned to George Henry. "So, a hard-working railroad man that knows medicine? We can sure use more like that on the C&O. What's your name, boy?"

"George, sir. George Henry McConnell."

"And you was on the lining bar gang when we jumped the tracks?"

"Yes, sir, seen the whole thing."

Mr. Marshall tried sitting up in the bed. "Can't ever get comfortable with that God-awful contraption pulling on me. Here, stuff this pillow back of my head, would you?"

George Henry pushed the pillow under Mr. Marshall's head. "That good?"

"Fine, fine. Now, tell me about yourself. Nurse says your daddy taught you doctoring."

"Yes, sir, he was with the 350th Machine Gun Battalion. The French, they gave him a medal during the war."

"Well, bully for him. And what about you? Got yourself a wife? Any young'uns?"

"No sir, ain't married, but my brother keeps after me to find a good woman."

Mr. Marshall laughed. "Stay single long as you can, boy. Once you's married, you's married for life. No sense rushing headlong into that trap."

Visiting this old white man sure beat losing what few coins he might have gambled in that dice game. George Henry smiled. "I ain't in no hurry to marry, Mr. Marshall. I'm looking to get me a better position first, maybe one of them Pullman jobs, so's I can keep a woman and pay the bills."

"You got a good head on your shoulders, George Henry. I expect you'll do just fine. Listen, you come back and visit me again, you hear?"

"Don't want to be no bother, Mr. Marshall."

"Hell, you won't be any bother. Truth is, a man can go plumb out of his mind just laying here. I'd be pleased for the company."

"Then maybe I'll stop by from time to time, bring you

some of Lorinda Jane's chicken soup."

"Say, speaking of vittles and such, you know them Johnson boys? They have that place out on Dry Creek."

"The ones running that corn mash still?"

"Sh-h-h." Mr. Marshall glanced at the door. "We don't talk about that around here, but yeah, they're the ones. If I was to give you some money, you think you could sneak me some of them squeezings next time you come?"

"I'll see what I can do, Mr. Marshall."

"And if you was to tell 'em I sent you, maybe they'll cut you in on the action, let you run some of their stock. You could make a right pretty sum to put away for that bride you'll be finding."

"That sounds real good, Mr. Marshall. Now, you'd best get yourself to sleep so's you'll mend proper." George Henry backed toward the door.

"Hold up, boy. One more thing . . ."

"Sir?"

"Just wanted to say thanks to you and that daddy of yours for saving my life."

Chapter Eight

You have two outstanding citations, Mr. Corsini." The strap on the Smokey hat tugged at a sunburned, cleanly shaven roll of flesh on the back of the trooper's neck. He ripped the top page from his ticket pad and passed it through the open window. "This will make three. My advice to you, Sir, is that you'd best take care of those pronto or you'll be facing arrest."

"Thanks, officer," I said as I took the ticket. "I sure will." I forced a smile. After he turned toward his patrol car, I wadded the ticket and tossed it in the back seat. A moment later, the blue lights stopped flashing in my rearview mirror. The cruiser pulled onto the interstate and disappeared into traffic.

"Okay, what'll go wrong next?" I craned my neck and stared into the cloudless sky. "Any more surprises?"

Only twenty minutes to my exit. If I held it under seventy-five, everything would be cool. I touched the accelerator.

A horn blared from behind.

"Holy—" I stood on the brakes. The driver of a pearl-white Lincoln Navigator flipped me off as she swerved around my '63 Impala.

I pushed back on the steering wheel and slowly exhaled. "Okay, chill. No more tickets, no accidents, just get to the damned hotel." I glanced over my shoulder and then eased the car onto the highway.

Eighty-seven in a sixty-five. Yeah, that'll run a few hundred bucks, at least, and Erica's college—another two, three grand? And that child support crap . . . Detective what's-his-name made it sound like a slam dunk that I'd flunk the DNA test. Man, if that went south on me, I'd be paying for that little crumb snatcher for the next eighteen years.

Speaking of the detective, what was all that Sicilian nonsense he was tossing out there? I knew nothing about Dad's family, except that he was an only child. Go figure, Italian and an only child. What are the odds? I laughed. Of course, any chance he had of doing the big family thing for me blew up when that Vietcong mortar found his foxhole.

Patches of snow clung to the shaded side of the median. Maybe Erica and her friend just got turned around during a sudden snowstorm. Hell, it probably happened all the time. They would have holed up somewhere, cold, but safe. Did they have a tent, or food?

We'd camped in the backyard once, just the two of us. She must have been five or six. We cooked hot dogs and marshmallows on the grill. She said she was scared bears would get us, but I'd never seen her laugh so hard as when I told her how I'd wrestle them—just like Davy Crockett. We'd been close once; maybe I was even her hero back then. What in the hell happened? How'd I screw it up so badly?

I reached into the folder on the seat and pulled out the fax. After checking my mirrors, I studied his grainy black and white photo. Closely cropped hair, a coat and tie, glasses— jeez, the boy looked almost geeky. What was she thinking? He'd better not have touched her . . . .

* * *

Thursday 11:17 AM

"Sir, your room won't be ready for another two hours," the pimply faced kid behind the front desk said. "I can hold your bags here behind the counter, if that would be a help."

"How about a place to eat," I said. "What's good around here? Also, where's your local newspaper office?"

"You want Italian, try Leonardo's down on Ridgeway Street. Newspaper's over on Main, but they're not open today." The kid handed me a one-page Chamber of

Commerce flyer with a map in the lower corner. I could probably walk the entire town in less than an hour.

"How about the police department? Are they open?"

By the look he shot me he must have thought I was being a wise-ass. "Main Street, behind the town hall," he said.

"Thanks." I grabbed a mint from the bowl on the counter as I headed out.

"Sergeant Johnson," the kid hollered.

I paused by the door and turned.

"He's the one to talk to about them hikers," the kid said. "He does all the crime investigations. My brother-in-law, he got his pickup stolen Christmas, a year ago." He leaned over the counter. "Sergeant Johnson figured it was them Dawson boys out on Route 220. He had that truck back in two days."

"Sergeant Johnson? Thanks, I'll look him up." I'd try the police department before lunch—maybe it would give me something to chew on besides Leonardo's ravioli.

The road into town followed railroad tracks that ran alongside a mountain creek carrying runoff from melting snows down to the Jackson River. On the right, winter-bare trees clung to the steep mountainside. To the left, wooden sheds, daylight peering through gaps in their weathered boards, dotted the rail yards. Modest bungalows, many with faded paint and dangling shutters, hugged the edge of the highway. A few had chicken wire fences enclosing their tiny front yards.

Thank God, Grandma'd had the sense to skip town before Dad was born. I'd have never survived growing up in that Appalachian hideaway. Heck, I didn't even own bib overalls.

Two old pickups and a minivan were the only other vehicles on the road. Noon rush hour? I glanced at my watch, then pulled in and parked next to a large brick building with a white columned portico and an imposing clock tower. The wooden sign above a side door read, "Police." Reporters have access to information a parent would never see. They didn't need to know I was Erica's father. The fact that her last name was now Gillespie made for an easy ruse.

An officer sat at a desk behind the counter. He wore a khaki shirt with a dark blue necktie. As I entered, he looked up from his paperback novel. "Can I help you, mister?"

"Name's Corsini, Richmond Journal News. You have a Sergeant Johnson here?"

"He's out." The officer put down his book. "Something I can help you with?"

"I heard a couple of kids were reported missing." I placed my notebook on the counter.

"You mean them college kids? Hell, we did a full search, dogs and everything. They ain't out there."

"You know that for a fact?"

"This time of year?" He laughed. "Anything that's out of place you're going to see it real easy—no leaves on the trees, ya know."

"And?"

"And what?" he said. "I told you, we didn't find nothing." He stretched, locking his hands behind his head. "You writing a story?"

"If there's anything to write about."

"Hey, will you put my name in that story? I got a sister down Richmond way, if you put my name in your paper, I'll call her and tell her to buy me a copy."

I smiled. "I'll see what I can do."

"You know what I think?" he said.

"No, but I'm all ears." Did I really give a damn what he thought? I put down my pencil and stared at the officer.

"They eloped."

"Really?" I said. "How do you figure?"

"Shoot, have you seen her picture? She's hot." He scanned the office and then lowered his voice. "Did you know the feller she's with is black?"

Okay, I could play along. I shook my head.

"It ain't for me to say, but if she was my daughter, I sure as hell would have raised her better." He folded his arms and gave what appeared to be a self-satisfied smile.

And if I'd been there for her, maybe none of this would

have happened. I jotted something in my notebook. "I'll make a note that you disapproved . . ."

"Whoa, hold on there." He waved both hands as though trying to erase the remnants of his words. "What I said was strictly off the record, you hear? Just between you and me. If you was to print that, Captain McConnell would have my ass." He glanced around before continuing. "His kind don't have a problem with mixing the races."

"His kind?"

He shrugged and nodded toward the wall behind me. Uniformed officers in a framed photo posed in typical military fashion, front row kneeling, back row standing. I tapped my finger on an African-American man standing in the center of the back row. He wore a navy blazer with an embroidered police badge on the breast pocket. "Captain McConnell?"

"Don't get me wrong," he said, "the captain's a real nice feller. College boy, you know. Word is, that's why he got hired." He pointed to my notebook. "Anyway, I need this job."

I slipped the spiral pad in my pocket. "No sweat, detective. Now, tell me about that eloping."

He fidgeted, tugging on his collar. "It's patrolman, but I'll be up for promotion in two or three months."

"Congratulations. Now, you said they eloped?"

"Maybe not eloped." He grinned sheepishly. "But I'd wager she's seeing that boy just to tick off her old man, get under his skin. Ya know what I mean?"

He had no idea how accurate he might be. I motioned toward the file cabinets along the back wall. "Do you have any investigative summaries, press releases, updated bios— you know, stuff the press hasn't already seen?"

"You're the only press sniffing around this one." He laughed. "This very minute those kids are probably shacked up, smoking joints and screwing their brains out, just doing what college kids naturally do."

I bit my tongue. "Will Captain McConnell or Sergeant Johnson be in later?"

"You might find Sergeant Johnson out at the diner. He took off to run errands and said something about grabbing some lunch. Captain McConnell has the day off. He's coaching the high school basketball team. They made the playoffs this year. You might catch him at the gym."

Day off? He was messing with some stupid basketball team while my kid was lost in those woods, probably scared to death and quite possibly injured? What kind of police department was he running? I almost said something I might have regretted, but instead I quickly turned toward the door.

"Thanks for your help, officer." I left the office and headed for my car. So, just out doing what college kids do, huh? That would mean she was safe, or at least not lying injured out in those woods somewhere, but there had to be a better answer.

Maybe it was time to find out if that diner knew the difference between grits and Cream of Wheat.

* * *

Thursday 12:10 PM

The cop was short and wiry, with jet-black hair slicked over in a style reminiscent of the 1950s. He set his cap on the counter and placed his mirrored sunglasses inside. A badge, partially hidden under his brown leather jacket, hung above his left breast pocket. He'd tucked the cuffs of his khaki trousers into his black cowboy boots. A navy blue necktie completed the uniform. As he took his seat at the counter, he caught his reflection in the mirror and brushed back a strand of hair.

The waitress brought a plate without waiting for him to order. He took a bite of what looked like a fried egg sandwich, washing it down with coffee.

I finished my burger. When it appeared he might be done eating, I picked up my glass of iced tea and ambled over to an empty stool beside him.

"Mind if I join you?" I set my drink on the counter.

He stared straight ahead. "It's a free country."

"Sergeant Johnson, right?"

"Who wants to know?"

"Name's Corsini." I held out my hand. "Mitch Corsini. I'm up from Richmond to do a story on those lost hikers."

After giving me a quick once over, he returned to his coffee. "You're wasting your time. There's no story."

I wiped my empty hand down the side of my trousers and straddled the stool. "One of your patrolmen, I didn't catch his name, he said he figured they'd left town."

"Could be. There's no sign of them around here." Johnson held his mug out to the waitress. "Hey, Molly, warm 'er up, will ya?"

"Initial reports suggested they were lost," I said.

"Initial reports are usually wrong," he replied.

"Still, you have no evidence that they came out of those mountains, right?"

Johnson set his mug on the counter and looked me up and down. "What's a big time city paper care about a couple of no 'count college kids anyway?"

"Just looking for a story." I sipped my tea.

"Where are you staying?"

"The motel out by the interstate. Why?"

Johnson snatched a toothpick from a shot glass on the counter and shoved it in his mouth. He rolled the pick from side to side and then poked at something between his teeth. "If something breaks on this case, I'll find you." He dropped the toothpick on his plate and dug a handful of bills from his pocket. "Hey, Molly, give me a Danish to go."

I dropped a couple of ones next to my empty glass. "What do your instincts tell you?"

He slid his sunglasses on, centered the visor of his cap low on his forehead, and studied his reflection in the chromed jukebox. "It was Corsini, right?" He smiled. "My instincts tell me you're wasting your time. You stay buckled up, Mr. Corsini, and you mind our speed limits, you hear?"

Chapter Nine

Thursday 1:46 PM

"The Alleghany Switchman and Weekly Journal" spanned the storefront window in antique gold lettering. I dropped a quarter in the box, pulled out a copy of the paper, and began to read. The boys' high school basketball team made the semi-finals. There was going to be a slide show next Saturday hosted by the historical society on the Civilian Conservation Corps' work at the nearby state park during the Depression. I searched for any mention of the lost hikers. Apparently, they weren't even newsworthy here. I folded the paper under my arm and continued my walk.

A dozen or more pair of tracks crossed the Jackson River and entered town from the southwest. Switches pinched the multiple tracks down to only two sets that crossed a small creek. Beyond the creek, the tracks switched out again, forming six or eight sets heading out of town to the east. I walked along the cracked sidewalk. Boarded-up buildings hinted at what that town might have been in its heyday. My great-grandfather ran trains out of there. He was probably buried somewhere close by. I could look him up, but did it really matter? I didn't even know his name.

Behind a crumbling warehouse, the hulk of an old truck sat in an overgrown parking lot, its dirt-encrusted split windshield staring vacantly at a world that had long ago passed it by. An old coal-burning steam locomotive hunkered on a siding in the rail yards. They'd probably put her out to pasture decades ago, around the time they shut down the Clifton Forge maintenance facilities. What a blow that must have been to a town built around the railroad.

According to my watch, McConnell would be at basketball practice, but he should have been out combing those woods for any trace of Erica. I'd head out there myself, but I needed a few specifics first, like where they were last seen. Turning away from the tracks, I followed a crumbling sidewalk that climbed through a tired residential neighborhood. On one corner sat a faded yellow gingerbread house, its front porch sagging. The old gal evoked pathos worthy of an eighty-year-old prom queen.

* * *

Thursday 4:45 PM

"Two-one-two, get the turnover, then work the fast break." The coach blew his whistle. "NO. Playing like that will NOT get you into the second round on Saturday." He waved his clipboard. "Gather up." The boys circled around a lean, muscular man about my age wearing shorts and a University of Virginia sweatshirt.

It hadn't been that many years since my playing days. I tugged at my waistband. Hell, a few months in the gym, maybe a shred of motivation . . . . Yeah, right. I slipped into the bleachers.

Practice ran another fifteen minutes, ending with the team running laps around the gym. The coach jotted a few notes on his clipboard and then turned toward the locker room door.

I scrambled from the bleachers and jogged across the court. "Captain, Captain McConnell." As I caught up to him, I sucked in my stomach. "Hi. I'm Mitch Corsini, Richmond Journal News."

He shook my hand. "I didn't know the big city papers cared about our little high school." He pointed to where I'd been sitting. "I saw you up there, had you figured for some assistant coach sent to scout us."

"Maybe I should be running laps with your team. I could sure use the exercise." I took a deep breath and patted my stomach.

He stared, seeming to study my face. "Do I know you?"

"No," I said, "I'm up here looking into those college kids who went missing. One of your patrolmen said you'd done some initial checking on the case and he mentioned I might find you here."

He continued to stare at me for a moment, and then shook off whatever seemed to be bothering him with a laugh. "Yeah, police captain, basketball coach," He shrugged. "I'm never sure which job demands more of my attention. Come on, we can talk in my office."

In the locker room, the musty aroma took me back to my days playing college football. Sweaty jock straps and gym shorts—probably hadn't been washed in weeks—aromas I'd never forget. We passed rows of metal lockers and wooden benches. Wire reinforced windows on the coach's office overlooked the locker room on two sides.

"Have a seat. It's Mitch, right?"

I nodded and sat down. "This sure brings back memories." I took in the locker room with a sweep of my hand. "Last time I was in a coach's office, I was getting my butt chewed for missing a block."

McConnell laughed. "As a charter member of the coaches' protective association, I'll have to believe you deserved it." He tossed his clipboard on the desk. "You said you were doing a story on those missing kids."

"Yes," I said. "This could be nothing, but my editor thought I should at least check it out."

He frowned, seeming to study his hands. "He might have been more right that he knows."

"You mean there is something to this story?"

McConnell kicked his feet up on the desk and clasped his hands behind his head. "Something doesn't fit—they didn't just vanish."

"So, instead of searching for them, you're off running a basketball clinic?"

"Look," he said, "nobody wants to find those kids any more than me." He tapped his finger on the desk. "Give me a clue, anything, and I'm out there with a search party, but we're talking over a hundred square miles of forest. I don't have that kind of manpower—and we don't even know that they're in those woods."

Anger—was it because he hadn't found Erica, or was because I'd called him out for conducting a half-assed search? Hell, I was angry too. At least we had something in common. I pulled out a pencil and flipped open my notebook. "The police report mentioned a jacket. It had blood stains?"

"Maybe. I haven't heard back on the lab tests. It might have belonged to one of the missing students, who knows?"

"So, where's the disconnect?"

"That's just it." McConnell shrugged. "You ever walk into a room you've known all your life and had that feeling that something, maybe some piece of furniture, a picture on the wall, something had been moved? You look around, but you can't put your finger on it. It's just—different." He shook his head. "You heard about the car?"

"No," I said. "What car?"

"Registered to that young man. We found it near the trailhead."

"The black boy?" I asked. "What can you tell me about him?"

McConnell stared at me for a moment. "The young man is an honor student. ROTC, tennis, cross county . . ." He counted off on his fingers. "He sings in the church choir."

"Any reason to believe they were dating?"

McConnell seemed to flinch. "Does it matter?"

"I suppose it shouldn't, but your deputy seemed to think something was going on."

He gave me a long look and exhaled. "How about a tour of the crime scene?"

"I didn't know there was one." I shoved the pencil in my pocket. "Let's go."

Chapter Ten

February 1936

"That egg money was to buy us bacon and flour." Lorinda Jane turned away from the blackened skillet on the small wood stove. Her lower lip trembled as she clutched her stomach. "The good Lord done provided them laying hens so's we could pay for this here baby, and all the while you's down on your knees, shooting them craps and doing the devil's work—where's your mind, Willie T.?"

George Henry wiped a biscuit around his tin plate, sopping up drippings from the fried eggs. He popped the morsel in his mouth and pushed back from the table. "I reckon this here ain't none of my concern. I'll just mosey on outside and leave you two to your conversations."

"None of your concern, George Henry?" Lorinda Jane wagged a long wooden spoon. "And just where was you last night? You's supposed to watch over your little brother, not give him all them lame ideas. You might as well put them dice in his hands yourself, what with all that talk about heading down to Richmond and getting one of them Pullman jobs."

"I . . . I was at the hospital last night, and ain't nothing wrong with Richmond. I hear they has good jobs." George Henry edged toward the door.

"My Willie can't go running off to no Richmond town, he has a family. He has responsibilities." Tears welled in her eyes. "That man needs to stay right here and take care of this baby and me. How's about you explain him that?"

"I warned him not to play in that game." George Henry glared at his brother. "Some folks is just too thick-headed for their own good."

"We earned us that extra pay," Willie said, "almost a full week's worth. Ain't you forgetting?" He wrapped his arms around Lorinda Jane's waist.

She pushed him away.

"Come on, babe. Was just a couple of dollars—ain't like it was my wages." He reached for her again.

Lorinda Jane stepped back. "It was a dollar and seventy-five cents, all the money I had, and we needs every penny." She wiped her eyes on the hem of her apron. "You wants to raise our baby in this drafty, nasty old chicken coop of a shack? You look around here, Willie T. McConnell. Is this here a fitting and proper place for rearing our young'uns?"

Willie glanced at George Henry. His eyes seemed to plead. "I fixed that leak like you told me, and me and George Henry, we's gathering scraps from down around the yards so's we can build your baby a fitting nursery."

"And we seen a used crib in the window at the mercantile," George Henry said. "What with our extra money from the train wreck, we has enough to buy it right now and set it in that there nursery."

Lorinda Jane sat at the rough-hewn pinewood table. She smoothed a checkered napkin and folded it into a triangle. "You boys used to talk about when you was young'uns up there in Philadelphia, with that big house and all them bedrooms and gas stoves and indoor plumbing and electric lights and schooling I ain't never had . . ." She snapped the napkin open and began folding again. "That's what I wants for my baby."

"And we'll have that again," Willie said. He took her hand. "I promise."

"He's right," George Henry added. "This here depression ain't lasting forever. Mr. Roosevelt, he's a smart man. He'll be putting this country to rights soon enough, and when he does, you and me and Willie here, and that baby, we can all move up north and buy our house back from the bank." George Henry set his foot on a chair and leaned across his knee. "We has family up there. That child will grow up with cousins and aunts and uncles, and me and Willie, we can start our furniture business again."

"You really think so? I mean, you boys ain't just telling Lorinda Jane stories, is you? Tell me you ain't spinning no tall tales."

"Babe, me and George Henry is going over to the yards next day off and we's borrowing that mule and cart from old Samuel. We's gonna load up all the scraps we can find. Then we'll be putting a fine nursery room on this here cabin—"

"And we'll be setting a fine baby crib in there too," George Henry said. "And maybe find us some storybook pictures to nail on them walls."

Lorinda Jane folded into Willie's arms and nuzzled against his chest. "I growed up poor. I knows about being poor, and right now, we's about as poor as I've ever knowed. It ain't right, birthing no baby into a life like that."

* * *

Willie stomped his foot on the hard packed snow in front of the shanty. "We can start up the business again right here."

"Come on," George Henry said, "we's gonna be late again." He shoved his brother down the path toward the rail yards.

"I's serious," Willie said. "We has the skills. Shoot, we was as good as any there was up north."

"And now we's as broke as any there is down south." George Henry scowled. "This ain't no time for walking away from no paying job, even if they ain't paying fair dollar."

Willie kicked up a cloud of snow. "We could start small, just a few jobs—after work, days off, such like that."

"You got your tools?" George Henry asked.

"You know I sold them. They's what paid for my train fare to Virginia."

"And you has how much money saved to buy you some new ones?" George Henry glanced sideways at Willie.

"Aw, you know I don't have nothing saved—but if I did, you and me, we'd be making us some big time money."

George Henry smiled. Their Grandpa Isaac had taught

61

them well. Those Society Hill ladies up in Philadelphia used to line up to buy their nightstands and highboys, their fine cherry tables, and especially their beautiful oak chifforobes. Was Grandpa still alive? He'd have to be close to one hundred years old. Even with that old copper ear trumpet, he could barely hear, and he spent his time in a wheelchair, but right up until the day they'd surrendered the keys to the bank and headed south, Grandpa Isaac still had an eye for craftsmanship.

"You ain't lying, little brother. We was a mighty fine pair, and Grandpa was sure enough proud of our work. The day's coming, when Mr. Roosevelt gets all this depression behind us, we'll open a shop again, and folks'll seek us out for all their fine furnishings.

"Dawn'll be topping them mountains in another hour. We'd best hustle." George Henry pointed toward the east.

George Henry latched onto a broken pallet as they crossed the rail yards, dragging it behind him until they reached the crew shack. It would be there come evening; those pine slats would do fine on a nursery wall.

"We's the first ones in today," Willie said. "Mr. Beckerman's going to be pleased."

"There ain't no pleasing that man." George Henry replied. He entered the shack and started a pot of coffee. One by one, other gandy dancers arrived, slumping into chairs or gathering in small clusters.

A whistle sounded outside the shack. "Grab your bars and line it up," Beckerman bellowed. "There's two miles of track a-waiting."

The track crew cleared the room, picking up tools from the pallets outside the door.

"Straight pay, standard shift. Load 'em up." Beckerman pointed toward the flatcar on the siding.

"But, Boss, we was working that wreck," George Henry said. "What happened to our bonus money?" He glanced at the others lined up beside him. Would they stand as one? Would others speak out?

"You." Beckerman pointed at George Henry. "You and

62

your brother, get over here."

George Henry glanced at Willie, then followed their boss to the far end of the crew train, out of sight of the others.

"You sassed me for the last time, boy." Beckerman shoved George Henry. "Both of you are off my crew. If I catch you on railroad property again, I'll shoot your black ass for trespassing."

"I wasn't sassing you none, Mr. Beckerman. We needs these jobs—" George Henry stepped forward.

Beckerman drew his pistol and thumbed back the hammer. "You got trouble hearing, boy? I said you're fired."

Chapter Eleven

The headlights swept the gravel clearing as McConnell turned the car into the small parking lot carved from the surrounding wilderness. He killed the engine and we were immediately engulfed in darkness the likes of which I've never known before. Slowly, as my eyes adjusted, the murky edges of the forest came into view.

"We found their car over there." McConnell pointed, then stepped out and shined a flashlight at the far end of the clearing. A glow-in-the-dark silhouette of a hiker reflected from a wooden sign posted beside a trail that disappeared into the woods. "The dogs picked up a scent and followed it for a few miles and then it just ended."

I left the door open and walked to the front of the car. My breath hung in the night air like a frozen cloud. Was Erica out there somewhere? It had been what, four days? How long would she be able to survive in that cold? I zipped my coat and shoved my hands in the pockets as I peered into the darkness. "Trails don't just end."

"This one did." McConnell shrugged. "And I wasn't all that surprised. It happens—rain, snow, strong winds, trails doubled back on, trails covered up . . ."

"Lost hikers don't cover their trail."

"Now you're starting to get the picture. You want to walk in a ways and see what we can see?"

I squinted at the shadowy forest. "I'm not much on this outdoors stuff."

"Worried about Bigfoot?" McConnell smiled and raised an eyebrow.

"A little daylight wouldn't hurt."

He turned toward the car. "Tell you what," he said, "I'll meet you out here tomorrow morning, say seven-thirty?"

"A.M.?"

He laughed. "How about something to eat? I'll give Sukey a call."

"Who?"

"My wife." McConnell climbed into the car. "She loves to cook. She works at the hospital in Covington, but she ought to be home by now, and she's always eager to set another place at the table." He pulled his cell phone from his pocket.

A six-pack and a pizza would have done me just fine. The last thing I needed was a plate of collards and ham hocks—or any warmed over hospital food. "Thanks, but she's not expecting me. I don't want to impose—"

"Nonsense. The woman always cooks too much anyway, and she'd be offended if you turned her down."

Trapped. Okay, maybe I could manage an hour or so. Afterward, I could still pick up a six-pack and head back to my room. "You sure? I can grab something at the diner out by the highway, but I wouldn't want to offend."

We drove by the high school. I picked up my car and then followed McConnell into what appeared to be an upscale neighborhood. Two-story brick homes set back from the street on wide, manicured lawns. A few Big Wheels and Radio Flyers dotted the sidewalks. McConnell pulled into a driveway. The doublewide garage door swung open automatically and a light turned on, revealing a Lexus in the other parking space.

I parked in the drive and followed McConnell through the garage and into the house.

"Nice pad," I said, glancing at the tiled floor and custom cabinetry. "They must pay cops well in Clifton Forge."

He laughed. "Come on, I want you to meet my better half."

We entered the kitchen. A beautiful woman, petite, with dark skin and closely cropped hair turned from the stove. She smiled and extended her hand. "Welcome, Mitch. I'm glad to meet you. When Bill called, it made my day. I've been dying to try out this new recipe, and I needed a guinea pig."

"Nice to meet you, too." We shook hands. Something on that stove had my mouth watering. "That sure doesn't smell like hospital food."

"Hospital food?" She cocked her head.

"Your husband mentioned that you worked at the hospital. I guess I assumed it was in the cafeteria."

She laughed and glanced at McConnell. "This is the only kitchen I labor in."

I'd stepped in it, but I wasn't sure how. "Sorry, but when your husband said you worked at the hospital and that cooking was your specialty, I put two and two together. Guess my math isn't so good."

"Math wasn't my strong suit either," she said, patting my forearm, "and that was an easy enough mistake to make." She glanced at McConnell. "Some people put more stock in my cooking than in my career."

"That's not so." He put his arm around her and kissed her cheek. "I just enjoy your cooking more."

She slapped his stomach and pushed him away. "You'd best stop enjoying it so much or I'll be seeing you professionally, fatso."

"Internal medicine." McConnell jerked a thumb toward his wife. "She's the department head."

A doctor? Hell, I hadn't just stepped in it, I'd done a belly flop. "Mrs. McConnell, I mean Doctor McConnell, please accept my apologies—"

"Hush. It's Sukey, and did that nasty husband of mine bring you here so he could play tricks on you? Shame on him." She snatched a wooden spoon from a crock on the island and wagged it at McConnell. "No dessert for you, young man."

He laughed. "She's a hard woman. You ready for a glass of wine?"

I followed him to the living room. McConnell held up a bottle of red and raised his eyebrows.

"Perfect." I settled into an armchair facing the fireplace.

He poured the drinks, handing me one glass and raising the other. "Here's to unsolved mysteries, the lifeblood of journalism."

I toasted and then set my glass on the coffee table. "Speaking of unsolved mysteries, I met your Sergeant Johnson this morning."

He gave a low whistle. "How'd that go?"

"He wasn't exactly a font of useful information. Have you warned the Chamber of Commerce about him?"

McConnell scowled as he walked to the fireplace and took a framed photo from the mantle. He studied the picture as he spoke. "He's okay, just a little rough around the edges. We went to school together, played on the same football team. His family goes way back in these parts."

"That sure makes me feel better," I said.

"What?" McConnell replied.

"Knowing the two of you are old buddies."

The photo was a faded black and white of laborers beside some railroad tracks. I'd seen it before, but where?

"There's a wall around Walter Johnson that I've never been able to penetrate." McConnell returned the picture to the mantle. He paused, as though measuring his words. "The man's an enigma, a mystery refusing to be solved."

"I'll leave that one for you; he's not the mystery I'm chasing." I lifted my glass toward the mantle. It had come back to me—Grandma had that same photo. "What's the picture?"

Handing me the brass frame, he pointed to a young man in the center holding a long pole. "That's my granddaddy, William Terrill McConnell. Folks called him Willie T. I was named for him. He and his brother worked for the railroad. They disappeared back in the thirties. If you want a mystery, try finding them."

"Sounds intriguing. What happened?" I studied the man behind the glass. He had broad shoulders and what looked to be a ready smile. He leaned against a taller man with a similar build and the same smile. Why would Grandma have had that picture? Had she known William, or Willie T., or whatever his name was?

"I won't bore you with ancient rumors," McConnell said, "not tonight anyway. Right now, I'm worried about those kids. They're the ones I want to find." He took the picture from my hand and returned it to the mantel.

"He never mentioned that you found the car." I sipped my wine. Merlot? I'd been on the hard stuff for so long that I'd forgotten how nice a glass of wine could taste.

"Who never mentioned?"

"Johnson," I said. "I asked him what information he had, and he didn't say diddlysquat about any car."

"The state troopers towed it away. I asked them to have their crime lab go over it." McConnell chuckled. "I had the feeling that Walter was more than a little rankled about having to share with the big boys." He picked up the bottle. "You ready for a refill?"

Ann's presence seemed to lurk somewhere behind me, watching over my shoulder. "No thanks." I raised the almost full glass. "I'll be driving, and I'm not confident I can depend on our friend to show me any compassion."

"Good point," McConnell said. "I'm not sure I'd show you any either."

"Are you gentlemen finished with all your crime talk, or shall I put my macadamia mahi mahi on slow simmer?" Sukey leaned against the doorway waving a spatula.

McConnell shot me a quick glance. "I don't know about the newspaper guy, but I'm starving."

* * *

Thursday 10:14 PM

The message light on the phone next to the bed flashed as I entered my hotel room. I picked up the receiver and punched the button.

"Just checking," Ann's voice said. "Did you find out anything more about Erica? When you get this, give me a call. Take care—and behave yourself."

I'd worked with that woman for years, and yet what did I really know about her? Nothing. Apparently, we'd even made love, but I had no memory of it. How could that even happen? She was another mystery to be solved. I dialed her number. She answered on the sixth ring.

"Before you say a word, I've only had one glass of wine and it was with dinner. I'm as sober as a judge."

"Based on the few judges I've known in my time," she replied, "that's not exactly a comforting thought."

"Listen," I said, "something's going on, I'm not sure what, but my antennae are on overload."

"Do the police have any leads?"

"I just had dinner with their head cop. Nice fellow, but his investigation smells worse than last week's mullet. I'm getting ready to head out to one of the local watering holes to see what else I can find."

"You're going to a bar?" Her voice softened. "Is that such a good idea?"

"Ann, this isn't about boozing. Erica's out there somewhere, and I'm going to find her."

"And how're you doing?" she asked. "Are you holding up okay?"

I wasn't, but whose fault was that? "I'm putting up a good front. Nobody here knows I'm her father. They think I'm just here to do a story."

"Mitch, you sound like hell. How about I come up there and give you a hand?"

Ann—here? That night we'd spent together must have given her ideas.

"Mitch, hello? Are you there?"

"Huh? Yeah. Look, everything's fine. I've got it under control."

"Right," she said. "I'll see you tomorrow."

Chapter Twelve

Thursday 11:10 PM

"Is this seat taken?" Her miniskirt slid up dangerously high over firm, slender thighs as she sidled onto the barstool beside me.

Blonde, nice body, and—cowboy boots? Now, that was an interesting fashion statement. I looked around the dimly lit honky tonk that seemed to pass for the only nightlife in town and realized I shouldn't be surprised. I took a sip of my beer.

"You're that reporter fella from Richmond, right?"

"Sorry miss, you seem to have me at a disadvantage."

"My name's Justine." She played with a button on her blouse, exposing more of an already tempting cleavage than I needed to see. "You're Mitch Corsini, right?"

I glanced at the front of my shirt. "Am I wearing a sign?"

She waved to the bartender. "Hey, Ernie, how about a draft?" Then she pointed to my glass. "Are you ready for another?"

"No thanks," I said, shaking my head. "I'm fine."

She smiled. "I'll bet you are."

I've had many a hooker put the moves on me, but none as straightforward as that. I slid my hand to my back pocket. Thank God, my wallet was still there.

"So," she said, "rumor is, you're writing a story about our city. Is that true?"

"Just looking into a couple of missing kids. You know anything about that?" I checked her reflection in the bar mirror. She played with her hair, twisting a strand around her finger. If she noticed that I was watching, she gave no hint.

"Word is, they blew into town, spent a day or two, then,

poof, they vanished."

"Vanished?" I said.

"You know," she said, raising her eyebrows. "They just disappeared."

"But their car didn't."

"You heard about that?" She glanced at me, took a sip of her beer, and stared into the glass. "Folks are saying they left that car to throw everybody off."

I turned and faced her. "It's Justine, right?"

"You remembered!" She grabbed my forearm and squeezed.

"Yeah, well, tell me why I should believe that." I extracted myself from her grip and picked up my beer.

"Believe what?"

"That they'd leave their car to throw everybody off. For what reason, and why abandon a perfectly good car? That's not normal behavior."

"So, who says they're normal?" She giggled.

What was her angle? Was she simply parroting something she'd heard, or did she really have knowledge of what had happened? "On the surface, all evidence seems to point to those woods. They went in. They didn't come out."

"I can tell you this," she said, "if they was in them woods, Sergeant Johnson and his men would have found them. They skipped town, that's for sure, and now they're shacked up somewhere, having themselves a good old time and laughing at all of us here in Clifton Forge."

That seemed to be the prevailing theory. I shrugged. "I guess that makes as much sense as Sergeant Johnson and his dogs missing them."

"Those weren't Walter's dogs."

"Walter?" I glanced at her.

"I meant Sergeant Johnson." She brushed her bangs from her face. "They weren't Sergeant Johnson's dogs. They belonged to the Dawson boys out on Route 220."

"Great," I said. "The dogs weren't Walter's? And I suppose they weren't trained tracking dogs, but that still doesn't explain the car, or where those kids are now."

"Do you think they're still in the woods?" She raised an eyebrow and frowned. "Is that what you're gonna say in your paper?"

"Look," I said, "I don't have a clue where they are. If the story's in the woods, I'll focus on the woods. If they've headed off to Las Vegas, I'll call my editor and see if he'll let me chase the story out there."

"Would you like some company?"

"Huh?" I turned on my bar stool and faced her.

"Vegas," she said. "I've never been there."

When was the last time a gorgeous twenty-something hit on me in a bar? Hell, had that ever happened? I smiled. It sure did the ego good, but life was already too complicated, and nothing in that bar appeared to hold any promise of helping me find Erica. "Vegas is a fast town," I said. "Way too fast for the likes of me."

"Are you saying you couldn't enjoy it for a weekend?" She hooked her finger inside the front of my shirt.

I removed her hand and turned toward the mirror. "Look, maybe you'd do better on down the bar. I'm not shopping—I'm just here for the beer."

She slammed down her mug and stormed out.

What in the hell was that? I caught my reflection in the mirror. It stared back, sober, alone, and just a tad confused. I checked my watch; if I hurried, I could still catch the end of the ballgame on the tube. I tossed down my beer, threw a buck on the bar, and headed outside.

"What took you so long? It's freezing out here." Justine leaned against the driver's side door of my Chevy. She pulled her coat tight and acted out an exaggerated shiver.

She was sure a looker, but in twenty years on the beat, I'd learned that beauty queens didn't generally fall into my lap, not even for money. Besides, lately I'd become a magnet for unwanted complications, and Justine, with her faux leopard skin coat, miniskirt, and suspicious questions suddenly seemed very complicated.

"Can I drop you somewhere?" I nudged her aside and unlocked the car.

She walked her fingers up my chest. "I thought maybe we'd drive around, you know, enjoy the stars. It's a gorgeous night. Then, if you're a good boy, we might end up back at your place."

"Tell me something, darling," I said as I looked her over.

"What's that?" She batted her eyelashes.

"Are you out of high school yet?"

"I'm twenty-four," she said with a huff, "and I've been to New York."

"There's a resume for ya." I held the door open. "Okay, sweetheart, slide in. It's not my night for stargazing, but I'll drop you off at your place."

She scooched to the middle of the seat. I climbed in beside her and started the car. "Okay, where's home?"

"Drive. I'll tell you when to turn." She slid over to the window and folded her arms.

We pulled onto the country road. "Did you grow up around here?" I asked.

"Grandma says our family's been in these parts over a hundred and fifty years."

"I guess that makes you a certified local, doesn't it?" I forced a smile. "Did you attend Clifton Forge High?" I glanced at the headlights growing larger in my rearview mirror.

She nodded. "There's a service station a half a mile up. Turn left there."

A blue light flashed in the rear view mirror. The car behind us gave two quick bursts on the siren.

"Hell, not again." I looked at my speedometer. Forty-eight in a forty-five? "Do they ticket for three miles over in these parts?"

She glanced nervously behind us and shrugged.

I pulled to the shoulder and opened my glove box. The registration was right where I'd left it after my last encounter with law enforcement.

White light beamed into the car and bounced off the window, blinding me to whatever was outside.

"Sir, kindly roll down your window and keep those hands

where I can see them."

Did he want to see my hands, or should I roll down the window? I put my hands on the steering wheel.

The officer tapped my window with his flashlight.

If I reached for the handle, would he think I was going for a gun? I held my hands in front of the window and turned them over, then pointed toward the window crank.

"Open the damned window," he yelled.

I cranked down the glass. "Evening, officer. Is there a problem?"

"License and registration please."

I passed him the documents.

He studied the driver's license for a moment, then leaned and shined his light on Justine. "Evening, ma'am."

She smiled.

"Sir, I gotta ask you to step out of the vehicle." He opened the door. "Will you please come with me?"

I turned to Justine. "Everything will be okay. I'll be right back." I followed the officer to the patrol car.

He opened the back door and motioned for me to get in. I obediently complied. He closed my door and settled into the front seat. The instrument panel had the look of an airplane cockpit: lights and dials, plus a computer screen angled toward the driver's seat. My DMV photo filled one side of the screen. Damn, I was going to hear about those overdue tickets again. I needed a wife, or a secretary— somebody to keep track of all that crap, write the checks, and remember to mail them.

The officer talked on the radio; I couldn't hear the conversation. Finally, he got out and opened my door. "Sorry to keep you, sir. Just a routine check." He handed me my license and registration. "You were going a tad fast back there. Try to hold it down. These mountain roads can sneak up on you flatlanders." He smiled.

"That's it? No ticket?"

"I was going to let you off with a warning, but if you'd rather . . ." He pulled out his citation pad.

"No thanks." I waved away his book. "That warning will

do just fine."

"Take care, Mr. Corsini." The officer tipped his hat. "And drive careful, ya hear?"

I climbed into my car and fastened my seat belt.

"Speeding?" Justine smoothed her miniskirt and crossed her legs.

I shook my head. "I have no idea what that was all about. Your law officers have some mighty peculiar ways." I pointed ahead. "To the gas station and turn left, right?"

Chapter Thirteen

"Lorinda Jane's gonna kill me. She's gonna kill me and nail my hide to the door." Willie dropped the broken pallet he'd been dragging along behind him and faced George Henry. "You couldn't shut that big mouth of yours just this once so's I could keep my job?"

Morning sunlight edged over the far mountain tops and danced in the mist rising from the river. George Henry tossed aside his load of scrap wood and sat down amongst the tall grass. He plucked a dried stalk and chewed on the tip. "Today was our day to be fired. Didn't have nothing to do with what I said. That man wasn't looking for an excuse, his mind was made up."

"But why us?" Willie sat beside him. "Why does we have to be fired? We works hard, and there ain't nobody on that line can move track like you."

"A man fights what he don't want to hear. When I says the white man's getting paid more for the same work, he already knows that. He don't want to hear it, but he knows it's true. He can't say, 'You's wrong, George Henry,' 'cause he knows I ain't."

"He's been scared of you right from the start," Willie said, "but then you had to go and show him up during that train wreck. Maybe, if you'd kept quiet, we'd still be drawing our pay today."

George Henry shook his head. "You know we couldn't carry them injured all that way—more folks would a died. Let me tell you how it is." He turned toward Willie. "You know the Widow Harrell over there on Tenth Street? The one has that big black dog?"

Willie nodded.

"What's that dog do when you walks by her house?"

"You mean how he's running the fence, acting crazy and all like he wants to take a bite out of my leg?" Willie said.

"That's for sure. Now, don't you suppose that dog is doing exactly what Widow Harrell wants him to do? He's protecting her yard. A man can't fault the beast for doing his job, right?"

"I reckon . . ."

"But when you walks by that house and that dog's doing what the Widow Harrell wants him to do, you gets angry just the same, right?"

"Damn right," Willie said. "I throwed a rock at him once when there weren't nobody looking."

George Henry slapped his brother's shoulder. "That's exactly what Mr. Beckerman done this morning."

"He throwed a rock?" Willie frowned.

"Exactly. Mr. Beckerman knows we was right, like you knows that dog's doing his job, but it makes him angry just the same. He can't stomach us being right, but he can't argue neither, 'cause he'd lose, so he throws a rock."

"And that makes him feel all better, but we's still out of work."

"Maybe not," George Henry said. "I know folks what might pay us some real good money for selling moonshine; could be as much as we was making on the tracks, maybe even more. Least ways it'll hold us until I get down to Richmond and see about one of them Pullman jobs." The morning sun warmed the damp field. George Henry leaned on his elbow.

"Little brother, it's time I took me a nap. When I wake up, we'll roust about and find us some more scraps for that nursery. There's no sense going home early and getting your bride all twisted out of sorts. She don't need to know we got fired. I'll visit the Johnsons tonight. You act like nothing happened. When I get home, we'll have us those jobs." George Henry pulled his hat over his face. Maybe they'd do all right, but he had to square it with the Johnsons before they mentioned anything to Lorinda Jane.

* * *

A hunched figure stepped from the cabin porch with a lantern in his raised hand. He peered into the golden light that bathed the small clearing on the mountain. George Henry dove behind a woodpile.

"That nigger's raiding our hooch," the man yelled. "Come around this way, Chester. You'll get a clear shot!"

George Henry hugged the wet ground as a load of buckshot tore into the woodpile, showering him with bark and wood chips. He should have gone home with Willie. He sure should have reconsidered climbing that trail up Dry Branch Creek at night with those crazy Johnson brothers chasing around, blasting anything that moved with that damned scattergun.

"Hey, Mr. Johnson." George Henry waved his hat above the woodpile. "Mr. Marshall sent me to buy him a bottle."

A shotgun blast blew a hole in the hat's brim. George Henry pulled down his arm and pressed his body against the muddy snow. Would the logs protect him? Maybe, but not for long. If he stayed put, he'd die for sure.

"Mr. Marshall don't send niggers to buy his whiskey," Chester said. "You's looking to steal our fixings. Now, show yourself, boy, and let me shoot your thieving black hide."

George Henry glanced through a gap in the logs toward the cabin. The lantern cast too much light to make a break in that direction. Maybe he should race straight into the woods. At least there, he'd have a chance.

"Stand and be shot, boy. It won't hurt much a-tall, least ways, that's what the last feller said 'fore he died." Chester gave a high-pitched cackle.

"Mr. Johnson, if you shoots me, that'll be murder. Mr. Marshall knows I come up here, he'll witness against you at your trial."

"For shooting a nigra? I don't think so. Besides, he's all laid up from that train wreck. He ain't in no condition to testify."

The light moved to his left, casting a glow on the trees behind the woodpile. No place left to run. "Mr. Marshall sent me to fetch him a bottle and while I was here I was to ask you about me and my brother moving some 'shine for you. We could sell to the lining bar crews, make you some extra money."

"Sell my liquor to the nigras? Hell, where would they get the money?"

George Henry slowly rose to his feet, his hands in the air. The night might have been cold, but beads of sweat trickled from his brow. "Lots of 'em already buys blackberry wine from Momma Pearl, that old colored woman back east along the river."

"I know who she is—witch doctor's what I heard."

"Yes, sir, some says she's a haint. That's the one. Well, sir, Mr. Marshall, he'll be needing some of your good stuff, not none of her sipping wine, and I promised him I'd talk to you about sneaking him a pint every now and again. I has the money right here." George Henry patted his inside coat pocket.

"And you's saying you can move our 'shine amongst the colored?"

"Sure enough, Mr. Johnson." George Henry stepped from behind the woodpile, his hands still raised. "I reckon we can move a couple of cases a week, maybe more. Bring you back your empties too."

"How much?" Chester Johnson lowered the shotgun.

"A nickel?"

"A bottle? Hell, I can get a white boy to move it for that."

George Henry took a step toward the Johnson brothers, now both standing in front of the cabin.

Chester leveled his gun. "That's close enough."

He'd be shot or he'd be hired. George Henry lowered his hands. "Your white boys, they moving six, eight cases a week amongst the colored?"

"You'll bring back my empties?" Chester asked.

"Rinsed and ready."

"It'll cost you, boy." Chester pointed at George Henry. "One penny for every bottle you lose."

"That's a fair price, Mr. Johnson. Me and Willie, we won't let you down."

"You do, you're a couple of dead niggers." Chester cocked the shotgun.

Chapter Fourteen

March 1936

"Papa, you're acting like a child. Stop your fussing and please do as I say." Rebecca raised the spoon to his lips. "This chicken soup will help mend those broken bones."

"It didn't help the chicken none." He turned away.

"I declare, you are impossible." She set the bowl on the nightstand. "How are you to recover your strength if you don't eat?"

"That Ella Jenkins cooked it up, didn't she?"

"I beg your pardon?" she said.

"That concoction." He wagged a finger at the bowl. "There's too much pepper, it has Ella Jenkins' markings all over it."

"She's a sweet woman, Papa. She only wants to help."

"She's a man-hungry old witch."

"Sh-h-h. Someone will hear—"

"Then someone oughtn't be leaning their nosy ears against closed doors." He threw a tissue box at the hospital room door.

Nurse Hadley did manage to meddle every now and again. Rebecca smiled as she lifted the spoon. "Just a sip, then you may have one of my oatmeal cookies."

Papa opened his mouth, but held up his hand before the spoon found its mark. "It weren't cooked by that Jenkins woman—I got your word?"

"I was up past eleven last night," Rebecca said. "I did the cooking after I finished my studies. You'll be pleased to know I'm earning extra credit just for putting up with all your cantankerous fussing."

"That woman's had her sights on me since before your momma passed, God rest her soul. She's husband-hunting."

"She's just lonely, and she cooks for everyone in the hospital, not just grumpy old railroad engineers."

"When are the funerals?"

Rebecca recoiled. "What funerals?"

"Axel Brown and Dan Potter, them two that was killed in the wreck. I need to get free of this contraption and go to their funerals." He reached for the ropes holding his leg in the air. "I knew their families."

"I knew them too," she said. "I conveyed your regrets and your sympathies. They buried them the day before yesterday. Now, leave those pulleys be, you'll ruin your alignment."

"Why didn't you tell me, child?" He let go of the rope and flopped onto his pillow. "Nobody tells me anything. I should have been there. That's the least I can do for fellow railroad men and their families."

"You were out cold most of the day, sleeping like a newborn, and I did tell you. Don't you remember how hard it rained? I talked about what a nasty day it was to bury a loved one. You just grunted."

"Where's my cookie?"

"Not until you take your soup."

"It's a curse, you know, being as good looking as I am. She wouldn't be chasing me if'n I was homely like them Johnson boys up on the mountain."

"Eat." She shoved the spoon into his mouth.

* * *

The small classroom filled as young women in starched uniforms took their seats. Rebecca opened her notebook and pulled a pencil from her pocket. "I'm going up there today, right after class," she whispered.

"Then you're a fool, Rebecca Marshall. No self-respecting girl, at least none that's young, white, and unmarried, has any business nosing around those colored shanties." Irene scanned the room, and then focused on

Rebecca. "What if something happened?"

"You're being silly. Nothing will happen. I'm just going to find the man that helped my papa and give him a proper 'thank you.' He deserves that much."

"And he'll see those blonde locks and figure he deserves a whole lot more than a thank you."

"Why are you always so negative?" Rebecca said. "They're just folks, same as us. What'd the coloreds ever do to you?"

"I'll tell you what they did." Irene leaned across the aisle. "Momma said when she was young, one followed her home." She lowered her voice. "He stayed back a half block or so, but he followed her every turn, right up to Grandpa's house."

"And then?" Rebecca frowned.

"Well, nothing, I mean, he didn't actually do anything, but wouldn't that be creepy, having one of them trailing you, like some jungle beast on the prowl?" Irene's eyes opened wide.

"And I suppose he was still there waiting when your momma came out the next morning?"

"No, silly." Irene shook her head. "Of course not. Momma said Grandpa chased him off with his shotgun. That colored boy didn't dare show his face in our neighborhood again."

Rebecca retrieved a brown paper sack from beneath her chair. She held it open. "Want an oatmeal cookie? I baked for Papa and had extras. It's too much work to mix up a small batch when, with hardly any extra effort, you can have a few dozen."

Irene laughed and took the cookie. "You know what'll happen if Doctor West catches us eating in class again?"

"Bedpans?" Rebecca giggled.

"Oh yeah." Irene smiled. "Sh-h-h. Here comes old 'Iron Pants' Hadley." She tucked the cookie into her handbag and opened her textbook.

* * *

Irene skipped down the hospital steps, falling in stride beside Rebecca. "It might be dark when you're ready to come off that mountain. You can't be up there alone after dark."

"Then come with me. It'll be fun, an adventure." Rebecca grabbed Irene's arm.

"No way I'm going up there," Irene said. "If my daddy was to find out, he'd tan my hide."

"Your daddy's too feeble, and you're too old for a spanking anyway. Come on." Rebecca tugged her sleeve. "We'll only stay long enough to say 'thank you.'"

"No, and you'd better not go either," Irene said. "I've a mind to tell your papa. That's what I ought to do."

"Fine. Then go on home and be done with it. But, if you ever tell a soul . . ." Rebecca shook her finger.

"Oh, stop worrying. I won't tell."

"Promise?" Rebecca cocked her head and scowled.

"Promise—but you be off that mountain before nightfall, you hear?" Irene poked her in the ribs.

"Yeow." Rebecca pulled away and laughed. "I'll tell you all about it tomorrow. Now, remember, mum's the word."

"And home before dark?"

"Cross my heart." Rebecca drew an "X" across her breast. Irene waved and turned the corner.

Rebecca walked alone for several blocks. The houses ended where the concrete sidewalk turned into a footpath beside the river. She and Irene had played there as children, racing through the fields and ducking into the forest in search of castles and knights in shining armor. Now, the trees formed a boundary beyond which proper ladies never ventured. The snow-covered path intersected a cart track that disappeared into the forested mountainside. She shifted her books to her other arm and began the climb.

The cart track wound up the pine-covered slopes. Rebecca paused at a switchback and caught her breath. Once, as a child of eleven or twelve, she'd come this far. It had been easier then. Mountains were always easier when they held dreams and fantasies. How could it be so warm in the dead of winter? She fanned herself and loosened her cloak. A breeze stirred. Rebecca took a deep breath and continued.

Eventually, the path ended in a small, rock-strewn clearing surrounded by winter-bare hardwoods and a few evergreen pines. Smoke curled from a stovepipe jutting like a broken spear through the tarpaper roof of a scrap-wood shanty. Tin sheeting covered a portion of the front wall. On one side, a room addition had been framed, but not yet enclosed. Chickens scurried about the yard, pecking at clumps of grass protruding through the snow. A ramshackle henhouse leaned against the hillside, seeming almost too tired to stand on its own.

So, this was where he lived. She was no stranger to poverty, white or black, but she'd never been so close to such a shanty. Maybe Irene was right. Maybe she had no business that far up the mountain. What if George Henry didn't care to hear her gratitude? She started to leave.

"Afternoon, Miss Rebecca. Is you lost?"

Rebecca turned.

A slender woman stood on the porch. Shadows hid her face. As she stepped into the sunlight, she lowered a scarf from her head, uncovering tight cornrow braids. Her ebony complexion glistened. Her features were more beautiful than any Rebecca had ever known.

"Have we met?" Rebecca asked.

"No ma'am." The woman stepped off the porch. "But I knows you. I works for Miss Nelson, your neighbor lady. I cleans her house, does some cooking. I sees you out the window when you's coming home from that hospital."

"Yes, that's where I know you from." Rebecca nodded. "I've seen you sweeping her porch, but always at a distance, and you always have your head covered."

"Keeps the dust off."

"I . . . I'm not lost." Rebecca wrapped her arms around her books, pulling them close to her chest. "I'm looking for a man named George Henry."

"He in trouble?" She placed her hands on her hips. "Did he speak out of turn, say something he got no right saying in front of a white lady?"

"No, no, nothing like that." Rebecca waved aside the accusation. "You seem to have me at a disadvantage. You know my name . . ."

"Sorry, ma'am. They calls me Lorinda Jane." She smiled. "So, why is you looking for George Henry? He gets wild sometimes, but he's a good man. He don't mean no harm."

"I wanted to thank him."

Lorinda Jane squinted and raised her hand, shielding her eyes. "What for?"

"For saving my father's life. Papa was injured in a train wreck. His leg was broken and he had severe bleeding. The doctor said he would have died, had your George Henry not known what to do. He patched and splinted Papa as good as any doctor would. Because of him, Papa is alive today."

"He done all that? Lord, that boy don't talk none about his railroading job. He must have forgot all about how he mended your pa."

"Well, if he is here, I would like to thank him and then I'll be on my way." Rebecca glanced around the clearing. "I should be off the mountain before dark."

"Lord, Miss Rebecca, there's days I wished I was off'n this mountain before dark." She laughed. "I suppose I knows what you means. But he and my Willie, they ain't up from the yards just yet. If'n you'd like, I'll tell him you stopped by to say, 'thank you.'"

"No, for saving Papa's life, I need to tell him in person. I'll wait. That is, if it's no bother."

"Then come on and set a spell." Lorinda Jane returned to the porch and pulled two wooden chairs into the sunlight. "I can use the rest myself. Now that I's expecting, I gets tired so easily."

"You're pregnant? My, it doesn't show."

"Maybe it don't show none, but I sure feels it. Now, you set on down and tell Lorinda Jane all about that nursing school. Someday, when this here young'un is all growed," she patted her tummy, "I'm gonna get me some schooling too, learn my letters and such, so's I can be educated, like George Henry and my Willie."

Chapter Fifteen

Friday 7:28 AM

The phone jarred me awake. I rolled over and glanced at the clock. Who'd be calling at that hour? I buried my face in the pillow as I lifted the receiver and dropped it back on the cradle. It was bad enough I'd spent the night tossing and turning, trying to remember the last time I'd seen my daughter, now some clown was dialing wrong numbers at the crack of dawn. I pulled the pillow over my face and closed my eyes.

The phone rang again.

I could hang it up, but whoever it was, they'd probably just call again. I grabbed the receiver. "It's six AM. What the hell do you want?"

"It's seven-thirty, Mitch. Are you awake?"

"Who is this?"

"It's Bill McConnell. I'm at the trailhead, like we agreed, but I don't have all day. I have a playoff game tonight and I need to be at the school this afternoon."

Slowly, I sat up. "This is why I didn't join the Marines, McConnell. I don't do five AM reveilles."

"You've got ten minutes to shower and dress. I'll see you in about twenty." He hung up.

Twenty minutes? He needed to manage his expectations. I started a pot of coffee and shuffled into the bathroom.

* * *

Friday 7:38 AM

Sunlight glared through the Chevy's dirty windshield. I found a napkin in a wadded fast food bag on the floor and wiped a spot clean in front of the steering wheel. The road out of town meandered around the mountain. I kept an eye on the speedometer.

Ann's phone call played through my mind as I drove toward the parking lot by the trailhead. Was she really coming to Clifton Forge? Maybe she'd have word on that DNA test. Hell, if I lost that one, I'd be eating drive-through burgers for the next eighteen years. Maybe that Bridget woman would hit the bars again and pick up some rich jerk who'd marry her and adopt her little crumb snatcher.

A car appeared in the rearview mirror. I checked the speedometer again, glancing up as a squirrel darted in front of me. I swerved, sliding sideways, then regained control. The car behind me kept its distance. I turned on my blinker and kicked up gravel as the Chevy pulled into the small parking lot.

"Twenty minutes," McConnell said. He tapped his watch. "Right on the dot. Man, you look beat. Rough night?"

I took a sip of coffee, burning my tongue. "Nah, just a complication from back home that decided to follow me here. I'll have it settled soon enough." I removed the lid and blew into my cup. "You said your guys were all over these woods. What do you expect to find today that they couldn't?"

McConnell held up a small digital camera. He clicked my picture and then turned the camera around, holding the preview screen toward me. "See what I mean? Beat, as if you'd been up all night. You really should have slept in this morning."

"What? Don't I remember somebody waking me around six?" I raised an eyebrow.

McConnell laughed and tucked his camera in a small waist pack. "It was seven-thirty, and I don't have any expectations about finding anything, other than a few Styrofoam cups my deputies might have tossed. However, you never know. Ten people can walk under the same tree and never see the black snake curled on the limb."

"You had to bring up snakes?" I rubbed my neck.

"Relax," he said. "It's too cold. They're still hibernating."

"Smart critters." I crumpled my empty coffee cup and tossed it in the Chevy.

"Ready?" McConnell broke off a dead limb to use as a hiking staff and headed down the trail. "You should see this place in a couple of months." He pointed with his stick. "Dogwoods, azalea, rhododendron— almost overnight these dull winter woods transform into the most amazing palette of colors you'd ever want to see."

"Sounds like a great story—all that springtime in the mountains azalea blossom crap." I took a deep breath as the trail turned uphill.

McConnell glanced over his shoulder. "I don't mean to take anything away from your flat country, but it's really something special when these snow-fed streams are tumbling through a forest splashed with flowering pinks and reds."

"Great. Send me a picture." I bent over and clutched my side, gasping for air.

The trail climbed, steeply at first, and then it leveled for another quarter mile or so. The deputy had been right; with the trees bare of leaves we had good visibility throughout the forest. Features such as rocks and shrubs were easy to pick out, even a hundred yards away. Any bit of clothing or man-made material not camouflaged to blend in would be visible as well. Had Erica come this way? What if she really was shacked up, as the deputy said, doing what college kids do? I tried to wipe the image from my mind. Why couldn't she be back at school, doing what college kids were supposed to do?

"Hey, Bill," I called. "You know a girl named Justine? She would have graduated high school seven or eight years ago, if she graduated."

McConnell glanced my way. "Not a blonde, by any chance? Nice figure, cheerleader face, cowboy boots?"

"Yeah, that's the one. There can't be two of them in a town this small."

"Actually," he said, "she's a twin."

"No kidding? Wow, talk about one of life's little fantasies."

"I'm not one to judge," McConnell said, "but if I had to

call it, I'd say she's the evil twin. How in the world did you run into her?"

"She tried to pick me up. Is she turning tricks, or something?"

McConnell stopped and turned to face me. "Are you sure she was trying to pick you up?"

"What do you mean? You don't think a young, good looking girl could possibly go for a guy like me?" I patted my stomach. "I'm in pretty descent shape—for a guy my age."

McConnell rolled his eyes. "No, it's not that. I'm sure there are plenty of twenty-something-year-old women who would see you as a good catch: seasoned, wealthy, sophisticated man of the world . . ."

"You can forget that wealthy part; I have an ex-wife."

He laughed and continued up the trail. A few moments later he stopped again and motioned to me. "Mitch, come here."

I caught up to him, then put my hands on my hips and gulped in several deep breaths.

"Look." He pointed toward something just off the trail.

A clue the police had missed? I came closer and searched the woods to our front. "What?"

"There." He poked the end of his stick into a blackened mound of . . . . "Bear scat," McConnell said. He gave me what looked to be a very self-satisfied smile. "It's not too early for a few of them to come out of hibernation, especially if they're second year males."

"And that matters because . . . ?"

McConnell leaned on his hiking staff. "First hibernation without mama. They're kind of lonely, I suppose, plus those hormones start working. You know, they wake up with an itch that needs scratching."

I unobtrusively scratched myself. "The poor guy needs a crisp twenty."

McConnell raised an eyebrow.

"Then he could hook up with Justine. I'll bet she could put a smile on old Smokey's face."

"You have her pegged right, but for the wrong reasons."

McConnell tipped his ball cap back on his head and started out again.

I stared at the bear poop. What distinguished that unspectacular collection of fecal matter from what a deer might deposit, or a wild dog, or even a mountain lion? Hell, did they have mountain lions up here? I quickly scanned the woods behind me and then I ran up the trail. "Hey, McConnell, wait up."

"Trash over there." He picked up something and put it in his pocket. "Energy bar wrapper. Careless hikers. Look at how the leaves are disturbed, even off the trail." He tapped his stick on the side of the trail. "A fair sized group came through here—our search party, most likely."

"One of your officers mentioned that the boy had hiked the Appalachian Trail before. Is this it?" I unbuttoned my collar. Winter in the mountains was warming up. I should have worn a lighter shirt.

"The AT's several miles to the east. He might have hiked this trail before, no way of knowing, but it's not a part of anything bigger. See that blaze?" McConnell pointed to a small slash of orange paint on the trunk of a tree. "The AT blaze is white, spur trails off the AT are blue. We're on a local route, and not one that gets much traffic."

A deer crashed through a tangle of brush below us and dashed across the trail, disappearing over a ridge to our front.

"Something sure spooked her," McConnell said. "Must be a dog or coyote running that creek bed."

Or a mountain lion? I drew closer to McConnell as I searched the forest. "So, if they came up here to hike and the bloodhounds tracked them along this trail, how was it the dogs never figured out where they went? Am I missing something?"

"They weren't bloodhounds," McConnell said, "just local hunting dogs Sergeant Johnson calls on from time to time. He said it wasn't unusual for them to lose the track; wild animals cross the trail and mix the scents, rains wash away the smells, or the dogs just lose interest."

"You're kidding, right?" I said. "How do you tell those

kids' parents that the damned search dogs lost interest?"

McConnell walked faster. "We've been all over these woods. My people are doing everything they can."

"Whoa, slow down." I hurried to catch up. "I'm not criticizing you, but I don't have a lot of confidence in the dedication of your Sergeant Johnson."

"He's not bad; you just have to take him with a large dose of salt. Back in high school he was the guy who always had the inside information, the hot scoop, the straight skinny. You know the type?"

I nodded. "It seems those are the ones who always manage to land in my lap, like process servers . . ."

McConnell glanced at me.

"It's a long story." I waved the back of my hand. "Tell me about Justine. You said I had the right read on her, but for the wrong reason. What's that about?"

McConnell pulled a plastic bottle from his waist pack and took a long drink. He wiped his mouth on his sleeve and looked me in the eye. "She's no angel, Mitch, not by a long shot, but I'll guarantee you she's no hooker."

"She could have fooled me." I took off my hat and ran my fingers through hair damp with sweat. "At least now I don't have to worry about getting hauled in for cavorting with a woman of ill repute."

"No, that cute little number you were messing with isn't for sale." He offered me the water bottle. "Justine Crawford is Sergeant Johnson's woman. He won't put up with her running around, and that's a fact."

Chapter Sixteen

March 1936

Moonlight shimmered on the mountain beyond the Jackson River. Lorinda Jane pointed down the path. "Look yonder, Miss Rebecca. Here they comes."

"Where?" Rebecca peered into the darkness. Two men emerged from the shadows, one tall and muscled, with broad shoulders, the other shorter, but with a similar build. They trudged silently, slumped from what must have been a long day working the rails.

Lorinda Jane waved. "George Henry, George Henry, come on up here. You has a visitor."

The taller man pushed his hat back and straightened, seeming to peer into the gathering darkness.

"Come on," Lorinda Jane said, "she won't bite none." She turned to Rebecca and smiled. "He'll be on his best behavior, I give you my word. If he ain't, I'll take my skillet to his thieving skull." She winked.

The men stopped in front of the cabin.

"This here's Miss Rebecca Marshall," Lorinda Jane said. "You done saved her daddy's life and didn't bother telling me nothing about it. She come to thank you." She turned to Rebecca. "Me and Willie's going to step inside. I has to check on that pullet I has roasting. You's welcome to stay for supper, if'n that would please you."

Rebecca glanced at Willie and George Henry. Two men home from a hard day of driving steel didn't need to share their meal with a stranger, especially a white woman. Besides, she'd probably feel even more out of place than she did right then. "Thank you, no. I must say my piece and be gone. Folks down the mountain are expecting me." That wasn't true. Would Lorinda Jane see through her fabrication? If so, she didn't let on.

"Miss Rebecca said she wanted to be off this mountain 'fore dark," Lorinda Jane said. "Since the two of you sauntered on up here like you had no place to be, the least one of you can do is make sure she gets home safe."

"That won't be necessary," Rebecca said. "I know my way." She looked into George Henry's eyes. "I came to thank you for taking care of my father, Clarence Marshall. The doctor said you saved his life."

George Henry snatched off his hat, twisting the brim as he clutched it. "Just done what any man would do, ma'am."

"Not according to Doctor West. He said it took a great deal of skill to splint up Papa's leg and stop all that bleeding. He tells us nursing students we should take a lesson from what you did."

"Don't reckon there's much I could teach no nurses, but I'm glad your pa's mending good and proper."

"Yes, he is healing quite well, thanks to you. Oh, and here." She handed George Henry the paper sack. "I baked oatmeal cookies for Papa and there were extras. I thought you might enjoy them." She glanced at Lorinda Jane, who stood in the doorway, her arms folded. "Well," she said, "I really must be going."

Rebecca stumbled as she stepped off the porch. George Henry caught her, lifting her as though she were a small bird and gently setting her on her feet in front of him. He towered above her.

"Miss Rebecca needs escorting down that mountain, George Henry. You make sure she gets home safe, and don't you be disrespecting her no way, you hear?"

"What are you talking about, woman?"

"I'm talking about no colored man being seen walking beside a fine, upstanding white woman, especially at night. You minds your manners, you walks a step behind, and you gets her home safe. If I hears different, my flapjack skillet will be finding that skull of yours."

* * *

96

"Come, walk beside me." Rebecca motioned George Henry forward. "It feels strange having you trailing along back there."

"Lorinda Jane said I shouldn't disrespect you none—"

"And that was sweet of her, but I need that lantern shining on the path ahead, not the one I've already stumbled over."

George Henry came alongside Rebecca.

"Does she really come at you with a skillet?"

He laughed.

"I'm serious, George Henry. Even a small woman such as her could cause a concussion, or worse."

He glanced at her and smiled. "That's just her way of talking, ma'am. She ain't a hard woman. Shoot, she has to look the other way every time she snatches up one of her hens and twists off their little heads for the roasting pan."

Rebecca laughed. "She seemed so strong, like she wasn't a woman to be trifled with."

George Henry ducked under an overhanging branch. "I don't reckon I understands a whole lot about women, but I figure a man's got to know when to be trifling and when to just shut his mouth and walk a step behind."

Was that the old south talking? She'd grown up around many coloreds, but knew them only in passing. They'd always been polite, extremely so at times. Why had she never given it a thought? Was she supposing that it was simply as things were meant to be? Yet, to fit into her world, people like George Henry had to bite their tongues, swallow their words, and quietly walk a step behind. She sighed.

A golden circle of light from George Henry's lantern bounced along the tree trunks, casting shadows across the path.

"How long have they been married?" she said.

"Who's that, Miss Rebecca?"

"Willie and Lorinda Jane. How long have they been married?"

"Be two years this May. They met at a social over at the Second AME Church, knew right from the start they was going to get hitched. Was like the good Lord done chose them for one another, and now they's having this baby. Me and Willie, we's building a nursery onto the house."

"I saw the construction," she said. "It appears to be coming along nicely. When is the baby due?"

"June, most likely. Me and Willie figure we'll have that nursery done by April, if we has the money."

"I'm sure Lorinda Jane will appreciate that." Rebecca gathered her coat close around her as a chill wind carried up from the river. "Papa said you told him you had medical training in the army. Is that right?"

"Not exactly, ma'am. Was my pa had the training. He was in France during the war; was a field medic. They gave him a medal. I have it in a box up at the house."

"You should be proud of that. I'd like to see it one day. Well, you certainly learned a lot from your papa. Doctor West was very impressed."

George Henry seemed to scan the star-filled sky, then he stopped and pointed toward the opening in the trees ahead. "Cart path yonder goes on down to the river, ma'am. It'll take you to the footpath."

"You won't walk with me the rest of the way?"

"Lorinda Jane said don't disrespect you none by being seen with you, so I'll say my goodnights right here. Evening's plenty bright. I'll shut off the lantern and keep watch until you's out of sight."

Moonlight glistened on his dark skin, highlighting his chiseled features. "It isn't disrespectful for a man to escort a lady home on such a dark night. I appreciate your company."

"Just the same, ma'am, I'd best be watching from here."

She nodded. He might walk a step behind, but not out of weakness. George Henry took command, that much was apparent, even in matters such as this, where, at least in society's eyes, she was supposed to hold all the power.

"Very well. Thank you for escorting me down the mountain and thank you again for helping my father."

"No trouble, ma'am."

"Give my best to Lorinda Jane. Oh, and please ask her to

come see me next time she's in town."

"I'll do that, ma'am." George Henry tipped his hat. "Y'all watch your footing. The snowmelt will be freezing again in this cold. Could get a mite slippery."

Rebecca left the woods and turned toward the lights of town. Patches of snow around clumps of dried grass sparkled in the moonlight. Wind swirled through the open fields, carrying dried leaves aloft. She clutched her books and walked faster.

Once on the sidewalk, Rebecca turned and looked toward the woods. Had he watched her all the way or was he already climbing that mountain? No light flickered in the dark tree line. Had he only carried the lantern for her benefit? Of course he'd find that path familiar, whether by moonlight or in the dark of night.

* * *

"You's coming from the wrong direction."

She jumped and turned toward the voice as Chester Johnson stepped from the shadow of a railroad building.

Rebecca gasped. "Chester Johnson, what in blazes has gotten into you, popping out at a girl that way? You like to scared me to death."

"You ain't coming from the hospital. Hospital's yonder."

"Yes, Chester. I think I know where the hospital is." Rebecca turned and continued walking.

"You wasn't coming from no hospital and there ain't no houses yonder." He hurriedly caught up, falling in step beside her. "Where's you coming from?"

"I don't see where that's any of your concern." She quickened her pace.

"I got my pickup running again. This coming Saturday, you want I should come by? We could catch us a moving picture show over in Covington. There's a new Gene Autry picture playing." He reached for Rebecca's schoolbooks. "Here, let me carry them."

She pulled free from his grasp. "I don't need any help, thank you."

"*The Big Show*, that's what they's calling it. The fellers down at the gas station was saying how it's the best picture he's done yet: six-shooters blazing and fists a flying." Chester sparred with an imaginary foe.

"Whatever are you talking about?"

"The Gene Autry moving picture show. Tell you what, I'll throw in an RC Cola and you can have your own sack of Milk Duds."

"I told you, I have studies. If I finish my studies, I'll be at the hospital with Papa. I'm sorry, I don't have time for picture shows." She walked faster.

"You been studying today, Miss High-and-Mighty?"

Rebecca glanced over her shoulder. Chester pointed toward the mountain. "What was you studying yonder in them woods?"

A man like him wouldn't understand, and it would be best for George Henry if he never found out. She turned on her heel and hurried home.

Chapter Seventeen

"How'd you and Sukey end up together?" I asked. "Were you a washout from medical school or something?" I settled against a tree and bit into my granola bar.

McConnell perched cross-legged on a flat rock. "We've come about two miles, maybe one more to go." He sliced an apple with his pocketknife.

"Ah, you don't want to answer?"

He laughed. "You almost had it right. We did meet in college, but I would never have been accepted to medical school—can't stand the sight of blood." McConnell handed me a slice of apple. "I was a starving graduate student, English major, just trying to make ends meet. One day I saw a poster in the student union asking for volunteers to serve as practice patients for the med students. The gig paid a small stipend, plus free meals in the cafeteria on days you volunteered, so I became a pin cushion for hire."

"She listened to your heart, found it to be pure, and the rest is history?"

"Not quite." McConnell cleared his throat. "This doesn't get repeated, right?"

I drew an "X" over my heart.

"There wasn't a girl within two hundred miles even half as pretty as Sukey, not in pre-med or in the English department, so when she needed to practice drawing blood, I jumped to the head of the line."

"Very touching," I said. "She saw you and it was love at first sight."

McConnell glanced at the ground and shook his head.

"When she stuck me I passed out—fainted dead away."

"Clever." I nodded in feigned approval. "Good first impression. I'll have to try that one of these days."

"Right," McConnell said. "Anyway, she loosened my collar, wiped my brow, did whatever wannabe doctors do when their patients go belly up." He took a bite of apple. "After I regained consciousness she pulled a chair beside my cot, held my hand, and smiled the most beautiful smile I'd ever seen."

"And then you got her phone number?"

"No, then I puked in her lap. If I recall, the cafeteria had chili dogs that day."

"Nice touch, McConnell." I chuckled. "I never would have come up with anything that creative."

"Laugh all you want," he said, "it won me the sympathy vote." He folded his knife and slipped it in his pocket. "You ready for a little more walking?"

I braced against the tree and pushed myself up, then brushed leaves and dirt from my trousers. My legs seemed to be asking what the hell I thought I was doing. Ann was right—time to cut the booze and burgers and hit the gym. Yeah, easier said than done.

We settled into a steady gait. The trail, such as it was, followed the crest of a ridgeline. Flat ground—finally.

"I'm curious," McConnell called over his shoulder. "Did she say she wanted to make it with you?"

"Who?"

"Justine. You said she was coming on to you. It doesn't make any sense."

"Thanks, I'd almost started feeling good about myself again. I appreciate that reality check."

McConnell laughed. "Not what I meant." He tapped the downhill side of the trail with his hiking staff. "It drops off sharply for the next mile. You slide off; you're on your own. I don't have ropes and I don't much feel like climbing all the way down to haul your carcass back up."

"Gee, McConnell, whatever happened to 'serve and protect'?" I inched closer to the uphill side of the trail. The foot or so of leeway might have been fine if the drop was only eight feet, but one slip there and I'd bounce a long way before a river rock broke my fall. With one eye on the drop-off, I followed McConnell as the trail wrapped around the next point.

Finally, McConnell held up his hand. "We're here."

On our left, the ground rose gently toward the crest of a ridge, creating a broad, forested plane, while to the other side an almost vertical drop of sixty feet or more ended in a rocky creek. Beyond the creek, the ground rose again, though not as steeply, forming a ridge parallel to the one we had hiked.

"The dogs went crazy right here," McConnell said, "then they lost the scent." He poked the trail with his walking stick. "Sergeant Johnson took the dogs up the trail another hundred yards or so and found what might have been a scent running a few miles that way to a dirt road." McConnell pointed. "But he didn't think the dogs had a good lock on those kids after they left here."

I tossed a pebble and counted to myself. On 'four,' it landed in the creek below. "How about there? Did he take the dogs down there too?"

"No, but if the kids had fallen or, more likely, if one had fallen and the other somehow climbed down to help them, don't you think there'd be some visible trace, blood on the rocks, scattered clothing, or gear, or something?"

"Two hikers," I said, scratching my head. "One gets hurt, the other goes for help—there's a blood trail. They get attacked by bears—there are at least bodies. What am I missing?"

McConnell glanced toward the sky. "I don't know, helicopters? UFOs?"

"Did you take the dogs up there?" I pointed to the flat, open high ground.

"There, and everywhere else we could get to within two hundred yards."

"What's up ahead?" I said.

McConnell shrugged.

"You don't know? You grew up here, you hike these

woods, you study the stupid bear poop, and you don't know what's up that trail?" I raised my hands in disgust and turned away.

"Never went up there." McConnell pulled a map from his pocket. "According to this it runs south another four or five miles, then ends on one of the county roads. The forest service cut the trail years ago. Apparently, somebody thought it was a good idea, but between the hiking over at the state park and the trails just across the valley in the Blue Ridge, this one never caught on."

"How much farther to the road where they lost the scent?"

McConnell nodded toward the trail ahead. "It's a few more miles, but keep in mind, for every mile we go in, we're adding that to our hike out. You sure you're up for it?"

My legs ached. I'd spent most of the morning catching my breath and trying to keep up. However, Erica might still be out there, somewhere.

"I'm fine." I waved dismissively. What the hell, maybe just around the bend we'd find the clue we needed.

The trail continued with the ridgeline on one side, the creek on the other. We headed downhill. I tried not to imagine our return journey. I was a journalist, not a mountain climber. I interviewed people, took cryptic notes concerning newsworthy events and then wrote compelling stories. Somehow, I didn't sense an interview pending at the end of the trail.

"You notice anything different?" McConnell said. He seemed to be almost jogging as we clambered down the slope.

"Yeah, we're going downhill," I shouted. "Other than that, I see the same damn trees, the same dead leaves . . . oh, wait, this is different." I bent and peered behind a boulder.

McConnell hurried to my side. "What is it? What'd you find?" He craned his neck.

I straightened and started walking again. "Nothing. I thought I'd discovered some fresh dinosaur dung, but I guess I was wrong."

"I'm going to enjoy the hike back, Corsini, I really am." He laughed and whacked me with his walking stick. "I've been going easy on you, but no more."

"Can I ask you something?" I said.

He shrugged, as though trying to make up his mind, then said, "Shoot."

"Do you follow NASCAR?"

"NASCAR? What kind of question is that?"

"Well, do you?"

"No."

"Not at all?"

McConnell hooked the trunk of a tree with one hand and swung down a rocky step. "Let's see, they line up a bunch of noisy machines, go around in a big circle, and then do what?" He didn't wait for my answer. "Oh, yeah, they do it all again. Now, if you put in a foul line and a three-point circle you'd have my attention, but a bunch of good ol' boys racing hotrods is not my idea of entertainment."

Ann had to be abnormal, but then I couldn't recall anything about her that fit the stereotype. She'd better not be pregnant. I needed a solution to one unintended pregnancy, not the addition of another. She'd really taken advantage of me that night.

"This trail's getting almost too overgrown to continue." McConnell banged at the tall weeds with his stick. "And I need to be heading back. I have a ballgame to get ready for."

"How far have we come?"

McConnell studied his map. "Since our last stop? About a mile."

"Where are we?" I looked over his shoulder.

"Right about here." He pointed on the map. "See this? It's an old wagon path coming from town. It crosses this trail somewhere up ahead. We're no more than a mile or so from Clifton Forge as the crow flies." He looked up, seeming to search the woods ahead. "Rumor has it moonshiners set up a still around here fifty or sixty years ago, probably used that old road to move their booze."

"Anything there now?"

McConnell folded the map and tucked it away. "Maybe a cabin or two. I haven't been there in twenty years." He pointed across the ridge on our left. "Had family over that way; forest fire burned them out in the Fifties."

He turned toward the direction we'd come. "Look," he said, "I really need to get going. Are you ready to head back?"

I shook my head. "Leave me the map. I'm going to poke around for awhile, maybe see what's up there."

"Right." McConnell folded his arms across his chest. "I already have two college kids missing. My reputation will go in the tank if I follow that by losing some big city reporter."

"I know my way out. I've been paying attention. The cars are that way." I pointed.

McConnell drew back, seemingly startled. "Lucky guess."

"I get paid to observe and report." I described our route to the parking lot.

"Okay," he said, "but take the water and the map—and you give me a call the minute you get to the hotel." McConnell studied the sky. "You have maybe another hour, then you need to be heading out or you'll lose daylight, you got that?"

I checked my watch and nodded.

"And watch the poison ivy." He pointed to a vine beside my foot, smiled, and then headed up the trail.

I searched out a tree with no offending plant life clinging to it and settled for a few moments' rest with the map and a granola bar. If Erica and her friend had come this far, which direction would they have gone? Up to the wagon path and back to town? What about their car, they'd still need to get to the parking lot. Did they have a plan, or were they just exploring? And what about those cabins McConnell had mentioned? I stood and brushed myself off. Maybe I'd find something up ahead that would give some hint as to where they'd gone.

Knee high brush tugged at my legs as I followed the overgrown path. Any landmarks to help me on the way back? I searched the woods—nothing but trees. Great, everything looked the same. I'd best stay on the trail.

I hiked another thirty minutes, then stopped and leaned against a tree as I scanned the woods. Nothing remarkable, just more of the same. McConnell had said I had about an hour. If I turned around now, my hour would be up about the time I got back to where he'd left me and I'd still have enough daylight to make it to the parking lot. I uncapped the water bottle and took a drink.

Movement flashed across the edge of my vision. An animal? I scanned the woods along the path, finding nothing . . . except a sudden uneasy sense that I was no longer alone. I ducked and then peered around the tree. There, two hundred yards distant, a flash of color, dull red. Had McConnell mentioned how long ago that bootlegging had ended?

Could be hikers, possibly hunters. I looked again. A long way off, someone peered from behind a tree. Was he pointing a gun at me? A poacher hunting out of season, maybe a bootlegger? Either way, it seemed prudent to get the hell out of there.

I ran up the trail, tripping over rocks and cutting across switchbacks. I glanced over my shoulder. Was he still there? I couldn't see anyone, but that doesn't mean I'd lost him.

I pushed on. The slope seemed steeper than what I'd recalled. Had Erica wandered down here too? Did that mountain man and his damn popgun play any part in her disappearance? I walked as fast as I could, glancing back occasionally into what appeared to be empty woods.

After a mile or so, I slowed. He must have been just a hunter, or possibly some kid plinking tin cans. I grabbed my chest. I couldn't breathe. I needed a break, but then something caught my eye. Were my eyes playing tricks, or had something darted across the woods behind me? I scrambled over a rock and took off again. The trail turned and leveled out. Thank God. I ran until I couldn't go any further and then I dropped to the ground clutching my sides.

A branch above my head shattered, followed by the crack of a rifle echoing across the gorge.

"Shooting tin cans, my ass." Somebody didn't want me there. I scrambled across the ridge, picked up the trail, and ran in a low crouch. Finally, after what seemed like hours, I staggered into the parking lot and collapsed across the hood of my car.

Slowly, my lungs filled with air. I leaned on the fender, raised my head, and puked. I squeezed my eyes shut as the world spun around me. Was my "friend" still out there watching? Would he be satisfied that I was miserable or would he decide that a bullet was still necessary? I took a measured breath and opened my eyes.

Oh hell, a flat? Maybe someone was trying to kill me, but I wouldn't get far on that tire. I knelt and ran my hand over the tread. Must have picked up a nail. I opened the trunk and pulled out the jack and the spare.

Fix the flat and then go talk to the police.

Chapter Eighteen

March 1936

"That was Cole Porter with 'It's De-Lovely' on your Lucky Strike Hit Parade. Now, for a change of pace, let's swing to the melody of Cab Calloway . . . ."

Rebecca kicked off her shoes, flopped into Papa's easy chair beside the floor model Philco radio, and rubbed her feet. She ought to run the carpet sweeper around the small living room, but the heavy cleaning would have to wait for the weekend. Her Anatomy II midterm was next week, and the time spent at the hospital with her father had put her behind in her studies. Rebecca bit into her corned beef sandwich, washing it down with a gulp of milk. Only ten minutes to relax and enjoy a little music, then she'd turn to those books. She closed her eyes and crossed her ankles on the hassock, waggling her feet in time to the music.

A soft knock at the back door was barely discernible above the radio. She rose and peered out the kitchen window. A woman in a threadbare cloth coat huddled in the dim glow of the porch light. Her head was wrapped in a scarf—or was that a man's bandana? Rebecca opened the door.

"Evening, Miss Rebecca," Lorinda Jane said. "George Henry said I should come by to see you." She rubbed her bare hands together and stomped her feet.

"Yes, come in out of the cold." Rebecca stepped aside and gestured toward the living room. "You look half frozen. Can I fix you something, a hot cup of tea, perhaps a sandwich?"

"I don't want to be no bother, Miss Rebecca, I finished my chores next door and saw your light was still on."

"And I'm glad you did. Please, have a seat," Rebecca said, pointing to the sofa. "I'll just be a minute." She hurried into the kitchen and started a kettle warming on the gas range. "Is corned beef all right?"

"No need, ma'am. I eats when I gets up the mountain."

"Nonsense," Rebecca said. "It will be ready in no time, and it gives us a chance to talk." She pulled a cup and saucer from the cupboard. "I hope the music suits you. Do you enjoy 'The Hit Parade'?"

"Ma'am?"

"On the radio, 'The Lucky Strike Hit Parade.' It's all the rage with the girls at school. I listen most evenings after I finish my studies."

"We don't have no radio up on the mountain."

"Well, if you were interested," Rebecca said, "you might find a used one cheap. I've seen them from time to time at the church bazaars."

"It don't matter none," Lorinda Jane said. "We ain't got none of that 'lectricity up there neither."

Rebecca buried her face in her apron. How stupid, how could she have not known? She sighed and removed two slices of bread, then rewrapped the loaf and returned it to the breadbox. "Do you take sugar in your tea?"

"Yes 'm. Sugar'd be nice, real nice."

Rebecca entered the living room and placed the sugar bowl next to the teacup and saucer on the end table. Lorinda Jane glanced at her, seeming to hesitate.

Rebecca nodded.

Lorinda Jane scooped a spoonful of sugar into her cup. She followed with another, and then another.

"Do you like cheese with your sandwich?"

"I reckon, ma'am. We can't afford no store bought cheese, but last year, Willie and George Henry, they bartered a man over by Covington—fixed the legs on his table and he give 'em a small wheel of cheddar. M-m-m." She rubbed her stomach. "I done some fine cooking that week."

Rebecca went to the kitchen and returned with the sandwich on a small dinner plate. "I hope you like it. I have so little time to cook anymore. I don't know what I'd do without ready made foods in the ice box."

Lorinda Jane stirred a fourth spoonful of sugar into her tea. "Ma'am, George Henry said you wanted to see me?"

"Yes." Rebecca sat on the sofa beside her guest. "I know you already work next door and I don't want to take you away from any arrangements you might have. However, I was wondering if you had time to come by here as well, perhaps twice a week, and do some light cleaning and possibly a little cooking?"

"You wants me to come work for you?"

Rebecca held up her hand. ""Before you say no, it would only be one or two days a week and just while Papa is convalescing. I simply cannot keep up with this house, tend to him, and finish my studies."

"I'd be pleased, Miss—"

"I can't pay much, money is tight, but I have a little saved. I think I could afford, say four dollars a week for two days work? If you think it needs to be more, I'll see what I can do."

"Four dollars?" Lorinda Jane clasped her hands to her chest and laughed. "Miss Rebecca, that sure enough beats the egg money my Willie is all the time losing in his foolish dice games."

"So, he's a gambler?"

"No, ma'am. Gambling's when you has a chance of winning. Willie ain't never won a roll of them dice in all his natural days." They both laughed.

Rebecca sipped her tea, peering at Lorinda Jane over the cup. Her voice softened. "And George Henry, does he favor the dice?"

Lorinda Jane set her plate on her lap. "This here bread is mighty tasty. We don't get no store bought, just what I bakes from the corn meal we trades our eggs for."

Rebecca cleared her throat. "I'm . . . I'm sorry. I feel ashamed, sitting down here worrying about our little problems when others are having it so much worse."

"Hard times is all around, Miss Rebecca. Ain't none of

your doing." She took a bite of her sandwich, wiping her mouth with her hand. "Willie and George Henry done lost their railroading jobs, but I suppose you knowed that. Money's tight, but Willie says Mr. Roosevelt, he'll be calling an end to this here depression soon enough, and when he does, we's moving to Philadelphia."

"They lost their jobs? Why? There's plenty of work to do on the rails."

"Willie didn't say. I 'spect one of 'em forgot and let his mouth run on. Wouldn't be the first time."

Rebecca studied the woman bundled on the couch. "Perhaps I can find five dollars a week." She forced a smile. "Now, what's in Philadelphia?"

Lorinda Jane bowed her head. "You has to understand, I's a country girl, born and bred. I knowed poor my whole life. Ain't had no schooling, but them boys," she nodded toward the mountain. "They ain't like local colored."

"What do you mean?"

"They has educations, trades too. Their daddy graduated college. He was what you call a professor at one of them schools in Philadelphia, and them boys both has diplomas."

"That's wonderful. I would never have guessed . . . ."

"They hides it. They don't want folks knowing."

Rebecca set her cup down and leaned forward. "Having a high school diploma is a good thing. Why, many here about, and I'm talking white folks too, they'd give their eye teeth for such learning. Why on earth would anyone hide that?"

"Educated white man, he gets them good, white man jobs." Lorinda Jane scowled. "Colored man with book learning, he's still just a nigger, and sooner he gets used to that, better off he'll be."

"That's not so—" Rebecca stood, balling her fists on her hips.

"Don't mean no disrespect, Miss Rebecca, but white folks gets scared if'n they sees a colored what has schooling." She gazed at the ceiling and smiled. "I surely do wish you could have heard them boys talk when they first come down to Virginia. They sounded just like them university men what

112

come here every summer to study the railroading business."

"I don't understand," Rebecca said. "They shouldn't hide their diplomas."

Lorinda Jane frowned. "You think educated colored boys has a hard time fitting in with white folk? Shoot, that ain't nothing, Miss Rebecca. You ought to see how the coloreds treated 'em when they was talking fancy."

"That's awful. Why should a person be punished for bettering himself?" Rebecca walked to the window. Snow flurries swirled beneath the porch light.

"I ain't no learned woman, Miss Rebecca, but I'd say folks, white or colored, they don't like being reminded of what they ain't got. When them two educated colored boys figured that out and started acting like what folks wanted them to be, instead of what they was, life got a mite easier."

The mantle clock chimed. "It's past nine o'clock," Rebecca said, "and the snow's starting up again. I don't mean to hurry you, but you ought to get up that mountain before it begins sticking."

"I reckon you's right, ma'am. Snow gets slickery on them trails, specially climbing the rocks. And it ain't as easy as it used to be." She patted her stomach.

"Then it's agreed. You'll work for us. How would Mondays and Thursdays be?"

"I'll be here sunup Thursday."

"That's too early," Rebecca said. "I was thinking more like noon until around seven, and you could have your lunch here, so don't bother bringing one. If those hours work, it will more than suffice for what I need, and it won't take too much time from your chores at home."

"Tomorrow," Lorinda Jane asked. "Is that Wednesday or is it Thursday?"

"I believe tomorrow is Thursday."

Lorinda Jane looked away and smiled. "Miss Rebecca, you reckon I can have me another white bread sandwich for my lunch tomorrow?"

Chapter Nineteen

March 1936

"You ain't nothing but a cheating bastard and you ain't getting away with it this time." Chester waved his revolver at the stub where the old man's arm used to be. "Turn around so's I can shoot your thieving ass, you lying one-armed polecat."

George Henry backed away. Whatever was between those two, it was none of his concern. He only wanted to pick up his whiskey and make his deliveries.

A single bulb from a broken fixture above the bolted warehouse door cast pale light on the gravel parking lot. Chester's pick-up sat next to the warehouse with its headlights off but the motor running. Two other trucks were parked in the lot, both large freight haulers with canvas covers over their cargo beds. From the dust across their windscreens, it appeared they'd been parked there for some time.

"I didn't cheat you, Chester, honest. I done sold six bottles here local and another eight to a man in Covington. All the money's right there." The bearded old man pointed to a cloth sack Chester held.

"I already looked," Chester said. "You shorted me two dollars." He tossed the money bag onto the seat of his truck. "I warned you last time, Stumpy, you steal from me, there'll be the devil to pay." He grabbed the man's lapels, shoved the pistol barrel in his mouth, and cocked the hammer. "You, boy," he called to George Henry. "Get over here."

Oh, Lord, he didn't want trouble, and especially not that kind. Just wanted to sell a few bottles, pocket some money to help Willie and Lorinda Jane. George Henry raised his hands as he shook his head. "No need for this, Mr. Johnson."

Chester removed the pistol from the old man's mouth. "Hell, I ain't going to shoot him, not tonight least ways." He laughed and pushed Stumpy aside. "That old pirate's been stealing from me for years. I'm letting him off this time because if I shoot him I'll have to shoot you too, and I'd rather you sell some bottles to your nigra friends first."

"Don't need no shooting, Mr. Johnson. I won't cheat you none, and Mr. Stumpy, he ain't cheating neither."

"Did you hear that, old man?" Chester laughed. "MISTER Stumpy had best give you a lesson in what happens when you steal my money." He smashed the revolver into the side of the old man's face, knocking him to the ground, then turned and pointed the pistol at George Henry. "You'd best learn your lesson well, boy. Stumpy here, he worked the yards with my daddy until he lost his arm coupling boxcars. He's like family. You, on the other hand, well . . . nigras don't get a second chance."

George Henry stared at the chrome-plated revolver, then at the man holding it. A .38 Special might have given him courage, but it sure didn't make him a man.

Chester coughed and looked away. He pointed to the case of whiskey on the ground. "Same time next week—and you'd best hope you're better at counting than that old fool." He swung up into his truck, tugged the shift lever into gear, and spun the tires as he pulled out of the parking lot.

George Henry wiped his brow and slowly exhaled, extending an outstretched hand to the old man on the ground. "He treat all his family this way?"

Stumpy got to his feet and brushed himself off. "Ornery, he is, sweet talking like a preacher one minute, bringing that Smith and Wesson down on you the next. You watch him, boy."

George Henry picked up the old man's hat, dusted it against his trouser leg, and handed it to Stumpy. "Maybe I was wrong to get mixed up with that man. Could be I'd do better sticking with work I know, laying tracks or working wood."

"Too late for that, boy."

"How's that, Mr. Stumpy?"

"Name's Morris, Daniel Morris." He held out his hand. "You's one of the gandy dancers, ain't you? I've seen you 'round the yards."

"I was, Mr. Morris. Been three years moving track, before Mr. Beckerman fired me."

"Hear me, boy, don't you quit on Chester Johnson. Nobody quits once they start working for that man."

* * *

George Henry climbed the steps to the ward on the second floor. He pulled off his hat and peered at the woman behind the counter at the nurse's station. "Evening, Miss Hadley. He sleeping?"

"Oh, good evening." She glanced at the clock on the wall. "Visiting hours ended thirty minutes ago."

"Yes' m." He lowered his head. "Had some errands needed doing. I won't be long, I promise."

She raised her eyebrow but smiled. "That old fuss wouldn't have settled anyway until he'd had a chance to see you. I declare, I don't know what it is, but once he lays eyes on you he snuggles down and sleeps like a new born. She waved. "Go on, but only for a few minutes, you hear?"

"Yes' m. I'll be quick. Thank you, ma'am." George Henry hurried to Mr. Marshall's room and knocked on the open door.

"Where you been hiding, boy? I thought for sure you'd forgotten all about me." Mr. Marshall pulled himself upright using a bar that hung from a rope above his bed. "Come on in, take a seat."

George Henry slid a chair beside the bed. "You feeling better, Mr. Marshall? You was looking a might peaked the other day."

"Doing much better since Rebecca commenced to bringing my meals. It was that hospital food, you know. Would have sallowed even a strong young buck like yourself. Now tell me, how's the new business?"

"I'm moving three or four cases every week," George Henry said. "I have my regular customers on a schedule, plus some from over Covington, white folks too. I expect it won't be long before the refreshment business will pay better than railroading ever did."

"That's sure good to hear. Now, you save your money until you have enough to buy you a new suit of clothes, store-bought, with a fancy silk shirt and a shiny red cravat. You do that and all those fancy colored women down in Roanoke will be rushing to Clifton Forge, looking to make you their husband."

George Henry twisted the brim of his hat and smiled. Mr. Marshall must have been talking to Willie. He wasn't looking to marry, not yet anyway, but when he did, it wouldn't be to any fast-talking city girl.

"Rebecca tells me you aren't local," Mr. Marshall said. "She says you came from Philadelphia. So how's a Yankee, and a colored one at that, end up in Clifton Forge?"

"Reckon you could say it was the depression, sir. We had us a business up north, a good cash and carry business. Depression come along and folks just stopped buying. The bank foreclosed. We lost everything, tools, furnishings, savings."

"Business, huh? What kind?"

"Custom furniture. My grandpa opened the shop after the war, the war of southern rebellion—"

Mr. Marshall chuckled. "In these parts we like to think on that as the war of northern aggression, but go on . . . ."

"Well, sir, Grandpa learned his furniture-making from the best there was, and folks up north, they seen the quality of his work. Business was good. He built himself a big house with a wide covered porch and six bedrooms, plus a stable and a steam powered workshop. He taught me and Willie all there was to know about making furniture, and we done right well too, until that stock market crash."

"And now you're a bootlegging gandy dancer." Mr. Marshall laughed. "It's a strange world, ain't it?"

"Yes, sir, sure enough is." George Henry held his hands

in front of him, studying the calluses. "But someday I'll be turning chair spindles and dovetailing dresser joints again. That's my dream. It's in my blood."

"Then I hope you do. A man needs dreams. Mine was to drive trains. I remember when I was a boy standing beside the tracks, seeing those big old smokestacks puffing and belching through the trees, and feeling the ground shake, then that engine would come into sight." He drew his hand across an imaginary horizon. "The other children would all back away, but I'd close my eyes and stand fast. I loved to feel the wind and steam rush against my face as the locomotive roared by." He took a deep breath and lay back against his pillow. "Dreams, I've lived mine, and once this gets mended," he slapped his leg, "I'll have a few more years up in that cab, highballing down to Norfolk, scaring cows along the way."

George Henry nodded. "Sounds like a fine way to make a living, Mr. Marshall."

"It is, boy, and so is turning a piece of cherry wood into something some blushing bride will cherish on her wedding day and hope to pass along to her grandchildren."

"Yes, sir. Dreams like that is worth having."

"Tell you what," Mr. Marshall said, "when I'm out of this damned hospital I'll pull some strings, get you up in the cab for a run to Norfolk. Be warned though, you'll shovel so damned much coal you'll think your back's going to cave, but every now and again, when that firebox is crackling and the steam's whistling, you can lean your head out the window and I swear, it's like God Himself is kissing your cheek."

George Henry smiled. "I'd be pleased to make that ride."

"Then it's done," Mr. Marshall said. "Now all I need do is heal up, and I'm heading home tomorrow, so I'm on my way. You bring me any medicine?"

George Henry turned his gaze toward the door.

"Old Iron Pants—that's what the girls in the nursing school call her—she's most likely forcing an enema up the mayor's butt," Mr. Marshall said. "He's two doors down, complaining of some intestinal malady. When she gets done with him, he'll wish that was all he had." He winked.

"Sir," George Henry said, "what do you know about them Johnson brothers?" He pulled a bottle from his pocket and filled a small silver flask he'd taken from the bed table.

"Johnson boys? Their daddy worked the yards, that is, until he got fired—took off a man's arm while they was coupling up a train—drunk on the job is what I heard. He died six, seven years ago. Some said it was murder, but nobody was ever arrested. Why'd you ask?"

"Ain't nothing," George Henry said. "It just seemed like that Chester fella, he has him a touch of mean, is all."

"I only know him to buy a bottle from every now and again, so it wouldn't be Christian to speculate, but I'd advise you not to turn your back on him. What I've seen sometimes in them eyes of his I wouldn't exactly call human."

Chapter Twenty

"Grab a seat," Johnson said. "Captain McConnell ain't here. Guess I'll have to do." He showed me into his cramped office. On the paneled wall behind his desk a framed certificate hung along side several photos. One photo showed Johnson shaking hands with what must have been a few local dignitaries; another was of Johnson posing beside a deer hanging from a thick, curved limb on some massive old tree.

"Okay, Mr. Corsini, what's your problem?" He propped his cowboy boots on the desk and crossed his legs.

I pointed at the picture. "Nice buck."

"Eight-pointer—weighed in right about a hundred and fifty pounds." A broad smile crossed his face. "Biggest deer bagged in the whole damned county that year. I took him with a Marlin 336 in .35 Remington. You familiar with that rifle?"

I shook my head.

"I didn't think so." He picked up a letter opener fashioned to resemble a miniature cavalry sword, complete with a tasseled hilt. He pulled the saber from its scabbard and twirled it in his fingers. "You said something about a shooting?"

"Yes, sir," I said. "Up there in the woods. I thought you'd want to know." I flipped open my notebook.

His eyes widened. "This ain't no damned interview . . ."

"No," I said, tapping the page with my pencil. "Just my notes. McConnell and I went hiking this morning. We checked out that trail where those college kids disappeared and somebody shot at me."

"Why bother me with this?" Johnson asked. "Captain McConnell already has that information, first hand."

"He wasn't there."

"I thought you said—"

I waved him off. "McConnell had to leave—a ballgame, or practice, or something. This happened after."

"I see," Johnson said, "so somebody shot at you, huh?" He poked the point of the letter opener into the palm of his hand, seemingly fixated on how far he could push without drawing blood. "You do a fair amount of hunting down there around Richmond?"

"No," I said. "Actually, I don't hunt."

"But you do spend a goodly amount of time in the woods; you're what you'd call an avid outdoorsman, right?" His stare seemed to pass right through me.

"Look, Sergeant," I said, "I don't know where you're going with all this. I'm not a hunter and I don't spend any more time outdoors than is absolutely necessary. I do know this—I know when I've been shot at."

"Oh, I see." He smiled. "You're some kind of combat veteran or something? When was the last time you was shot at?"

"I've never been shot at before. What kind of stupid question is that?"

"Just establishing the facts, Mr. Corsini. You being a big time city reporter and all, you ought to appreciate that." He tapped the sword on the desk. "So you don't spend much time in the woods?"

"No."

"And you've never been shot at before."

"That's correct."

"So you ain't got a clue what it's like getting shot at, am I right?" Johnson slid the letter opener into its scabbard and leaned his elbows on the desk. "Tell me, Mr. Corsini, how's hearing some kid popping off at a squirrel different from somebody trying to kill you?"

"He wasn't shooting at a squirrel, he was shooting at me."

"He hit you?" Johnson cocked his head and looked me over. "You bleeding?"

"No," I said, "but I saw him. He pointed his rifle directly at me and I heard the shot when the bullet hit the branch right over my head."

"Oh, you seen him? Why didn't you say so?" Johnson picked up a pad and a pencil. "Now we have something. Go on, give me a description." His pencil hovered over the paper as he looked at me.

"Well, he was pretty far away," I said. "I didn't get a really good look."

"Hair color? Height?" he asked. "What kind of rifle?"

I shook my head. "I couldn't tell from that distance, and he was behind a tree."

"But you know he was aiming at you?"

"He pointed the rifle right at me."

"Couldn't have been aiming at a squirrel?"

"I didn't see any squirrel," I said. My stomach tightened. Not the time to lose control . . . .

"You sure it was a 'he'?"

I paused. I'd assumed he was male. Could he have been a she? I formed the hazy image again in my mind. "I can't be one hundred percent certain. I suppose there's a chance he could have been a woman with her hair tucked up under her hat."

"And this man or woman, whatever your sniper was, I suppose he or she was white?"

"Yes, yes sir, of that I'm pretty well certain, he was white." I poked my finger on the notepad.

"Couldn't have been a fair-skinned black person?"

"Well, I suppose that's possible, but—"

Johnson pushed his pad away and tossed the pencil on his desk. "Okay, Mr. Corsini, let's see if I have this right, a white male, or possibly a female, who might also be black, was in the woods. You heard a shot, and then a tree branch fell to the ground, is that about right?"

I nodded.

"Of course, you might have noticed there was more than

one branch on the ground—they do drop off the trees every now and again—they don't need bullets to get 'em started neither." He steepled his fingers and tapped his fingertips on his upper lip. "Are there any pertinent facts I might have missed?"

This had been worse than useless. I'd been bested in a chess match where I was supposed to be the better player.

Johnson folded his hands and smiled. "Mr. Corsini, I can see where someone unfamiliar with our woods and not used to hunting might be confused, even frightened by something as innocent as a young boy squirrel hunting with his .22."

"Yes, sir, I suppose I might have overreacted." I stood. "I am sorry to have taken up your time, Sergeant Johnson. Please accept my apologies."

Johnson walked me to the door. "No need to apologize, Mr. Corsini. I'm glad I could help straighten all this out before any rumors got started." He patted my shoulder. "We look to hikers and campers to boost our economy. No sense in scaring off potential revenue, right?"

* * *

Friday 7:30 PM

"Weren't no puncture, Mister. She was just low on air." The garage attendant pointed to the valve. "Stem's fine too, I checked it out. Somebody just let out your air."

"Okay," I said. "Thanks." I tossed the tire in my trunk and paid him.

As I headed for the hotel, rain splattered on the windshield. Thank God I was out of those woods.

So, I was shot at and somebody let the air out of my tires. Sounded like a message. I strummed my fingers on the steering wheel then flipped open my cell phone and punched in a speed dial.

Ann answered on the second ring. "Mitch, I was just getting ready to call you. I'm on the road. Should be there in another hour."

"Good," I said. "This morning McConnell and I checked out the trails where the kids were last known to be and somebody tried to shoot me."

"What? Are you okay?" Her voice seemed to fill with fear.

"Yeah, yeah. Just a warning, at least that's what I think it was."

"Are the police on it?" she asked. "You reported it, didn't you? And who's this McConnell character?"

Hadn't I told her about him? "Bill McConnell, he's the head of the local police department. He's a black guy—"

"Does that matter?"

"Huh? No, of course not," I said. "I just thought you'd appreciate knowing. He seems to be a good guy—and he hates NASCAR."

"Shall I ask Abe if this counts as your annual diversity and sensitivity training?" She seemed to laugh. "Maybe we could do a feature for the society page: Mitch Corsini, resident bigot at the <u>Richmond Journal News</u>, discovered that he can, in fact, play nicely with the local colored boys."

"Give it a rest, Ann. You'll like him. I'd fix you up, but he's already married."

"That never seemed to stop you. Speaking of which, did you ever get back in touch with that woman's lawyer? They're pushing for a court date PDQ, and your little friend came back around yesterday with another subpoena."

"What'd it say?" I didn't have time for any more legal nonsense, my kid was missing and apparently, somebody didn't want me finding her.

"Hey," Ann said, "it's not my lawsuit; I didn't accept it."

Suddenly, the skies opened and blinding torrents of rain washed across my windshield. I turned on my wipers and slowed to around fifty-five. "So where's the subpoena?"

"Beats me," Ann said. "Maybe he went over to your place and hung it on the doorknob."

An eighteen-wheeler roared past, throwing a wave of water across my hood. I swerved and gripped the wheel. "There's nothing for you to do up here, Ann. How about you go on home, find that subpoena, and then give me a call?"

"No thanks," she said, "and speaking of calls, Sandra was looking for you. You'd said not to give her your cell number, so I didn't."

"Did she have any news?"

No. She was hoping you did."

I took a deep breath. "I'll call her if and when I know anything. By the way, how are you doing?"

"Me?" Ann said. "I'm doing great. Abe has me working a front-page feature, and as of yesterday, my driver is ahead in the points total. Life couldn't be better."

"I mean, about that night, you know when you came over." How could I ask without sounding like a jerk, but I had to know. I needed to put it to rest. My world was complicated enough without another kid.

"Are you talking about that night you attacked me with the peanut butter sandwich?" she asked. "Honey, I forgave you days ago, put it right out of my mind."

She couldn't be pregnant, she wouldn't be kidding around. But then, maybe she didn't know yet, maybe she hadn't tested.

"Mitch? Hello, can you hear me . . . ?"

A crackling filled my ear. The call dropped. Maybe just as well, Ann was obviously playing coy, so she couldn't be worried about anything . . . unless her plan was to wait until the dust settled on the other case before she sprang her news on me?

I dialed her number again, but didn't connect. Was it the storm or just a blind spot in the mountains? I tossed the phone on the seat. Just as well, some conversations were meant to be had in person.

Chapter Twenty-one

Friday 8:45 PM

The search dogs had drawn a blank. The cops had too. I grabbed a slice of pizza, propped one of the hotel pillows behind me, and opened my notebook. Erica'd been missing for five days and I wasn't any closer to finding her. How long could they survive without food or shelter? Maybe they were shacked up somewhere, like the deputy said, but that didn't explain leaving their car. Besides, she wasn't the type. That other kid? Yeah, he was probably into drugs or something, but Erica? No way. Sure, she'd been ticked off at me, but she wasn't going to morph into some gang banger just to get back at her old man—

A loud knock at the door interrupted my train of thought. Probably that pizza guy wanting to argue his tip. Hell, he took forever to get here and the damned pie was barely warm. I wiped grease from my chin and opened the door.

Ann barreled past. "Glad I caught you in," she said. "That storm nearly blew me off the highway." She draped her raincoat over the armchair and flopped on the bed, then reached for the pizza. "Do you mind? I'm starving."

"Nice to see you too." I closed the door.

She raised an eyebrow and motioned toward the box.

"Yeah, sure," I said. "Help yourself." What was going on? My bed, my pizza—she was making herself mighty comfortable. I eased into the desk chair and rested my feet on the bed.

"Any word on Erica?" She leaned over the box as grease drizzled off the slice of pie. "M-m-m, this isn't bad."

I shook my head. Maybe I didn't have that Sicilian

pedigree, but I knew my pizza, and that cardboard crust just didn't cut it. "The cops haven't found anything," I said. "That kid she was with probably kidnapped her or tricked her into doing something she wouldn't normally do. I bet he tried to get her hooked on drugs."

"And you think that why . . . ?" Ann's look seemed to hold a challenge.

"Come on," I said. "Erica was raised better than that."

She rolled her eyes.

"Okay, so maybe I wasn't the best role model, but I never did drugs."

"Do the police suspect drugs?" She dropped the pizza into the box, waving her hands as though they'd somehow become contaminated. "Too greasy. Was that the best you could find?"

Shacked up and doing weed—weren't those the deputy's words? I handed Ann a paper napkin. "The cops don't suspect anything. She's missing and they don't have a clue."

Ann flipped the box closed and rested on my pillow, folding her hands behind her head. Her sweater stretched across her small breasts. "What do we know?" She said. "Give me a run down."

She was a looker, that was for sure, but it could get complicated if I let her move in with me.

She glared and folded her arms across her chest. "Mitch," she said. "Are you listening to me? Think about my question. I'll be right back." She slid off the bed and headed for the bathroom. The door closed, followed by the hum of the exhaust fan.

What the hell, if she wanted to move in for one night, I could handle that. I unbuttoned my shirt, stretched out on the bed, and fluffed the pillow beside me.

She returned a few moments later, gave me a quick glance, and then plopped in the chair. "You look tired, so make it quick," she said. "Who knows what?"

Was she talking cop stuff?

"Hello?" Ann waved her hand. "I was thinking of doing some checking on my own tomorrow, but it would help if I knew which stones have already been turned. Are you okay, or do we need to finish this in the morning?"

"Yeah, I'm fine," I said. "I was just recalling what had transpired since I arrived." I casually pulled my shirt closed. "Here's the scoop: the local gendarmes searched the woods, called out the dogs, and came up empty, well, except for a jacket. It wasn't Erica's, maybe that kid's. The state police have gone over the car. They didn't find anything. No credit card receipts anywhere since before they arrived in Clifton Forge. Apparently, they bought gas in town, paid cash, grabbed a bite at the diner, also cash, and then they went for a walk in the woods. Lost people leave a trail, a scent. These kids aren't lost."

Ann patted my ankle. "And how's her daddy holding up?"

Daddy? Good question. I'd buried that identity too long ago to remember. The fact of the matter was I was confused—and scared. I shook my head. "Some things you can't solve by stroking a check. This is new territory and I'm worried."

"Anything I can do, other than just being here?"

God, could I have been any more of a jerk? She'd spent the last two years pushing my buttons—and loving every minute of it—but she'd always been a friend. While she was worrying about my kid, I'd been trying to con her into bed. Damn, I bet she had horrible memories of that night, I'd been pretty drunk . . .

"Get some rest," Ann said. "I'll see you in the morning."

"Hold on." I sat up and grabbed her hand. "I'm not all that tired, just a little scared." I stared into her almond eyes. "Look, as a father, I've been kind of a dud."

She raised her eyebrows.

"Okay, for sure a dud, maybe worse," I said. "And if she concocted all this to get back at me, I deserved it, but my gut is telling me this wasn't for payback. She's missing, and that pothead friend of hers is probably taking advantage of her this very minute."

Ann sat beside me, placing her arm around my shoulder.

"No one can take advantage of Erica unless she lets them, and you can't stop being her daddy—no matter how hard you try."

"Can I ask you something?" I said.

What happened to Ann's wise cracking sister routine? I'd been comfortable with the old Ann. She'd fire, I'd fire back. I knew those rules. This was different, unsettling. Her expression seemed one of concern, even compassion.

"Ask away," she said. "Anything you'd like." Her voice softened.

"This will sound awful. I guess I'm not very good at being serious, but I need to know, that night at my house, how . . . how bad was it, I mean, how bad was I?"

She laughed and shook her head. "What is it with you men and your egos?"

I shrugged. What'd she mean?

She took my face in her hands and gazed into my eyes. "I have a few questions for you, Mitch Corsini. This means yes," she moved my head up and down, "And this means no." She turned my head side to side. "Are you with me so far?"

I nodded.

"Good. Now listen carefully. Do you respect me as a person?"

I nodded.

"As a journalist?"

I nodded again.

"And as a woman?"

"Yes, of course . . . ."

She put her hand on my mouth. "No talking, just nod. Now, have you ever known me to do anything totally off-the-deep-end stupid?"

I considered that for a moment and then shook my head.

"Good. And would you say I have a certain style, refinement, élan, perhaps?"

Yeah, she did. I had to give her that. I nodded again.

"So, could you imagine a woman with my class and sophistication debasing herself by crawling between the sheets with some pitiful, slobbering, knee-walking drunk?"

Well, I hadn't looked at it that way, but she had a point. I shook my head.

She lowered her hands and smiled.

"Wait. You mean . . . nothing happened?"

"Sure, stuff happened. You puked and you assaulted me with a sandwich, at which point I punched out your lights." She pounded her fist into her open palm. "Oh, and you have the lumpiest sofa I have ever slept on. Do you have any idea of the junk you had hidden beneath those cushions?"

We hadn't . . . ?

She wasn't pregnant?

I leaned against the pillows. "You mean, all that time, you led me on, let me believe . . . and you were just yanking my chain?"

Ann laughed. "You damned well deserved it, Mister God's-Gift-to-Women, and I enjoyed every minute."

"You are an evil, vicious, sadistic woman."

"And don't you forget it," she said as she laid her head on my shoulder.

I put my arm around her. "Do you have any idea what I've been through?"

"Afraid you'd lose standing amongst your Old South, 'Lost Cause' buddies?"

Yeah, maybe I was, but why? Laying there, her breath soft against my neck, all those black/white, what-will-people-think, twentieth century paradigms crumbled like a stale beer pretzel. I pulled her closer.

Ann patted my gut. "No funny ideas, tiger. You know I'm not that kind of girl."

I had to smile. "Would you believe me if I said I'm glad?"

"There's hope for you, Corsini." She kissed the tip of her finger and planted it on my forehead, then got up and walked to the door. "I'm in 203. Call me tomorrow. We'll do breakfast."

* * *

Friday 11:25 PM

I muted the basketball game on the TV. and pulled an old photo of Erica from my wallet. She wore her cheerleader uniform. I smoothed the corners. Eighth grade? She'd pretty much grown up without me—but there'd been a time . . . .

Another knock at the door. Ann again? I'd been surprised at how incredibly glad I was to see her. I hopped up and opened the door.

"Good evening, Mr. Corsini." Justine twisted her blonde hair around her finger and batted her eyes. "You gonna invite a girl in, or do I have to stand out here in the cold?"

What in the hell was she doing there? I glanced up and down the walkway outside my room. Had anyone noticed her? I hesitated and then stepped aside.

Justine sashayed into the room wearing a white miniskirt and a plum colored turtleneck under a leather jacket. She dropped her purse on the desk and sat on the edge of the bed. "I got to thinking maybe you were a mite lonely up here, all by yourself." She slid off her jacket and crossed her legs.

Great body—I wouldn't last two minutes if she started peeling off layers. I took another quick peek along the walkway and closed the door. "Loneliness isn't something I normally worry about."

She smiled. "A man like you, with all your big city charms, I can believe that."

"Look, I think you pegged me wrong. I appreciate you stopping by, but I'm not looking for company. I have work to do." I opened my laptop and hit the power button.

"Can I watch?" She stretched across the bed, propping her head in her hand. What little modesty that miniskirt was supposed to provide was negated by a salacious pose.

What was her game? This wasn't just some come-on, she was working an angle, and I was her target. I positioned the chair between me and the bed and stood behind it. "This isn't really a good idea. It's getting late and I still have a story to get to my editor. If you have information for me, maybe we could hook up tomorrow."

"But I thought we'd hook up tonight." She ran her hand down her thigh.

"Look, I'm in a relationship." Damn, where'd that come from? Why'd I say that? Still, maybe it'd get her to drop the come-on and just leave.

"Really?" She glanced around the room. "I don't see that your relationship is doing you any good right this minute—"

A knock on my door caused me to jump. Had to be Ann. How was I going to explain the bimbo on my bed? I motioned to Justine to be quiet and then I opened the door a crack.

"Was patrolling out this way, Mr. Corsini." Johnson craned his neck, peering past me, into the room. "Thought I'd drop by and tell you that the boy's father will be in town tomorrow."

I wedged myself into the space between the door and the frame. Had he seen her? "Boy's father? You mean the missing kid's? Great. I'd like to interview him."

"You got a problem in there?" Johnson stood on his toes and raised his head. I still had him by two or three inches.

"No. It's just late and I'm not fully dressed. When can I meet the kid's old man?"

"My office. Ten o'clock." He turned abruptly and walked away.

I waited until the patrol car pulled out of the parking lot, then closed the door and turned to Justine. "I hear the two of you are an item."

"When I want us to be," she said. She pulled her sweater over her head, then lay on her back, one arm draped across the top of the pillow. She fingered a catch on the front of her bra.

Lord, why me? I needed to get rid of her, not watch her strip. "I don't want trouble with any gun-toting boyfriends, especially ones who wear badges." I tossed her the sweater and pointed toward the door. "It's past your bedtime."

She wiggled into her sweater, grabbed her jacket and purse, and then turned as she opened the door. "Some men can't handle a real woman." Her eyes flashed to the empty bed. "Enjoy your relationship."

Chapter Twenty-two

April 1936

Willie plucked a flowering sprig from a dogwood tree beside the tracks. "You reckon Lorinda Jane will forget about that egg money if I brings her some flowers?"

"Did you lose her money again?" George Henry asked. "You ain't stupid, but I swear, there's times I wonder where your brain's hiding." He tossed his jacket into the boxcar and climbed aboard, then turned and held out his hand. "Grab a hold."

Willie clasped George Henry's wrist, planted a foot and clambered up.

"How much did you lose this time?"

The dogwood sprig twirled between Willie's fingers. He seemed to ignore the question as he glanced out the boxcar door. "Spring's busting out all across them mountains. Reckon that means my baby's coming real soon. You think it's a boy?"

"If it is," George Henry replied. "I hope he has the good sense not to gamble away his mama's egg money. It's hard enough keeping one of you out of trouble."

"It weren't but one dollar and twenty cents. She won't miss it none with all she's earning working for the Marshall's." Willie took off his coat and rolled it into a pillow. He lay on the floor of the boxcar and raised the pink flowers to his face. "You ever smell anything sweet as this here dogwood?"

"I'll plant them flowers on your grave after Lorinda Jane finishes with you," George Henry said. "By the way, I paid the balance on that crib at the mercantile. We can carry it up the mountain tonight. Maybe seeing that in the baby's room will lift Lorinda Jane's spirits and she'll forget all about her eggs."

The engine whistle sounded one long blast, then the car lurched and began rolling. Soon, flashes of red and pink azalea and dogwood blossoms flew past the open doors.

"We have another case what needs delivering tonight," George Henry said. "Folks from Covington are stopping out on the highway around nine o'clock. I told them one of us would be waiting with their order."

"I'll head out there with you," Willie said. "We can carry the crib up the mountain, grab a quick supper, and still be out on the highway in plenty of time to make the drop."

"Willie," George Henry asked, "how much have you told Lorinda Jane about this refreshments business?"

"Not a whole lot, why's you asking?" Willie said.

"Cause I figures our take on that whiskey we just delivered will square you with her egg money, but you have to promise me you'll put an end to all that gambling. Time's come for you to start saving for that baby."

"We'll have us some extra. She's making five dollars a week."

"Lorinda Jane can't be coming down the mountain many more weeks," George Henry said, "and once Mr. Marshall mends, that job's ending. Selling moonshine's all we got."

"We also got us this free delivery, thanks to the C&O," Willie said. "I figure we's doubled our business. Moonshine's all we got, but it pays a whole lot better than railroading, and I don't go to bed no more fighting the aches and pains." He rubbed his shoulder.

"Figure this," George Henry replied. "If Mr. Beckerman or them Pinkerton fellas catch us hopping rails to make our deliveries, we'll be on the jailhouse road gang for sure. No money to be made in that."

Willie laughed and cupped his ear. "You say something? Can't hear nothing over that locomotive."

George Henry smacked his brother with his hat.

* * *

Darkness closed around the narrow mountain path. Willie shoved his hands in his pockets and kicked a stone on the trail. "She didn't even ask about the money. You see her eyes get all big and wet when she seen that crib? Maybe now we can spend some of our liquor money on tools, or get us some hooks and line. I hear tell the bass are biting good down in the river."

"You's a darned fool, Willie Terrill. I'm telling you, don't mess with that woman's cash. She won't be satisfied to take her skillet to your skull; when she finishes with you, she'll be coming after me." George Henry shoved Willie, knocking him off stride.

"Full moon yonder," George Henry said. "We'd best watch ourselves out on that highway. If the sheriff catches us hauling whiskey, he'll lock us in chains." He gazed through the canopy of spring leaves above the path. Moonlight glistened on the tracks along the river, tracks polished by the hundreds of rail cars rolling across them every day.

"Where'd you hide the stuff?" Willie said.

"It's safe." George Henry replied.

"But if somebody was to find it, Chester Johnson will take it out of our hides."

"I said it's safe. You remember them trucks at the back of the warehouse?"

Willie nodded.

"I done some investigating. One of 'em has a busted axle. I bet it hasn't moved in five years. When I get our bottles from Johnson, I wait until he's out of sight, then I tote 'em over to that old Chevrolet and hide 'em under the canvas."

"That's why you'll do the managing when we open our woodworking shop again," Willie said. "You's the one has the head for business." He grinned, slapping George Henry on the shoulder.

George Henry glanced at his brother. He could mention about how gambling away egg money was no way to begin their new business, but no sense in plowing old ground.

They came to the footpath and turned toward town. Wildflowers covered the field along the side of the mountain, only hinting at their true colors in the moonlight.

George Henry plucked a stalk of grass and shoved it between his teeth. Even with what they'd spent on the nursery and the crib, and even with his brother's gambling, they'd still put aside enough to begin thinking about tools. Down at the mercantile there'd been a canvas satchel with leather loops—nice traveling bag. They'd start small, odd jobs and such. Someday they might have money to reopen their shop, but for now, tote bags and hand tools were all he could consider.

An automobile rumbled through the downtown section, the glow of its headlights sweeping the storefronts and lighting the tree-lined street. The road in front of the warehouse was empty. Business traffic had ended for the day. Most railroad workers would be home with their families. Nothing stirred as they entered the dimly lit parking lot.

"You wait here and keep watch," George Henry said. "You see anybody, toss a stone against that canvas cover. That'll be my signal to lay low, got it?" He stared until Willie nodded, then he scurried across the gravel to the rusted hulk in the far corner. Pausing momentarily at the tailgate, he scanned the trees on the hillside bordering the parking lot.

All clear.

George Henry threw back the cover and climbed into the bed of the truck. The dank stench of musty canvas filled his nostrils. He blinked, adjusting to the dark interior, then moved forward, stumbling over something in his path. The truck had been empty when he stashed the whiskey last night. Had someone been there since? Were their bottles safe? He kicked aside the obstruction and felt for the wooden case in the corner. There it was, right where he'd left it. He hefted the liquor. By the weight, all seemed proper. Whoever had tossed that other stuff into the truck hadn't discovered his twenty-four bottles of ninety-proof Chester Johnson home-brewed corn mash. Still, he'd best find another hiding place. This one was no longer private.

George Henry lugged the whiskey to the tailgate, stumbling again over that same object. He kicked. Whatever it was budged—heavy, but not solid. He set the case of booze on the wooden bench along the side of the truck bed and lifted the canvas. Moonlight fell upon an old man lying on his stomach.

George Henry gasped.

Had some old drunk climbed in there to sleep? He poked the old man's shoulder, but he didn't stir. He shook him roughly. Still no response. George Henry leaned out of the truck and whistled, then waved to Willie.

Willie trotted over. Grabbing the tailgate, he stepped up and peered into the darkened space. "What's wrong? Somebody steal our 'shine?"

George Henry drew back the canvas and pointed.

"Who's that?" Willie asked.

"Don't know."

"He dead?"

"Appears so."

"You kill him?"

"I didn't kill nobody. That's how I found him."

"Roll him over," Willie said. "Is he still breathing? Check his pulse or something."

George Henry rolled the man onto his back. Dried blood covered his beard and his chest.

Willie pointed. "Looky there, he's missing an arm."

"It's Mr. Morris . . . it's Stumpy . . ." George Henry knelt beside the man and placed his fingers on the bloodied neck. "Sure enough dead. Poor fella's juggler's been cut through and through. Somebody sliced him up bad."

"You sure? Check him again."

"Willie T., the man got no pulse," George Henry replied. "Somebody stuck a knife in his chest and slit his neck. They hacked him up so bad he never had a chance, and I reckon I know who done it."

"Who's you thinking?"

George Henry glanced at Willie and then picked up their whiskey. "We'd best git. Ain't nothing we can do for old Stumpy, and it ain't healthy for colored boys to be found hauling bootleg whiskey with a dead white man at their feet.

Chapter Twenty-three

An insistent knock pulled me from a deep sleep. I rolled over and glanced at the clock. It was too early for housekeeping. Rubbing my eyes, I wrapped myself in the blanket and stumbled to the door. Blinding sunlight greeted me as I cracked the door open. "Uh, yeah?"

"Are you hungry?"

I squinted and shielded my eyes. "Ann?" What accident of nature created such chipper morning people? "It's barely dawn. Come back in a few hours."

"Get dressed," she said. "I'll meet you downstairs in twenty minutes."

There was no sense arguing. Slowly I nodded in resignation and closed the door. Suzie Sunshine. Could that mean she hadn't noticed Justine leaving my room last night? Thank God for small blessings—one less complication—but what about Johnson? He didn't need to stop by. He could have called. He suspected something.

I hurried through my shower and got dressed. When I reached the parking lot, Ann was waiting beside my car.

I pointed to my watch. "Haven't you heard of brunch?"

She laughed as she slid into the front seat. "Isn't this a gorgeous morning?"

I grunted and turned the key. The Impala's V-8 kicked over on the second try.

Ann played with the radio. "There has to be a good Country station in a place like this. What passes for a civilized breakfast around here?"

Country and Western? Go figure. I shook my head. "How do you take your grits?"

"Butter and salt," she said. "No pepper."

"I know just the place."

The only other customers in the diner were an old man at the counter and a young couple huddled in a booth. We headed to a booth at the other end of the diner and took our seats. The waitress brought us coffee and took our order.

"What's the plan?" Ann peered over her mug.

"The boy's father will be at the police station this morning. Sergeant Johnson asked me to drop by."

"They still don't know that you're Erica's dad?"

"Seems a good idea to keep that under wraps."

"You want company?" she asked.

"That's up to you."

The waitress set our plates on the table. "Anything more I can get you, Hun?"

"No." I waved her away and then pointed to Ann's biscuit. "You gonna eat that?"

Ann raised an eyebrow, then shrugged and shook her head. "So, where are they?"

"Who?" I said, with my mouth full.

"The kids," Ann replied. "What's your gut telling you?"

Suddenly, my appetite disappeared. I dropped the biscuit on my plate. "Something's going on. I can't figure it out, but they're caught in the middle—and I'm not buying that lost hiker nonsense."

She leaned closer. "Sergeant Johnson?"

"Maybe . . . and his tramp girlfriend."

"Have you been keeping her a secret?" Ann locked me in a scowl.

Why the guilt? I had nothing to hide. "I told you about her. She's twenty-four, maybe twenty-five, blonde. She tried to pick me up one night, pumped me for information. Think cheerleader—"

"Or pole dancer?" She smirked.

"Yeah, that too. Look, none of this makes sense," I said, pushing my plate aside. I scanned the diner before I continued. No one new had entered. The couple sat too far away to eavesdrop. Besides, they were caught up in one another. The old man seemed transfixed on his coffee. "We need to check those woods again," I said. "I'm no expert, but I know when I've been shot at. Somebody out there has something to hide, and Johnson and that bimbo of his are up to no good. There's got to be a connection."

"So, shall I return to the hotel and change into hiking clothes?"

"Later," I said, tossing a twenty on the table. "The kid's old man will be at Johnson's office at ten. We have some time to kill. Come on, I'll give you the Chamber of Commerce tour."

* * *

Saturday 9:57 AM

McConnell was in Johnson's office when Ann and I arrived.

"Mitch, good to see you again." He stood and extended his hand.

"'Morning, Captain." I shook hands and then motioned toward Ann. "Captain Bill McConnell, Ann Richardson. The paper sent her up here to make sure I'm not padding my expense account."

"And to help him find the real story in this mountain mystery," she said. "Nice to meet you, Bill."

"Where's Johnson?" I asked.

Before McConnell could answer, a side door opened and in strolled Johnson, accompanied by a short, distinguished black man in tan slacks and a navy blazer. He wore a sky blue shirt open at the collar, revealing a pair of gold chains.

"Mitch Corsini, Richmond Journal News," I said.

"James Douglas." He smiled and nodded. "Peter's father."

His mustache and goatee formed a perfect circle around his mouth, as though drawn on with a marker. He sure didn't look like a brain surgeon, but he did have the look of money—street money, probably drugs . . . .

"Captain," Johnson said, "with your permission, let's get on with this."

143

McConnell nodded.

Johnson sat behind his desk and motioned toward the other chairs. "I'll tell you like I told Mr. Douglas," he pointed to me, "there's no evidence those kids are still around here and no indication of foul play."

"What about the car?" I said, glancing at Douglas.

Johnson shrugged. "What about it?"

"Hold on." McConnell held up his hands. "That's a question that does need answering, however the state police don't have a clue and neither do we. We're working on it."

"He's only had it a year," Douglas said. "Peter wouldn't just abandon it. I hate to even bring this up, but could they have been kidnapped?"

"Why'd you say that?" Johnson asked. "Did you get a ransom note?"

McConnell shot Johnson a stern look. He stood and leaned on the desk. "There's no evidence that would lead us to suspect that, Mr. Douglas. However, at this point we can't rule out anything."

"How about drugs?" I asked.

"Drugs?" Douglas replied. "My boy doesn't do drugs."

A smile crossed Johnson's face. "We did find dope."

"Only a trace of marijuana under the seat," McConnell said. "Maybe enough for a small joint. Nothing significant."

"College kids," Johnson said. "What'd ya expect?" He laughed.

"I expect answers," I said. I turned to the boy's father. "No offense, Douglas, but it sounds as though your kid might be into some illicit activity that could have caused this whole mess."

"And what makes you think that marijuana belonged to Peter?" Douglas banged the desk. "What about that white girl?"

"She wasn't driving." I stabbed the air with my finger. "And it wasn't her car." She couldn't be into that stuff, could she? How long ago had it been since I spent time with her? Did I even know her anymore?

"Mr. Corsini," Johnson said, "you seem to be taking a

sudden personal interest in this case. Is there something you want to share?" He drew his miniature sword letter opener from its scabbard and tapped the blade on his desk.

For once, Johnson was right. I'd lost my cool—but there was no way Erica was responsible for that dope. "Look," I said, "the car was abandoned and you found the boy's bloodied jacket. Just where do you draw the line on foul play, Sergeant Johnson?"

"He's right, Walter." McConnell waved as though clearing the air. "Something stinks in all this. Folks don't just disappear."

"Well, I didn't say we were closing the case," Johnson said. He dug the tip of the letter opener into the wooden desk.

"Peter knows the outdoors. He doesn't get lost." Douglas locked Johnson in a stare. "So where does that leave us, Deputy?"

"It's 'Sergeant'," Johnson replied. "And it leaves us right where we were—with no answers." He kicked his feet up on the desk. "But also no indication that a crime had been committed."

"Bull—"I stepped forward.

"Hold on a sec." Ann stood and walked behind the desk. She paused for a moment, studying the picture of Johnson's deer on the wall, and then turned toward the group. "What if someone borrowed Peter's car?"

"So what if they did?" McConnell asked. "That leaves us with what?"

"Peter loans his car to a friend," she said, "and the friend goes backpacking while Peter and Erica slip off somewhere together. They don't even know they've been reported missing."

Johnson laughed.

"Something hit your funny bone, Walter?" McConnell suddenly sounded like the coach putting the wisecracking student back in line.

Johnson wiped his eyes. "I was just picturing the two of them in some hotel, high on pot and too horny to notice their frigging car was gone."

"You're way out of line, Johnson." I leaned on his desk and glared. What made him think he could talk about Erica that way?

"Really?" Johnson smiled. "And I suppose you're saying they couldn't be shacked up?"

"You've searched the local hotels?" I asked.

"No, damn it." Johnson stood, wagging his letter opener at me. "And there ain't a shred of evidence suggesting they ever checked into any of our hotels."

"All two of them?"

"You're wearing on my patience, Corsini," Johnson said. He leaned over the desk. Our faces were inches apart.

McConnell stepped between us, pushing each of us away from one another. "Settle down, Walter." He looked at me. "We did ask the hotels if they'd had anyone by either name registered. They didn't. Also, neither Peter nor Erica has answered their cell phones since this all began."

"Peter wouldn't be smoking grass or shacking up," Douglas said. "He was raised better than that."

I spun around, facing the shorter man. "What the hell's that supposed to mean?"

"It means he's not impressed with your white, liberal, do-gooder trollops who think they can erase three hundred years of collective guilt by hopping in the sack with a black man."

"My Erica wouldn't be caught dead in the sack with your kind—"

"What the hell is that supposed to mean?" Douglas grabbed the front of my shirt.

Ann glared from behind the desk.

McConnell folded his arms, staring as though he was looking right through me, searching my very soul.

"This Gillespie girl, she mean something to you, Corsini?" Johnson circled the desk. He seemed to enjoy the turn of events.

"You've dug a pretty deep hole," McConnell said. "Maybe now's the time to come clean. What are you doing here?"

Douglas's eyes bulged. If he had his way, we'd replay the Watts riots right there. McConnell wasn't as aggressive, but his icy stare sent a chill up my spine.

"Look," I said, "I didn't mean to suggest that just because she's white—"

"And your daughter?" McConnell grabbed the case file from Johnson's desk.

"Okay, yes, I'm Erica's father." I tried to force a smile as I backed away. "Her mother and I are divorced. Erica took her stepfather's last name."

"Your press access has just been terminated." McConnell handed Johnson the file. "Sergeant, clear it with me before releasing any information, Got it?"

Johnson smiled and looked my way. "No problem, boss."

"So," Douglas said, "your daughter's too good to be caught in bed with a black man?"

"Like father, like daughter." Ann turned to McConnell. "Bill, do you mind dropping me off at the hotel?"

Chapter Twenty-four

April 1936

Rebecca awoke with a start. The textbook that had been resting on her chest fell as she rose from the sofa. She rubbed her eyes. The clock on the mantle read eight minutes before ten and she still had two chapters to go; she'd never get caught up.

There it was again, that sound. Someone knocking? Who'd be visiting at that hour?

Shuffling to the kitchen, she flipped on the light and drew aside the lace curtains covering the four-paned window on the back door. Outside, driving rain pelted a tall man standing on the porch. He faced away from the door, but his bearing struck a familiar chord. What brought him out on such a night? She opened the door.

"George Henry, is that you? Whatever is wrong? My goodness, it's Lorinda Jane, isn't it? She left here over two hours ago—has something happened?"

"Evening, ma'am." He smiled and doffed his hat. "Lorinda Jane's doing just fine. I left her and Willie up the mountain. They was fussing about egg money and she was fixing to take that skillet to his head again."

Rebecca laughed. "Where are my manners? Please, come in." She stepped aside.

"No ma'am. I don't want to mess your floors none."

"Don't worry about the floors, get out of that rain."

"Rain's just kisses from heaven," George Henry said. "The frogs tell me they's partial to it, and I didn't mind it none myself." He wiped his boots on the mat and stepped into the kitchen. A muddy puddle gathered beneath him.

"So, you talk to frogs?"

The chuckle escaped before he could cover his mouth. "I sure do, ma'am, many an evening down by the river. They has more intelligent thoughts to share than most people—and they'll listen to a soul all the night long."

"I must remember to try that some evening after I've finished my studies." Rebecca brushed aside her bangs. "Well, I'm supposing those frogs didn't suggest you come out on such a night just to be sociable, so what brings you to our door at ten o'clock?"

"Sorry, ma'am. I lost track of the hour. I don't own no clock." He pulled a checkered bandana from his back pocket and wiped his face. "I come by to see Mr. Marshall. Is he still awake?"

"What sort of business do you have with my father?"

"Is he up, ma'am. I won't keep him, I promise. I only need a minute or two."

Rebecca crossed her arms and leaned against the jamb of the door leading into the living room. "Papa is asleep. I'd rather not wake him unless it's an emergency. Is there something I can help you with?"

George Henry hesitated, twisting the brim of his hat as he held it in front of him. "Reckon it can wait 'til tomorrow. Sorry to disturb you at such a late hour." He turned toward the door.

"Now just one moment," she said. "You wake me from a sound nap, drip water all over my clean floor, the least you can do is be sociable." She pointed to the table. "Have a seat and let me fix you some hot tea to take the chill off." As she held the wooden match close, the flame under the kettle sprang to life.

"Don't mean to be no bother, Miss Rebecca." He shook his head as he stepped toward the door. "The evening's late. I'd best be getting on so's you and Mr. Marshall can get you rest."

"Are you always this stubborn, or did the frogs put you up to it? The water's still warm. It won't take but a minute to bring it to a boil."

George Henry pulled out a chromed metal chair and sat

by the kitchen table holding his hat in his lap.

"So, are you going to tell me about this business with Papa, or do I have to fetch my own flapjack skillet?"

His eyes widened, then he nodded and laughed. "Nothing important, Miss Rebecca. I just run errands for him every now and again. Railroading business, and such."

"I see, so you aren't going to tell me, are you?"

His head lowered. He poked the toe of one boot at the mud caked on the other.

"Very well," she said, "then you must tell me something else, something only the frogs have heard."

"Ma'am?"

"Tell me about Philadelphia," Rebecca said. "Lorinda Jane says you were a master carpenter with customers from Baltimore to Trenton and you even had pieces in the New York stores. Is that true?"

The tea kettle whistled. She poured a cup and set it in front of George Henry.

"Lorinda Jane shouldn't be bothering you none with any of that." He blew into his mug and took a sip. "That was before. A man oughtn't waste his time looking back."

She slipped into the chair across the table. His mug of tea seemed lost within those large, powerful hands. Light from the electrified chandelier above the table glistened on his dark, chiseled cheeks. Her throat tightened. How cruel to have owned your own business in a big city only to find yourself a gandy dancer, lining railroad track in the Virginia mountains.

"You are absolutely correct," she said. "We must look ahead. Mr. Roosevelt was saying pretty much the same thing just the other night on the radio." She studied the handle on her cup, then looked up, gazing into his eyes. "I have a personal question."

His eyes blinked rapidly as he scanned the kitchen, as though searching for an escape route. Apparently finding none, he lowered his head. "Don't know about personal, but if you has a question, ask away."

"It's about your brother."

"Willie T.?" Relief sounded in his nervous laughter. "Shoot, that ain't personal, what do you want to know about old Willie?"

She smiled and draped her arm over the back of her chair. "I've known men named Willie, I've even known white men named Willie, but I've never heard of anyone named Willie T." She raised an eyebrow.

His mouth twitched, then grew into a mischievous grin "You mean, why does we call him that?"

Rebecca nodded.

"'Cause that's his name."

"T?"

George Henry chuckled. "You don't know our Grandpa Isaac."

"Then tell me." She sipped her tea.

"He's a union man, through and through."

"Yes," she said. "Papa's in the union too, but I still don't understand—"

He bit his lip. Was he fighting back a smile, having fun at her expense?

"THE Union, Miss Rebecca, Third Regiment, United States Colored Troops," he said, "Mr. Lincoln's army. He still has his uniform, wears it every Decoration Day."

"Ah, a Yankee?" She giggled. "I'll forgive him that transgression, but what's that got to do with your brother?"

George Henry leaned toward her, resting his elbows on the table. "Grandpa Isaac was born and raised right here in Virginia on a tobacco farm down by the Carolina line. When he got his freedom papers, he headed north and joined the Union Army so's he could put an end to slavery, which he done."

"Papa runs trains all through there, South Boston, Danville. They haul a lot of tobacco up to Richmond."

"Yes, ma'am, that's the place. Well, when I come along, Grandpa said I needed to carry the name of a Virginian and a good Union man, so Daddy named me for General George Henry Thomas, Virginia born right there in Southampton County. They called him 'The Rock of Chickamauga' for that battle he fought over in Tennessee."

"Yes, I've heard him mentioned by some of the veterans at the hospital. And Willie?"

"Well, he come along later, so he got second pickings—General William Rufus Terrill, from over by Covington. Had a brother was a general on the rebel side, but Grandpa never bothered teaching us his name."

"So, all this time our fine community of beloved Confederate veterans and loyal sons and daughters of the Confederacy have had Yankee spies in our midst?"

"Sh-h-h." He held a finger to his lips. "War's over, Miss Rebecca. You won't be telling nobody, will you?"

She laughed. "Your Yankee secret is safe with me, General."

"That's good, 'cause I sure don't want that fracas kicking up again. Grandpa's nigh on one hundred years old, but that uniform still fits, and if he thought them rebels was stirring things, he'd be out of that wheelchair and packing his haversack." George Henry set his mug on the table and stood. "Thank you for the tea, ma'am. I'd best be getting on up that mountain now."

Rebecca gathered the dishes and placed them in the sink. "Thank you for stopping by. I enjoyed our visit and I promise, I won't tell a soul about your northern treachery." She covered her smile with her napkin. "Well, maybe, I'll tell the frogs."

"They already knows, ma'am." He laughed as he stepped outside.

"Good night, George Henry. Tell Lorinda Jane I look forward to seeing her in a few days." She waved and closed the kitchen door.

"What's all the racket? Can't a man get a decent night's sleep anymore?" Papa stood in his nightshirt in the living room doorway balancing on crutches.

"Papa, you shouldn't be up and about. Come, let's get you back to bed." She took him by the arm and turned him toward his bedroom.

"I heard voices. Who was here?"

"Well, since you asked," she said, "it was George Henry, and he said he was on an errand for you."

"He didn't tell you what for?"

"No, Papa, I couldn't get that out of him. He mentioned railroading business." She walked beside him, steadying his awkward gait on the crutches. "Now you tell me, what railroading business does a gandy dancer have up here at ten o'clock at night?"

"Beats me." Papa shrugged. "You know how those coloreds are, sometimes they get confused, might even make things up."

"Papa—"

With a dismissive wave, he climbed into bed. She reached for the lamp switch, then paused. Within the half opened nightstand drawer, a flash of silver caught her eye. "Papa . . ." She lifted the flask between two fingers. "What is this doing in my house?"

He pulled the blanket to his chin. "That's my medicine, child. Don't be bothering my medicine."

She unscrewed the cap, sniffed, and turned up her nose. "I've handled my share of drunken railway workers in the emergency room. I know the smell of corn whiskey. Where'd this come from?"

"Now child, you're getting into a man's business, nothing you need worry yourself over."

"George Henry—he's turned you to the spirits, hasn't he?"

His hand shot from beneath the covers and grabbed the flask. "George Henry wasn't no more than a babe in arms when I took up the spirits, and you've never seen me affected. I never missed a day's work, and it never come between me and your mama, God rest her soul, so don't you be getting all high and mighty, child." He tucked the flask under the blanket. "George Henry agreed to act as my go between, keep me supplied while I'm laid up, that's all."

"And that's enough." She clenched her fists. "I'll give him a piece of my mind next time I see him."

"Weren't none of his doing. I put him up to it, and that's

that. Leave the boy alone. Once I'm fully recovered, I'll be back to fetching my own. I swear, you'd think the prohibition was still on."

She tapped her foot. "Just how much of those spirits are you consuming every day?"

"A man needs a swig to settle his supper and another to settle him to sleep. I don't drink none before supper and never more than two, three swallows after."

"Fine." She reached beneath the covers and retrieved the flask. "Then I will make sure that neither you nor George Henry introduces any more of that vile brew into this house than is absolutely necessary." She slipped the flask into her pocket. "Tomorrow after supper, if you have the need, you can see me for your medicine."

Chapter Twenty-five

April 1936

"Nail your end, then toss me that hammer." George Henry held one end of the plank against the pine studs that framed the nursery and glanced at his brother. "When we get this finished I'm going after a cool glass of spring water and a patch of shade." He wiped his brow with his sleeve.

Willie set the nail with a tap of the hammer. Three powerful blows drove it flush. Moving to the center of the board, he pounded in three more, then handed George Henry the hammer.

George Henry finished his end and exhaled heavily. "Sure been a hot one. I never will get used to how these Virginia springs jump smack into the middle of Virginia summers. Philadelphia was hot, but it didn't hit you all at once."

"And we had them electric fans in the woodshop, don't forget that." Willie said.

George Henry dropped the hammer into his canvas tote and then scooped a dipper of water from the bucket on the porch, drizzling the cool liquid across the back of his neck.

"You remember back in January how you was saying you couldn't take them Virginia winters?" Willie asked.

Numbed fingers from winter snows and now summer sun baking the back of his neck—both were hard on a man, but he'd put up with anything that brought him closer to his dream. George Henry closed his eyes and imagined the smell of cherry sawdust, the warmth of finely sanded oak, and the sweet taste of maple turnings flying off his lathe. He wasn't living the rest of his life as some white man's beast of burden, hauling iron rails and driving eight-inch spikes—or selling someone else's moonshine whiskey.

"Lorinda Jane won't be up the mountain for another two hours," Willie said. "Supper won't be ready 'til after sundown. How about we grab our poles and head to the river?"

"Let me cool a spell first." George Henry pulled his sweat-soaked shirt over his head and spread it over a bush on the sunny side of the porch. "I heard the brownbacks are biting good on Junebugs."

Willie glanced around as though checking to see if anyone could overhear him, and then lowered his voice. "You hear any talk about Stumpy while you was in town?"

"Heard he was dead. You hear different?" George Henry pulled a rocking chair into the shade and sat.

Willie slapped him on the arm with his hat. "You'd best listen up, brother. They found his body in that old truck. Rumor is he was done in by a colored man. They's looking for a gandy dancer."

George Henry reached for the tin cup hanging from a nail on the porch. He dipped the cup into the bucket and took a drink. "We ain't working the rails these days."

"It don't matter," Willie said. "Colored is colored. Besides, somebody might a seen us in town that night."

"You know it weren't us. Johnson's the one, the same man we're selling for."

Willie soaked his bandana in the bucket and draped it over his head. Water drizzled across his face, mixing with the sweat on his bare chest. He dangled one leg off the porch and leaned against a post supporting the corrugated tin roof. "Don't you think we ought to be telling somebody, the sheriff, maybe? What if we was seen around that truck? Folks'll be thinking we done it."

"You already said they's looking for a colored. How long you reckon they'll keep looking once a black man walks into that jail and owns up to being in the back of that truck with that old dead white man?"

* * *

"You get on up the mountain. Here, take my pole. I have a delivery to make, but I'll be along shortly." George Henry glanced up the dark mountainside toward the cabin where Lorinda Jane no doubt had dinner waiting.

"You ain't meeting Johnson, is you?" Willie asked. "You need me to go along?"

"Ain't meeting Johnson, not tonight least ways." George Henry patted his jacket pocket. "Mr. Marshall's medicine."

Willie laughed. "Is that old fox mending any? Seems like he's taking enough of them medicinals."

"He don't drink all that much, just a few swigs every day, but he can't keep a bottle in the house, he says Miss Rebecca would find it. He has a small flask that's good for hiding and I bring him a refill every few days."

"You's spending more time over there than Lorinda Jane does. Maybe they need to hire you too."

George Henry shook his head. "Ain't looking for more jobs. After I sell off them two cases we stashed night before last, I'll be telling Johnson I'm done with his murder and his moonshine."

"He won't like that," Willie said. "We's making him too much money."

"And not making near enough for ourselves. But I can't rightly tolerate working for a man what done old Mr. Stumpy like he done—and if Johnson thought for one minute we had any suspicions on that, him and his brother would be grabbing their scatterguns and hunting us down."

"Best think on that before you up and quit. Chester Johnson's one hard man. I wouldn't want to be on his bad side." Willie turned toward home.

"And I don't much care to be seen on his good side, neither." George Henry waved and walked away. Chester Johnson was a hard man—and a bad one too. He had to get away from him, but he needed a plan. He'd worry on that another time.

The evening star sparkled beneath a crescent moon in the eastern sky. Bats flitted in the twilight, chasing unseen prey. George Henry slung his jacket over his shoulder and breathed deeply. Maybe Virginia was icy cold in the winter and steamy hot in August, but come spring, when the evening air carried the scent of dogwoods up the mountain, then it was enough to push thoughts of Pennsylvania clear from his mind. He followed the sidewalk past the business district, up the hill, and into a neighborhood with two- and three-story frame houses lining the street, their covered porches edged in hollies or flowering azaleas.

The light beside the front door of the yellow Victorian on the corner glowed brightly, illuminating two wicker rockers on the porch. George Henry walked past the steps and turned the corner, going instead to the darkened rear of the house. He knocked softly on the back door.

A light in the kitchen flickered on. The door opened. "George Henry, what brings you by this evening?" Rebecca motioned for him to enter.

He pulled off his hat and stepped inside. "'Evening, Miss Rebecca. Is Mr. Marshall up and about? I figured if I come early, maybe he'd be awake."

"Awake for railroading business?" She folded her arms.

"Yes' m. I 'spect so." He peered past her, into the living room.

"Wait here." Rebecca left the room, then returned a few moments later. "Is this what you came for?" She held out the flask.

She'd found him out. He smiled. "Mr. Marshall, he told you about our arrangement?"

"I want this understood, I disapprove of spirits, and I am disappointed to learn that you're mixed up in selling this poison." She sighed and handed him the flask. "He says it's helping his sleep, so I suppose that isn't such a bad thing. He does have a lot of pain, you know."

"Broke bones can be hard mending, but I wouldn't bring squeezings into your home if it was upsetting to you, ma'am." George Henry hesitated, the bottle half way out of his pocket.

"No, not upsetting, not anymore, and thank you for considering my feelings. Please, sit." She motioned toward the table. "Here, let me do that over the sink." Rebecca took the bottle to the sink and refilled the flask. "How much does he owe?"

"Bottle's all paid for, ma'am. If you wants, now that you knows about it and all, you might just keep it here. Then I won't be needing to stop by again, that is, until it's empty." He pointed to the brown glass bottle on the drain board.

Rebecca screwed the cap on the flask and put it behind some dry goods in the pantry. She picked up the bottle and glanced at the panty, then turned toward George Henry. "I know it means stopping by more often, but I fear having this in the house where Papa might find it."

"Yes, ma'am. I know just what you mean." He reached for the bottle, his hand overlapping hers. "Mr. Marshall, he might become too fond of his medicine if he was to have so much of it around."

She hesitated, then smiled and withdrew her hand.

"It'll be best if I comes by from time to time so's you can refill that flask." He slipped the bottle in his pocket.

"Thank you, George Henry. That would be a wonderful kindness. Are . . . are you hungry? Could I make you something, a sandwich, before you go?"

He held up his hands and stepped away. "Thank you, ma'am, but Lorinda Jane has supper waiting up the mountain. If I was to come home without my appetite, she just might go to fetching her skillet."

"Then hurry home to your supper, George Henry," Rebecca said. "I wouldn't want to be responsible for any harm coming your way."

She opened the door. "Oh, I almost forgot, I picked up something at the store today." She took a fresh loaf of bread from the breadbox. "Would you give this to Lorinda Jane? She's become fond of store-bought and I know she won't spend the money herself."

"That's mighty kind, ma'am. Lorinda Jane, she'll be pleased." He stepped onto the porch.

"Good night, George Henry." The door closed behind him.

He stood on the porch and took a deep breath. Her skin was smooth as hand-rubbed rosewood. A man couldn't allow himself such crazy thoughts, not about a white woman. But had he ever before touched anything so perfect?

Shoving his hat on his head, he ambled down the hill. A breeze up from the river carried the faint hint of creosote from the rail yards below. The ghost of a halo encircled the waning moon. Come morning, there'd be rain. He put on his jacket and softly hummed a tune they'd chanted while lining track.

A block beyond Rebecca's house a truck pulled to the curb beside him. "Boy. What's you doing walking around at night in the white folks' neighborhood?"

George Henry removed his hat and leaned over. "Mr. Johnson, that you? I was making a delivery. Now I'm heading back up the mountain."

"I hired you to sell liquor to the nigras, not to be running 'shine down this part of town. I got white folks to handle that."

"Ain't selling to the white folks, excepting for Mr. Marshall. You remember? He asked if I'd fetch his bottle until his leg mended."

"You owe me for two cases I gave you night before last. Pay up, boy, or I'll come looking for you." Johnson spit out the window.

"The railroad had the gandy dancers working the tracks late yesterday. I didn't have a chance to meet up with my regular buyers, but I'll get them bottles sold, don't you worry none."

Johnson leaned out the window, motioning with his finger. "Come here, boy."

He stepped closer to the cab. Suddenly, the barrel of a chromed, pearl-handled revolver loomed inches from his face.

"The railroad didn't work late tonight, but instead of selling my liquor to your no-count coloreds, you was off bothering a white woman. I seen you through the window." Johnson cocked the hammer. As the cylinder rotated, the silvery tips of the bullets glistened in the moonlight.

George Henry stepped back. "Weren't bothering Miss Rebecca none, just delivering Mr. Marshall's order. I'll be out tomorrow moving the rest of them bottles, and then I'll be waiting with your money at the usual place come Tuesday next."

Johnson lowered the pistol. "The usual place don't work no more. You bring that money up to my place—and don't even think about cheating me none, you hear?"

"Yes, sir. I hears just fine. Tuesday next, your place." George Henry put on his hat and started to walk away.

The truck rolled along beside him. Johnson leaned out the window. "And another thing, boy. I'd best not catch you up there bothering God-fearing white folks, especially Miss Marshall. Nigra's got no business in the white neighborhood after sundown. If I see you around the Marshall place again, I'll shoot you dead and be called a hero for doing it."

Chapter Twenty-six

McConnell's car had already disappeared by the time I reached the police station parking lot. No problem, I'd catch up with Ann at the hotel and square things with her there. She'd misunderstood. Hell, they all had. Erica wasn't prejudiced; she didn't have a hateful bone in her body, and what was wrong with a father wanting what's best for his kid?

Was the morning a little on the warm side, or did it only feel that way compared to the icy stares I'd been getting in Johnson's office? I climbed into the Chevy and rolled down the window. They had no call for getting all uptight while my daughter was out there in that wilderness suffering from God only knows what. I gunned the engine and pulled out of the parking lot.

If they didn't want to believe me, that was their problem. I'd been shot at. That was sure as hell no kid—and he wasn't hunting squirrels. Whoever it was, he was trying to hide something. He held the key. He had to know about Erica. So what if Johnson wasn't going to push it? Yeah, he might even be involved. I'd have to find that gunman on my own, and when I did, I'd make him spill his guts.

Exiting the interstate, I pulled onto a winding two lane. McConnell had come a different way, but the road markers looked similar. Then again, one tree-lined mountain road pretty much looked like any other. I should have grabbed a map.

The road twisted around the mountain, then straightened for about a mile. Gas station ahead . . . the turn off to

Justine's place? Yeah, the trailhead was only a few miles further. I hadn't screwed up after all.

Justine—now there was an enigma. Great body, but her 36 C's should come with a warning label. Messing around with those could definitely be hazardous to your health. Whatever her angle, I'd best keep my distance until I had her figured out.

A patrol car turned from the gas station onto the highway, paced me for a half mile, and then hit the blue lights. I glanced at the speedometer, fifty-six. What the hell? I hadn't broken any laws. My lawyer would hear about this— once I cleared up that past due payment he said I owed him. Okay, keep your mouth shut. Don't tick the guy off. Probably just a burnt out taillight. I pulled onto the shoulder.

The officer approached the car and peered in. "License and registration please."

One of Johnson's men, same guy who pulled me over before. I opened the glove box to retrieve my documents.

He craned his neck. "Whatcha got there?"

"Where? I'm just reaching for my papers."

"There, in the glove compartment." He pointed. "That bag."

"There's no bag in my glove box."

"Sure enough is. I can see it." The cop placed his hand on his pistol. "Sir, please step out of the car."

I kept my hands in plain view on the steering wheel. No sense giving him any reason to shoot. "Calm down, officer. I'm no threat and I have nothing to hide."

"Good. Then you won't mind stepping out of the car." He motioned toward the road.

No sudden movements. Don't give him cause to panic. I held up my hands and pointed toward the door handle.

He nodded. "Slow and careful, mister."

"Look, officer, there's been some mistake." After easing the door open, I raised my hands and stepped from the car. "My daughter's missing. I'm out here to solve a crime, not commit one."

"Face the vehicle and spread 'em. You know the drill."

What'd he take me for, a hardened criminal—some kind of repeat offender? What the hell, I'd seen it often enough on TV; I could play along. I widened my stance and leaned on the hood of my car.

He patted me down and then pointed to the Chevy. "You give me permission to search your vehicle?"

Burger wrappers, fossilized French fries, maybe a Jimmy Buffett cassette—I had nothing to hide. "Yeah, sure," I said. "Knock yourself out."

"Go stand beside the patrol car and keep your mouth shut." He pushed me away from the door.

The cop leaned into the front seat, looked around, and then walked to the other side and opened the passenger's door. He smiled as he reached into the glove box. "Well, well. What have we here?" He held up a small plastic bag of white powder.

Where the hell'd that come from? "Whoa, there's been some mistake, officer." I stepped toward the car.

"Stand easy, mister." He placed his hand on his holstered pistol.

I stopped in my tracks and raised my hands. Don't mouth off. Stay cool. "That's not mine," I said. "I've never used the stuff." I forced a smile. "I'm a scotch man."

"Right, and I'm a wide receiver for the Washington Redskins." He dangled the bag in front of me.

My jaw tightened. "Look, I don't know how that stuff got in my car."

"It ain't yours?" He laughed.

I snatched the bag and turned it over, looking for I didn't know what. "There's got to be an explanation." I shrugged.

"Yeah, like maybe you're running dope." He took back the bag, holding it by the top edge between his thumb and forefinger. "This might just buy you some hard time, mister."

I'd watched him search the car. He couldn't have planted it. How the hell'd it get in there? And how'd he know to look for it?

"You want to step back to the patrol car? Since I now got what you call probable cause, I'm gonna have to do a complete search." The cop locked a vise-like grip on my arm and led me to the squad car. He opened the rear door. "Make yourself comfy. I'll only be few minutes." He pushed me into the seat and slammed the door.

No door handles, wire cage between the seats—I couldn't get out, even if I wanted to. Since arriving in Clifton Forge, I'd spent considerable time in the back seat of cop cars. They'd changed a lot since my college days . . .

Cautiously, the cop poked around in the trunk with his nightstick as though expecting something to jump out and bite him. It'd serve him right. He slammed the trunk, glanced in the back seat, then returned to the squad car. He bent down and stared through the window, giving me the once over, as if trying to measure my character. "Looks like just the one bag. I'm no lawyer, but if you're lucky, you might could get off with simple possession. It's possible they won't go after you on intent to distribute."

Intent to distribute? Hell, I didn't have time for all that legal crap, Erica was lost, or kidnapped, or being forced into who knows what by that Douglas kid. I needed to get into those woods. I had a couple hundred in my wallet . . . .

"Hey, officer," I said. "Evidence gets lost all the time, right? It'd be a shame if that dope was to disappear."

"You offering me a bribe?"

I reached for my wallet. "I'd never do that, officer. That'd be illegal."

"You're funny, Corsini. A few days in the cooler might just do you some good."

"Hey, you could have planted that stuff." I banged on the cage separating us. "It's your word against mine. You don't have a case. I'll be out before lunch."

He turned from the driver's seat, dangling the bag as he smiled. "No case at all, just this dope with your fingerprints all over it."

* * *

Saturday 2:17 PM

"Phone call? Sure, you got a quarter?" The officer smiled.

He'd been on duty when I first visited the police station—Mister paperback novel—maybe he'd be reasonable.

"Look, I don't have the number with me; it's in my cell phone, with my personal stuff. Can you bring it to me?"

"You're supposed to use the pay phone." The officer glanced around the small, barren lock-up, as though making sure no one witnessed what was about to happen. "If I give you your cell phone, you make one call, then you give it right back, you hear?"

I nodded.

The officer left.

Two bunks rested against a wall made of steel boilerplate. Each bunk had a pillow and blanket, no sheets. The only other furnishings were made of stainless steel: a toilet, a sink, and a mirror on the wall. Iron bars wrapped in heavy mesh enclosed the other walls and the top of the cell, which was about a foot lower than the ceiling. Damn, no chance to tunnel out with my spoon.

The officer returned and passed my phone through the tray slot in the door. "I'll get in trouble if anybody knows I let you have that. Two minutes, no more. Got it?"

"Thanks, officer. I'll give a holler soon as I'm done."

Ann's name came up first on my contacts list. I highlighted her number and pressed "send." The phone rang several times and then rolled to voicemail. Coverage was rotten in those mountains, maybe it hadn't gone through. I tried again.

Voicemail.

Could be she was still fuming about that nonsense in Johnson's office. She'd probably seen my name come up on her phone and decided to play hard to get. That woman could be impossible at times.

"Hey, you done yet?" My jailer poked his head in the door. "Sergeant Johnson will be back any minute and I'm not getting my ass in a sling for nobody."

"One sec . . ." I held up a finger and dialed again. Her voicemail answered.

"Ann? It's me. It's Saturday afternoon and I'm in a mess.

I'm in the Clifton Forge jail. They're railroading me on some trumped up drug rap. Be a darling and come bail me out, will you? There's no way I can spend a night in this lousy joint.

"Yeah, and about that stuff that took place in Johnson's office, look, I'm real sorry. You know I didn't mean anything by it."

Chapter Twenty-seven

April 1936

Rebecca cleared the kitchen table. She set the dishes in the sink and then glanced at the clock. If they soaked until morning she'd have time to finish studying for her exam, but Papa was still awake and listening to the radio. Until he went to bed there'd be no quiet in the house anyway. She turned the spigot and filled the sink.

"Rebecca, do you have a moment?" Her father called from the living room.

"What is it, Papa?"

"I need my medicine."

Laughter crackled from the radio.

"Papa, what in heaven's name are you listening to?" Rebecca carried the silver flask into the living room. "I can't remember you ever laughing so hard. Is that Burns and Allen again?" Papa sat in his easy chair, his bad leg propped on the ottoman. He unscrewed the cap and took a swig from the small bottle, then recapped it and gave it a shake. "Almost empty. Where's that boy?"

"George Henry?"

"Yes. He hasn't been around here for days. You tell that girl working for you to let him know I need more medicine."

"I'll mention it to her, Papa. Now, when your show signs off, you get on to bed. Call me if you need any help. I'll be finishing the dishes and then studying." She tucked the flask in her apron pocket and turned toward the kitchen.

"Fibber McGee."

"I beg your pardon?" She turned at the kitchen door.

"You have to listen to this feller." He wagged his finger at the radio. "He's—what's that you kids are always saying?

He's a hep cat."

"I'm sure he is, Papa, but he won't get my chores done and he won't help me pass my exams."

She returned to the kitchen and placed the flask in its hiding place in the pantry. It had been several days since George Henry had stopped by. Lorinda Jane hadn't mentioned anything, so he must be all right; still, it wasn't like him to stay away. It wasn't that she was worried . . . or was it? She looked forward to his visits. Rebecca rolled up her sleeves and reached into the soapy water. Tomorrow she'd ask Lorinda Jane.

Her father's laughter continued in the next room. She smiled. He'd had a rough recovery, but Dr. West thought he was finally on the mend. In a few months he might even return to his beloved trains. She shuddered. If it weren't for the medical bills, she'd just as soon he took his retirement and got off the rails while he still could.

A soft knock at the kitchen door pulled her back to the moment. She rinsed the plate, wiped her hands on her apron, and flipped on the porch light. George Henry stood on the stoop, his hat in his hands.

Rebecca smiled as she opened the door.

"Evening, Miss Rebecca."

"I was beginning to think you'd forgotten us. Come in, George Henry." She untied her apron and hung it beside the sink.

"Been busy, and I didn't want to be no bother to you and your papa." He lowered his head.

"Bother? Where in the world would you get such an idea? Papa's almost out of his medicine, and I . . ." She paused and smiled. "Well, it's good to see you. Please, have a seat. Did you bring a bottle for Papa?"

He pulled a bottle from his pocket and set it on the table. She took it to the sink and refilled the flask.

"Lorinda Jane will be delivering soon," Rebecca said. "When do you suppose she'll need to stop working? I worry about her climbing the mountain in her condition."

"Don't know, ma'am. I expect she'll quit working when

the labor starts. She ain't one to be laid up sick for no reason."

"Rebecca," Her father called from the next room.

"Yes, Papa?"

"Somebody's knocking."

"Excuse me. I'll be right back." The swinging door closed behind her as she entered the living room. Her father waved toward the front porch without turning away from the radio.

"All right, Papa. Be patient, I'll get it." She opened the door a crack.

"Evening, Rebecca." Chester Johnson snatched off his hat.

"Chester. Good evening." She held the door open just wide enough to glance out. "What brings you out at this hour?"

"Got my truck, thought you might like to take a little ride up over the mountain. Moon's out; it's a real pretty night."

"Thank you, Chester, but I have studying to do and Papa to tend to."

"I brung him some whiskey."

"I beg your pardon?" Rebecca opened the door wider.

"Your pa, he's one of my customers. I heard tell he might be running low, so I brung him a bottle of my best squeezings."

"I see, and just where might you hear that my papa is in need of any whiskey?" She placed her hand on her hip.

Chester ran his hand through his hair and smiled. "Folks, they work for me, you know, and I decide where they sell, who they sell to. Your pa, he was buying from some nigra that weren't supposed to be up in the white neighborhoods, but don't you worry none, I straightened that boy out."

Was he talking about George Henry? She didn't hold with fighting, but that'd be one scrap she'd pay to watch. "Do tell?"

"Yes' m, he won't be bothering you no more. And you can tell your pa, anytime he's needing some squeezings, I'll fix him right up."

"Well, MISTER Johnson, I don't believe we need you, or anyone else, deciding who should or shouldn't visit our home. I'll thank you to mind your own business and keep your nose out of ours."

"Rebecca? Who's that at the door?" Papa called.

"No one, Papa. I'll handle it." She pushed the door closed.

Chester forced it open again. "You was all the time acting uppity, Miss Rebecca Marshall, but I seen you and that nigra setting there at your kitchen table. Maybe you won't be so high and mighty when word gets around that you're sweet on a colored boy."

How dare he? She threw herself against the door, slamming Chester's hand in the jamb.

He yelled and shoved the door open, knocking Rebecca back. Chester stood in the doorway flexing his hand, then he centered his hat on his head and pointed at her. "Time was if a nigra didn't know his place, he'd likely find it at the end of a rope."

"Chester Johnson, get off my porch this instant, and you leave George Henry and his family alone or I'll report you to the sheriff." She slammed the door and turned the latch.

"Rebecca?" Papa called from his chair. "What's all that commotion? You got trouble?" He turned down the radio and reached for his crutches.

"No need to get up, Papa. It was nothing, just some weasel sticking his nose where it doesn't belong." She turned off the porch light. "And I don't want you buying any more liquor from that Chester Johnson, you hear me?"

Papa answered with a blank stare as she hurried past him and into the kitchen.

"George Henry, did you get Papa's whiskey from Chester Johnson?" She crossed to the window and pulled the shade.

"Mr. Johnson? Yes' m. He's the one supplying my bottles, but I aim to quit the whiskey business after I finish selling my last load."

"Good." She peeked out the back door before pulling that shade too.

"Is there a problem, Miss Rebecca?"

"I'm afraid so." She took a step toward George Henry.

"What'd he do, ma'am." George Henry stood. "Did he hurt you?"

"He's been watching us."

"Watching us talk?"

"He thinks . . ." She lowered her head and laughed softly. "He thinks there's something going on between us."

"Miss Rebecca, I didn't mean to get you in no trouble. It was wrong, me coming by so much." He held out his hands. "I knowed all along it was wrong. From now on, Lorinda Jane can bring Mr. Marshall his bottle—"

Rebecca took his hands in hers and squeezed. "I won't be told who can enter my own house or who I should or should not see. I won't ask you to put yourself in danger, but neither will I cower before that filthy man."

"Ain't just me could be in danger, Miss Rebecca." George Henry pulled away from her grasp. "I should have told you, should have told somebody, least ways, but me and Willie, we was the first ones to find Mr. Morris's body in the back of that old truck."

"Stumpy? Yes, wasn't it awful? But I thought the police found him."

"Me and Willie seen him lying in the back of that truck just dead as can be three, four nights before the police discovered him."

"And you didn't tell anyone?"

"How'd you think it would look, two colored boys coming across a dead white man that's all cut to pieces? The police, they'd just put the cuffs of them colored boys and then tell the town they caught the killers."

"And you think Chester Johnson had something to do with that murder?"

"Can't say for certain, but Mr. Morris, he was working for Mr. Johnson, selling whiskey, and me and Willie, we seen them arguing about money."

"You need to tell the sheriff."

"Let me think on that," he said. "Maybe in a day or two."

Rebecca lifted the shade on the door and peered into the darkness. "He might still be watching. Maybe you'd best stay here. I can fix up the sofa—"

"Meaning no disrespect, Miss Rebecca, but if'n it's bad for me to visiting in the kitchen, what kind of trouble will get stirred up if somebody sees me spending the night?"

Her cheeks warmed. Had he noticed? "I suppose you're right," she said. "You and I know that we simply enjoy conversation and a cup of tea every now and again, but if you slept over, that would sure get the town to talking, wouldn't it?"

His eyes met hers and then he looked away, rubbing the back of his neck. "I'd best be getting on, ma'am. I'm sorry I brung this trouble down on you."

"Sh-h-h. You brought nothing down on me, and that Chester Johnson doesn't have any say in this household." She touched his sleeve. "Be careful."

He smiled. "I know the deer trails better than most. He won't find me." George Henry lowered his voice and looked into her eyes. "You take care, Miss Rebecca, and if he bothers you again, you tell me, you hear?"

"I will. Now go. Be safe—and talk to the sheriff." She turned off the porch light and closed the door behind him. The strength of his words lingered in the stillness.

Chapter Twenty-eight

Sunday 6:27 AM

Had I ever endured a more miserable night? I could blame it on those broken springs that squeaked and sagged beneath that crummy two bit mattress, but to be honest, it probably had a lot more to do with the hard truths I'd wrestled with all night long—truths I'd been ignoring for too many years. My defense had been that I only wanted what was best for my kid. Yeah, right. How much crap had I tried to whitewash by hiding behind that old saw? Erica sure deserved a hell of a lot better—and so did Ann.

Ann . . . Had she gotten my message? Of course she had. She was blowing me off just for spite. Damn, that woman could be infuriating.

I sat on the edge of the bed rubbing the back of my neck. Thank God I hadn't had any roommates—or was the correct term "cellmates?" Hey, maybe after the dust settled, I could write a gripping exposé on what it's like to pull hard time in the Clifton Forge slammer. I laughed.

The door to the outer office swung open and a cop entered balancing a tray and a cup of coffee. "'Good morning, Mr. Corsini. I brought you some chow." He slid the tray through the slot in the door and passed me the coffee. "Anything else you need?"

"Did I have any calls? You hear anything from a woman named Ann Richardson?"

He seemed to ponder my question and then shook his head. "Nope, but I just came on. The night guy didn't mention any calls, but he did say the magistrate phoned in, set your bond at five thousand dollars, so as soon as you can scrape together five hundred of that, you're free to go."

"Five hundred dollars? Hell, I can handle that right now. You guys take credit cards?"

"Right, and personal checks too." He laughed. "What do you take us for?"

"Listen." I moved closer to the bars. "I tried to get a call through last night, but it never connected. What's the chance I can phone out this morning?"

"According to the log, you had your one phone call. Talk to Sergeant Johnson when he comes in. He's usually here by nine, nine-thirty." He pointed at the coffee. "You take anything with that?"

I shook my head.

"Fine. Holler if you need a refill. We'll give you up to two refills, no charge."

"And after that?"

He paused by the doorway. "You don't want to run a tab on Sergeant Johnson." The officer closed the door.

The tray on my lap held an individual serving size box of corn flakes, a plastic spoon, a pint of milk, one cold biscuit, and one foil jelly packet. I punched open the perforations on the cereal box and poured in the milk.

Framed for drugs, a steel bunk that doubled as a torture device, and now this lousy food—I'd sure as hell let Johnson hear about it the minute he walked in . . . Hold on, what gave me the right to complain about some lousy cereal and a hockey puck some two bit sheriff was passing off as a biscuit? What about Erica? How long had it been since she'd eaten? What would she give right then for a taste of those soggy flakes? What if she was injured and laying out in those woods somewhere? The poor child was probably starving, just trying to survive on a stale granola bar and some slimy swamp water.

I banged the biscuit on the metal tray, then broke it in half, squeezed a glob of jelly between the stale pieces, and took a bite. Not bad . . . must have come from the diner, but not recently. So much for McConnell's breakfast buffet. I set the tray on the floor beside the cell door and sat on the bunk drinking my coffee.

"Hey, Corsini," a deputy yelled, poking his head through the doorway. "You made bail." He disappeared, then returned a moment later with keys and unlocked the cage. I followed him to the front counter.

"Got some paperwork," he said. "This is your hearing date. Sign here." He pointed. "And here's a copy of the receipt for your belongings. Car's in the parking lot. One of the officers drove it in for you." He handed me a pen.

My hand paused over the paper. Should I ask if they packed it full of dope? No, just shut up and get the hell out of there. I signed.

"That woman, the one that was in here with you the other day, she made your bail. You and her got something going?" The officer winked.

The clasp on the brown envelope was sealed with tape. I peeled it open and dumped the contents on the counter. Everything seemed to be there. I scooped up the loose change and keys and grabbed my copies of the paperwork.

"The captain wants to see you before you go." The deputy nodded toward a closed door at the end of the hallway.

It had better be a damned apology. That dope wasn't mine and he knew it, and his stinking jail accommodations were six stars shy of a five star rating. I knocked on his door.

"Enter."

McConnell waved me to a stuffed leather chair as he adjusted his reading glasses and scanned some papers in a folder. Finally, he sat on the corner of his desk and looked up. "Your stuff tested positive. Coke, low grade."

"It isn't mine."

"Time will tell." He closed the folder. "I've done some checking on you . . . a Pulitzer? That's mighty impressive."

I shrugged. I'd worn out my bragging rights on that one years ago.

"I also see here that your father was the son of one Rebecca—"

"—Corsini. Yeah, I know," I said, "she died last week. What's that got to do with my missing daughter?"

He stared, as though trying to memorize every scar and wrinkle on my face. What was going through his mind?

"Look, Captain, where's all this going? My kid's missing, but instead of looking for her, your cops are trying to hang some bum possession rap on me." I stood. "Are you finished?"

"Mr. Corsini, We're going to find your daughter. I've called in the Feds. One of their people should be here tomorrow. All I ask is that you lay low and stay out of trouble. We'll get to the bottom of this."

"Lay low? The only problem I seem to have is with your cops."

"Mr. Corsini . . . Mitch, look, I'm working some leads. I just need time."

"And that's the one thing Erica doesn't have." I stormed out.

* * *

Sunday 8:28 AM

I had to find Ann. That was first on my list. I needed to thank her for bailing me out and maybe even apologize for what I'd said the other day. I slid behind the wheel of the Chevy, cranked it up, and headed for the hotel. Maybe apologize? No, I'd better grovel. I'd been way out of line. I'd hurt her—probably a hell of a lot worse than she'd ever let on. I banged my fist on the steering wheel. Man, why did I always have to be such a jerk?

Blue lights filled my rearview mirror as I approached the highway on-ramp. What the hell? I pulled over beneath the overpass and turned off the engine, then I opened my glove box and reached in: maps, expired warranty information, broken sunglasses, but no surprises. Thank God for that. I pulled out my registration and sat quietly studying the patrol car in the side view mirror.

Sergeant Johnson jumped out of the cruiser and stormed toward me like a man who'd had his hemorrhoids painted with hot sauce.

I rolled down the window and held out my license and

registration. "'Morning, officer."

"Don't hand me that crap, Corsini. Get out the car." He planted his fists on his hips and seemed to spit the words through the window.

"Is there a problem, officer?"

"The problem is you. You gonna get out of that car, or do I have to drag you out?"

I slowly stepped from the car and straightened to my full height. Johnson's D.I. on steroids persona didn't seem affected by the fact that his spitting and spewing was now aimed at my chest.

"Sergeant Johnson," I said. "I'm over your Podunk town, your two-bit police department, and your wise-ass attitude. If you're filing charges, bring 'em on. If not, get the hell out of my way. My daughter's out there and you morons haven't done diddlysquat to find her, so now it's up to me."

Johnson pulled back. "What do mean, 'corrupt'?"

"I mean one of your cops planted that dope in my car—how else would he have known to pull me over?"

"You sonofabitch, you can't prove that."

"Then do your job. He's your cop, you prove it."

Johnson shoved me against the car. "Turn around and put your hands behind your back. I'm taking you in."

"Like hell you are." I pushed his hands aside.

He threw a punch. I blocked it and then locked his wrist in a vise-like grip. I might have been out of shape, but four years of playing Division I football still counted for something. I twisted until his knees buckled. "We can settle this right now, Johnson. It's your call. You want me? You think you got what it takes?"

"Justine." He uttered the name between clenched teeth.

I loosened my grip. "What about her?"

"You know." He pulled free. "I seen her in your room. No big city newspaper man is coming to my town and stealing my girl."

So that was it. I took a deep breath. "Nothing happened."

"Bull—"

"She came to my room looking for . . . hell, I don't even know what she was looking for, a way out? A new life? A chance at Broadway and big city lights? Your guess is as good as mine."

"And you dazzled her with all your college degrees and your fancy words." Johnson fidgeted like a bantam rooster prepping for a brawl.

"Look, Sergeant, she came on to me, I admit it, but nothing happened. My life's too complicated already. I can't afford any more entanglements."

"You and that Richardson woman got something going?"

"We work together, we're friends. That's all." He didn't need to know about any other thoughts that might have crossed my mind.

"Justine might be high strung, but she's not a bad woman. She's just young and easily led." He placed his hand on his holstered pistol. "If I ever heard of anybody filling her full of lies so's they can get into her pants, they'll pay for that mistake with their life. Do I make myself clear, Corsini?"

"You taking me in?"

Johnson threw up his hands and walked toward the squad car. He reached the front bumper and turned. "You're wearing on my patience, Corsini. You'd best finish your business and then clear out of my town—and if I catch you messing with Justine again, it won't end with talking."

Chapter Twenty-nine

Room 203. Her car was in the hotel parking lot, so she had to be in. Drapes pulled tightly across the window suggested she might still be sleeping. I knocked twice.

After a moment, the door opened a crack. Ann squinted and shaded her eyes. "Make it fast. I'm checking out."

"Hold on," I said, pushing my way into the room. "We need to talk." Clothes lay beside an open suitcase on the bed.

"You're out of jail," she said. "You're free. What else do you want?" She folded a dress over her arm and neatly placed it in the suitcase.

"I need you to hear me out." I pushed the desk chair out of the way and stood facing the bed. "Look, you were right. The other day in Johnson's office, you had me nailed, but you didn't know why."

She gave me a dismissive glance and then returned her attention to the suitcase, pushing items around as though measuring where they might go. "Mitch, I've had your number since day one, but I've been too stupid, or too bull-headed, to admit it. You thought it was all a game and I thought you'd change, or maybe you'd just realize the game wasn't funny any more."

"So," I said, "I get painted with the big white KKK brush because I want what's best for my kid, is that it?"

"When did you ever want what was best for that child?" She scowled and tossed a pair of shoes into the bag.

"So I should go to confession, bare my soul, tell the whole world what a lousy parent I've been, is that it?"

"Your words, not mine." She continued packing without looking up.

"Okay, you know it, I know it, and sure as hell Erica knows it—I earned a big fat 'F' in fatherhood. But that doesn't mean I stopped loving her, I just got caught up in a lot of other crap."

"I'm sure Erica feels much better knowing it was only a question of priorities." She pushed me aside and gathered makeup from the desk.

"Hey," I said, as I grabbed her arm, "you've known for years that I was 'missing in action' on the daddy front, that's not what's bugging you. You're worked up about that whole black-white thing, aren't you?"

She tried to pull away. "And you're saying I shouldn't be?"

"Is this about Erica, or is this about us?" I turned her to face me.

"We work in the same office, Mitch. We have lunch every now and again. That's it," she said. "There is no 'us'."

"How would your daddy feel if he found out you were seeing a white guy?" Maybe that was a stretch, but I had to separate her from her emotions.

"You mean if he were still alive? Ann said. "He wouldn't care, as long as the man treated me right. I'm free, black, and over twenty-one. I can see who I want, thank you. Now, if you're done, I need to finish packing. If I hurry, I'll be home by noon." She pushed me toward the door.

It was going nowhere, but I couldn't let her go—I didn't want to let her go. "What would he have said if you were younger, say just out of high school? You don't think he'd be worried?"

She folded a robe, then gathered it to her chest and sat on the bed. Her voice softened. "If he'd been there, maybe he would have cared enough to worry, but that's different—"

I sat beside her. "I won't pretend that I'd given this any thought at all, that is until last night." I took her hand. "A very wise and caring friend gave me the gift of a quiet evening in the municipal lock-up, all expenses paid. I had time to think, and what I thought about was how I'd really hurt the two people in this world that I cared the most about.

Last night I heard my words again, but through your ears, and they sounded hurtful—maybe even more than hurtful. Ann, I can't try to B.S. my way out this time. I screwed up—big time, and I'm sorry. I was a jerk—but then you ought to be used to that by now."

Tears welled in the corners of her eyes.

"It wasn't even about Erica seeing a black guy—well, maybe it was at first, but you want to know what the real issue was?"

She turned toward me.

"It was about the two of them," I said, "and what they'd face as a couple. I didn't want my baby to go through that."

She laughed and wiped her eyes with the back of my hand. "You mean having to face a world full of Mitch Corsinis?"

"Yeah, something like that," I said. "Our generation's gotten better, and maybe it's no big deal for the kids, but there's still a million jerks out there a whole lot worse than me, and I don't want my kid, or my grandkids, having to deal with them. It'd be different if she was older."

"You mean, like your age?"

"Yeah, my age," I said, "and a whole lot wiser. She hasn't thought it through. She doesn't understand the ramifications. She's not ready to face the consequences."

"Consequences?" Ann said. "You mean, like she's done something wrong?"

"No, you know darn well what I mean—like dealing with how others will react."

Her scowl seemed to be directed at me. "Like having to have that 'Guess Who's Coming to Dinner' talk with her daddy?"

"Hey, not fair," I said. "She could have that talk with me."

"Sure, Mitch Corsini, Grand Dragon of the Imperial Order of Parents Against Racial Harmony. Oh yeah, she'd feel real safe, and that Douglas boy? If he knew what was good for him, he'd wait on the front porch until she had you bound and gagged."

"Come on, I'm not that bad."

"No? You're worse." She shoved me over.

"They're still missing, and I'm through waiting on McConnell's Keystone Cops. It's time to tear those woods apart, tree by tree. I wish you were staying. I could sure use your help."

She stared at me for what seemed like an eternity and then slowly shook her head. "Damn it, Corsini. Why do I ever listen to you?" She stood. "Get out of here so I can change into some hiking clothes. Give me ten minutes. I'll meet you at your room."

* * *

Sunday 9:30 AM

Beer cans littered the small parking lot. It must have been one hell of a party. I spread a map over the hood of the car. "The trail starts here." I pointed first to the sign beside the trailhead and then to the map. "McConnell and I made it to about here," I said, tracing my finger across the map, "which is beyond the place where the dogs lost the scent. This is also where I was ambushed."

She folded her arms. "And when he starts shooting again, your plan is . . . ?"

"He'll see you first," I said, tugging on her red jacket. "You can distract him while I circle around and come in from behind."

"You're using me as bait?" She slapped my arm.

I laughed. "Look, here's the plan. We'll leave the trail right about here." I tapped the map. "From then on, it's cross country. Anyone worried about intruders will be watching the trails."

"I don't think I'll need this." Ann tossed her jacket in the back seat.

I grabbed the canteens she'd made me buy on our way out of town and then locked the car. "You take the lead," I said. "I'll tell you when to stop."

She started off at a fast clip. "How do you figure he got the dope into your car?" Ann asked over her shoulder.

"Had to be when he searched the glove box, but I was watching, I didn't see a thing."

"You can plead it down to simple possession. No jail time, maybe a fine. It'll haunt you if you ever run for governor, but other than that, it's no big deal."

I picked up a fallen branch and stripped it of its twigs and leaves. It made the perfect hiking staff. "It's the principle of the thing. I'm ticked off that he'll get away with it and that I'm the one who'll end up paying."

"Get over it," she said. "You've got more important things to worry about."

She was right, but it still stuck in my craw. I slowed as we climbed a gentle rise onto a broad, flat expanse. The trees stood farther apart and seemed to reach their barren branches higher into the sky. Pink flowers dotted the forest. Dogwoods? McConnell had pointed them out last time but I couldn't remember what he said they were.

I scanned the woods and pointed to the trail ahead. "I remember this stretch. Enjoy it while you can. In another half mile it's all uphill, that's when you'll need to carry me."

"I should have wrapped my red jacket around you." Ann laughed. "Your woodsman friend might find a stationary target a lot more entertaining."

"I'll be okay, but I won't pretend to be something I'm not. Don't forget, I have about eight years on you."

"And a hundred and thirty pounds," she said. "Don't I recall suggesting that you needed to join a gym?"

I sucked in my gut for just a moment, but what the hell, she wasn't looking anyway. I let it out and gave it a pat. "When we get home, I promise."

The trail wound uphill. Ann slowed, pausing several times as I caught my breath. Was she being kind, or should I drag her to the gym too? She wasn't breathing hard, but beads of sweat gathered on her forehead. With McConnell it was a different contest. That was guy against guy—and he'd enjoyed kicking my butt.

"It gets steep up ahead. Careful where you step." I tested the edge of the trail with my hiking stick. The ground rose gently to our left, while on the other side, a sixty foot drop ended in the creek bed. "This is about where McConnell said the dogs went crazy—before they lost the scent."

Ann checked her watch. "We've been hiking for about an hour and a half. How far have we come?"

"Three or four miles?" I shrugged.

Leaning against a tree, she studied our surroundings. "You and Bill kept going down that way?" She nodded toward the trail.

"Yeah, another couple of miles," I said. "That's where all the shooting happened."

"What's over there?" She pointed toward the broad ridge on our left.

"Don't know. We didn't go up there, but McConnell said they used the dogs all around here and came up empty."

"Is that another trail?"

I followed her finger as she pointed toward a rise. "I don't know. Wait a sec." I searched the map. "Nothing shows on the map. You want to check it out?"

"It can't hurt." Ann stepped aside and motioned me forward. "You go first."

On the crest of the ridge we found what appeared to be the trace of an old trail. "It looks like it runs down that way," I said. "Maybe it intersects the trail we were on."

"We must have walked right past it," she replied. "It doesn't appear to have been used recently. If Erica and Peter had gone there wouldn't the leaves be disturbed?"

"Beats me, but it could take us someplace they had been, maybe another trail junction, who knows?" I studied the faint trace as it meandered over the ridge and disappeared into the woods. "We know where the other trail goes and that's already been searched. I say we give this one a try."

Ann smiled and stepped aside again.

Staying on the ill-defined path took all my concentration. Even then, I had no confidence I'd be able to find my way back. McConnell had shown me the blazes for the other trail, but this one had no blazes—probably no more than a game trail—and not one the current crop of forest critters seemed to be particularly fond of.

We moved parallel to the other trail for a mile or so and then our path veered to the left. As the ground sloped toward a rock-strewn ravine our path followed a ridgeline a few yards below its crest. I stopped and took a drink from my canteen.

"Do you know where we are?" Ann asked.

Was that a look of concern, or just curiosity? I pulled out the map. "Here's the first trail, over there somewhere." I waved toward our right. "If we get lost, I think we can reconnect with the old trail by going across that ridge." Then I glanced at the scuffled leaves behind us and laughed. "Or we can simply backtrack. Our trail won't be hard to follow."

That seemed to put her at ease. We hiked another mile, maybe more. To be honest, I hadn't a clue.

"What's that?" Ann pointed, then hurried up the trail several yards and stopped.

When I caught up to her, I followed her gaze to where the dark, wet underside of disturbed leaves marked the route someone, or something, had taken coming down off the ridgeline. The track crossed our trail and continued into the ravine to an outcropping of large boulders.

I glanced both ways and shrugged. "Should we explore what's over the hill or check out those rocks?"

"We can see where the trail to the rocks ends," Ann said. "Let's check that first." She took off toward the pile of boulders.

I walked along behind. We still had miles to go to get back to the car. A wise man knows when to conserve energy.

"Mitch, come here, quick." She bent over a rock, waving frantically.

What the hell, it was only a few more yards. I broke into a jog. "What is it?"

Ann pointed to a dark opening beneath one of the boulders. "Is that some kind of cave?"

Chapter Thirty

April 1936

"I'm sorry to leave without making your lunch, but Lorinda Jane can fix it for you just as soon as she gets here. I need to get to the market before all the fresh produce is picked over." Rebecca pulled two dollars from the coffee can hidden in the pantry. "How's your leg this morning?"

"Itches to beat all," Papa said. "That girl should be here by now. What in tarnation's keeping her?"

"Stop your fussing, Papa. She'll be along shortly." She peered out the window. "Clouds are building to the south. There's a storm coming. Will you be able to pull those windows closed, or shall I close them now?"

"It's warming up a mite. You go closing them windows, you'll take away the only breeze I got."

"Maybe after lunch you can enjoy sitting on the porch. Miss Ella Jenkins might even see you sitting there and stop by for a visit." Rebecca winked.

"Lord, child, how can you bring ruination to something as pure and peaceful as a man enjoying a spring day on his own front porch? Now, if I even go out there, I'll be nervous as a cat in a room full of rocking chairs."

Rebecca smiled as she studied her reflection in the mirror and straightened her hat. A sudden clamoring on the front porch followed by a knock hurriedly drew her to the front door. When she opened the door Willie stepped forward, pulling off his hat.

"Miss Rebecca, you got to come quick."

"Willie, what is it? Whatever is the matter?"

"It's Lorinda Jane, ma'am. The baby's coming and she's in awful pain." He clutched his hat in both hands. "Please,

Miss Rebecca, can you come take a look?"

"The baby? It's way too early for that child. Something must be wrong."

"Can you come see?" Willie waved for Rebecca to follow.

"That's work for a doctor or a midwife," she said.

"There's no time, and they wouldn't come up the mountain no how. Please, Miss Rebecca, Lorinda Jane needs your help."

"Well, I have assisted with a few deliveries. Let's see what can be done. I'll need clean towels and boiling water. Do you have those?"

"I think so. I'll run on up the mountain and put a kettle on the fire—" He turned and started down the steps.

"Wait. Has the baby crowned?"

"Ma'am?"

"Can you see the baby's head?"

"I don't think so, ma'am, but I didn't look. She was cramping and crying and such, and I was scared for her. I come straight here to fetch you."

"You left her alone?"

"George Henry's with her, but he said Pa's army training didn't cover birthing no babies. He don't think she started delivering."

"All right, that's good. You get on up there, gather the towels, and start the water boiling. I'll be along shortly."

Willie gave a quick nod and raced down the steps.

Rebecca turned toward her father. "Papa, I need to get up the mountain right away. Lorinda Jane's gone into labor."

"I heard. You go on and tend to that girl. I'll fix my own sandwich. If I get desperate, I'll just set on the porch and wait for that old busybody, Ella Jenkins, to stop by with a basket of goodies."

"Papa, you're impossible. Now behave yourself. I hope to be home by supper." She blew him a kiss and pulled the door closed behind her.

* * *

"Hurry, Miss Rebecca," Willie called from the cabin door. "She's hurting bad and we don't know what to do."

Rebecca rushed inside. Lorinda Jane lay in a bed against the wall, her knees raised. Tears streamed down her cheeks as she clutched her stomach. George Henry knelt beside her.

"Bless you for coming, Miss Rebecca."

Rebecca glanced at George Henry and smiled. "We'll do this together. Has she started pushing?"

"No, ma'am, not so's I can tell."

"Good." Rebecca placed her hand on Lorinda Jane's forehead. She'd watched deliveries, even assisted, but would she remember all that she needed to do? What if there were complications? No, no—she mustn't allow her fear to take over. Rebecca took a deep breath. "I'm right here, Lorinda Jane. Everything's going to be fine."

Lorinda Jane's body tightened.

"Wait, don't start pushing just yet." Rebecca pointed to the lantern. "Willie, move that so it casts light over my shoulder. Good. Now, let's see . . . yes, you're definitely dilated. The baby's head is showing."

"That's a good thing, right, Miss Rebecca?" Willie peered over Rebecca's shoulder.

"Yes, it means the baby is in place for proper delivery. It won't be long now." Dear Lord, it's too soon, he's so tiny. I'm not ready to do this . . . please, give me strength—

Lorinda Jane's piercing scream filled the small cabin.

Rebecca glanced at George Henry. "It's time."

He squeezed her hand. "You'll do good, Miss Rebecca."

She forced a smile. "We'll do good." She turned to Lorinda Jane. "When I tell you, you breathe like this." She blew several short puffs.

"It hurts, Miss Rebecca . . ." Lorinda Jane squeezed Rebecca's hand.

"I know, I know, but it will be over shortly. Now listen to me." Rebecca wiped Lorinda Jane's forehead with a damp cloth.

"Head's showing." George Henry nodded to Rebecca.

"Good. George Henry, you be ready with a towel. Willie,

get behind her and help her sit up as she pushes." Rebecca glanced toward the ceiling. "Lord, please guide me . . . ." She wiped her sleeve across her brow and positioned herself at the end of the bed. "Now, with the next pain, I want you to take a deep breath and push."

Lorinda Jane tensed, then groaned and pushed.

"Good. Again."

Lorinda Jane pushed.

Rebecca looked up at her and smiled. "You're doing fine, Lorinda Jane, just fine. Now, again. Blow hard and push."

Lorinda Jane rose up on her elbows as she strained.

"Push again. Push. PUSH!"

How long had it been? Rebecca licked her lips. Her mouth was dry from coaxing Lorinda Jane through each contraction. How much longer could Lorinda Jane keep pushing?

"Come on," Rebecca said. "Give me a BIG push now."

Lorinda Jane sucked in a deep breath, gave a fierce growl, and squeezed her eyes closed as she strained to birth her child.

"He's here!" George Henry said. "Willie, your boy's here!" Lorinda Jane fell back against the pillow.

Rebecca cradled the tiny infant as he delivered, then lifted the baby by his ankles and slapped his backside as she'd seen the doctors do. An angry cry came from the tiny mouth.

A wave of relief swept over Rebecca as she wiped the baby's face then wrapped him in a blanket and laid him in the crook of Lorinda Jane's arm. "Here's your son. He's the most beautiful baby I've ever seen."

"He's so small." Willie said. "He going to be all right?"

"He is almost two months early, but I certainly hope so."

"He got all his fingers and his toes? He got—"

Rebecca placed her hand on Willie's arm. "I'll ask Doctor West to come up here and have a look. I'm sure he'll be willing."

Lorinda Jane cried softly as she clutched Rebecca's sleeve. "I ain't never been a momma before. That there was some hard doing."

Rebecca patted her hand as she stood. "Would have been a lot harder delivery if you'd let him grow to full term."

"Miss Rebecca," George Henry said, "we's grateful for all you done. Me and Willie, we couldn't a delivered that child ourselves."

She gazed into his large brown eyes. Was that a tear on his cheek? She smiled. "The good Lord had already made up His mind. You and Willie couldn't have stopped that child from being born."

George Henry seemed to recognize the truth in what she said. He smiled and nodded.

"Now, let's get a few things cleaned up and then we can step outside and give Lorinda Jane and Willie some private time to enjoy that wonderful new son of theirs."

* * *

George Henry rocked the chair back and crossed his legs. He whittled the end of a stick with his pocketknife. "Weather's coming."

"It certainly is." Rebecca rocked beside him on the cabin porch. "Looks to be building to the south. How long you reckon until it's here?"

"Hard to say." He pointed with his knife. "If'n the wind shifts, it could go east. If it blows north, be on us within the hour."

Her work there was done. She gazed at the darkening clouds through a break in the trees. The smart thing would be to head home, beat the storm, but she wouldn't mind the rain as much as the lonely walk down the mountain. She turned to George Henry. "You watch that baby's cord. Do like I showed you, and make sure Willie keeps it clean. It'll drop on its own."

"Willie says they's naming that baby after me."

"George Henry? That's a fine name for your nephew: strong, honest, just like your Yankee general. But what if you marry one day and have your own son, won't you want him to have your name?"

George Henry laughed. "Willie keeps trying to fix me up

with women. Guess I ain't found one to my liking yet."

Rebecca looked away. What was to his liking? She shouldn't ask. She shouldn't even care. "And what about your son?"

"Shoot, if I ever has me a son," he said, wagging the piece of wood he was carving, "I'll still name him after me. Can't be too many George Henry McConnells in this world."

She laughed. "You are so right."

He rocked in silence for a moment, and then turned toward her. "You done real good in there, Miss Rebecca. You're going to make a fine nurse."

"Thank you. I had some very good help." She patted his hand and smiled.

George Henry tensed, but didn't pull away. Why had she done that? What would he think? She quickly folded her hands in her lap as guilt passed through her like a hot wave—or was it something else? "I really must be going. Papa has been alone all day, and he'll be ornery as a blue jay if he doesn't get his supper."

George Henry stood. "I'll walk you down the mountain."

"Thanks, but that won't be necessary. Besides, if that nasty Chester Johnson is watching, it would be best if you weren't seen walking with me."

"He's bad people, Miss Rebecca. You watch out for that man." He raised his hand. "Wait here." George Henry stepped into the cabin. He returned a moment later carrying a yellow slicker. "Rain's almost on us. You'd best take this so's you doesn't get that pretty dress all wet."

"Thank you." She turned as he draped the slicker over her shoulders. "Tell Lorinda Jane I'll come back tomorrow to check on her. You and Willie take good care of her, and that little George Henry McConnell, too."

* * *

Rebecca pulled the hooded slicker tight as the wind drove sheets of rain against the rubberized cloth. Another four blocks and she'd be home.

"Evening, Rebecca. Out for a walk in the storm?"

Chester pulled alongside her in his pickup.

"What I am out for is none of your concern, Chester Johnson."

"I can give you a lift, get you out from the weather . . . ."

Rebecca faced the rusted blue truck. "Let me say this one more time: I don't want to ride in your truck and I don't care to have you following me all over town. Is that perfectly clear, Chester Johnson?"

"Slicker looks a mite big on you. You got it on loan from somebody?"

"That's none of your concern either." She began walking again, more briskly than before.

"Looks like what them gandy dancers wear." He drove slowly beside her. "You been visiting with that nigra up on the mountain?"

"For your information, I was delivering a baby for the girl who works for us. It was nursing business, and none of yours."

Chester gunned the engine, threw the truck in gear, and pulled away.

He knew she'd been up on the mountain. He must have known that was George Henry's slicker. Oh God, had she put George Henry in danger? In a fair fight, he'd crush that little weasel . . . except Chester Johnson wasn't one for playing fair.

* * *

Rebecca lowered the window and stepped over the puddle. "You were just going to let it rain all over the kitchen floor? I know you aren't as mobile as you'd like, but you sure seem able to get over to that stupid radio easily enough."

Papa cleared his throat. "Guess I missed that one. I was busy taking care of the ones in the living room. How's that colored girl?"

"She was resting comfortably when I left, and her baby seemed to be doing fine. He's so tiny, but he has a powerful set of lungs. I'm going back up there tomorrow to check on both of them."

"Don't you think that ought best be left to one of the others, maybe one of those colored midwives? I don't like you going up that mountain all by your lonesome without a proper gentleman escort. People will talk."

"They can talk until their tongues fall out. Lorinda Jane and Willie are our friends, and they don't have anyone else to turn to."

"She's our house girl. Friends are white folks."

"Papa, you know what I mean; they're good people. You care about Lorinda Jane, don't you?"

He shifted in his seat and waved with the back of his hand. "You know durned well I care, I just don't want you finding yourself too far out on a limb with no way to climb back."

Rebecca patted his shoulder. "I'll be careful, Papa, you know I will."

The clapper on the front door knocked rapidly.

Rebecca glanced at her father. "Who'd be out on such a night? You sit tight, Papa, I'll be right back." She walked over and opened the door.

"Sheriff Blakely, Good evening," she said. "Whatever brings you out on a night like this? Please, come in and dry yourself. Papa's in the kitchen. Can I fix you a cup of tea?"

The sheriff stepped inside the door, water dripping from his raincoat, and removed his hat. "Evening, Miss Marshall. Was you I come to see."

"Me? Goodness. Well, won't you have a seat?" She motioned toward the sofa.

"I'll stand, if you don't mind." He turned the brim of his hat in his hands. "You heard about old Stumpy Morris being murdered?"

"Yes, I did. Such an awful thing, that poor man . . ."

"An eyewitness come forward, says there's a colored boy been seen around here every now and again, one of them gandy dancers. He's the one done the killing."

Rebecca froze. George Henry? "Hold on," she said. "Your so-called eyewitness, he wouldn't happen to be Chester Johnson?"

"Sorry, ma'am. I'm not at liberty to disclose that information. I just need to ask you a few questions about this nigra that done the killing."

"Slow down, Sherriff," Papa said, hobbling in from the kitchen. "I know that boy. He does chores for me. He's no killer."

"Evening, Clarence. I got a witness says he is."

"George Henry did no such killing," Rebecca said, inches from the sheriff's face. She wagged her finger. "And if Chester Johnson says he witnessed it, you'd better be asking yourself what else he knows about that crime."

"Whoa, hold on there, I'm just looking for a few facts before I head up the mountain and bring that boy in. Don't go getting all high and mighty, I'm just asking questions."

"Sounds to me like you've set yourself up as judge and jury," she said. "George Henry is innocent."

"Then let's see his proof. I have a white man says he seen that boy do the killing and I aim to go up that mountain and bring him in." The sheriff pointed toward the door.

Rebecca crossed her arms and paced. Finally, she stopped beside her father's chair. "No," she said. "I'll bring him in."

"You'll do what?" the sheriff said.

"You and you deputies just stay off that mountain. His brother and his brother's wife just had a baby two months premature and they don't need a trigger-happy posse chasing around those woods. I'll bring him down in the morning, straight to the jail, no guns."

"You can't do that, child," Papa said.

She turned and stared. "Of course I can."

The sheriff rubbed his chin. "Your daddy's right, ma'am. He's already killed one man—"

"He hasn't killed anyone." She pushed the sheriff toward the door. "You give me until noon tomorrow or that judge and the newspapers will get an earful. And you can tell Chester Johnson for me that I'll see to it that he's the one who will be answering for murder."

Chapter Thirty-one

Rebecca pulled the hooded slicker over her head and stepped into the predawn squall. She clutched a basket filled with bread, jams, butter, and canned goods from their pantry. Lorinda Jane and Willie would need the extra stores, especially if George Henry was no longer there. Would he come down the mountain with her? Could she hire a lawyer, and how would that look, a white woman siding with the colored man who was accused by one white man of murdering another?

Lanterns in the rail yards bobbed and flickered as night crews assembled trains for the morning runs. She hopped over a puddle and turned onto Ridgeway Street. A few lights shone in the brick two-story C&O office building. Janitors? The bosses wouldn't be in for another three hours.

Once past the hospital, Rebecca followed the river around a horseshoe bend to a path leading into the forest. The familiar rocky, overgrown path followed a small stream up the mountain to the small clearing and Lorinda Jane's cabin. From within, a lantern flickered behind a broken window pane.

Rebecca knocked.

Inside, someone stirred, then footsteps. The door opened a crack.

"Miss Rebecca," Willie exclaimed, "What's you doing up here?"

"I came to see Lorinda Jane and the baby."

Willie peered past Rebecca to the woods behind her. "You come alone?"

"Boy," Lorinda said, "don't you be keeping Miss Rebecca

waiting out in that weather. Open that door so's she can come in and get warmed."

Willie stepped aside.

Lorinda Jane huddled beneath blankets in the bed closest to the wood stove. The bundled baby lay on her chest. "'Morning, Miss Rebecca. Best I can tell, my boy's doing like he should." She laughed. "He's hungry all the time, always rooting around for that teat."

Rebecca set her basket down. "And how's momma feeling?" She placed her hand on Lorinda Jane's forehead.

"Sore, but I've had worse pain. Willie's none too keen though, having to mess with the bedpan."

"You should be up and about in a day or so," Rebecca said. "I haven't talked to the doctor, but I hope to this morning. Once this storm lets up, he needs to see you and the baby." She opened the basket. "I brought you a few things, just to carry you until you're able to cook again." She held up the wrapped bread. "Store bought."

Lorinda Jane's face broke into a wide smile. "You and your daddy is too good to us. I'll have to send Willie and George Henry down the mountain to do my chores for you, until I'm up again."

"Where is George Henry?" Rebecca scanned the small cabin. "I thought he'd be here."

Lorinda Jane opened her robe and snuggled the baby against her breast. She lifted the nipple to his mouth. "See? That boy's just like his daddy. He knows where I hides the sweetness. Willie, go fetch some water and put a pot on the stove."

"Water's in the bucket. I brung it earlier."

"That's old. Go fetch fresh water for Miss Rebecca." She waved. "Go on now."

He grabbed the bucket from beside the stove. "Water's fine. I just brung it this morning." He shook his head and shuffled out the door.

"Come, sit beside me." Lorinda Jane pointed to the small wooden chair.

Rebecca scooted the chair next to the bed.

Lorinda Jane glanced at the door, then looked at Rebecca. "I'll speak my mind just this once, then I ain't talking about it no more."

Talk about what? Rebecca's throat tightened. Whatever could she mean?

"Miss Rebecca, you's a good woman. I sees a kindness in your heart—but you don't want no part of where that heart is pushing you to go."

"I . . . I don't understand."

Placing her hand on Rebecca's forearm, Lorinda Jane said, "I seen how you look at George Henry when you're thinking nobody sees. I ain't saying it's wrong, just bad, bad for you, bad for him."

How could she know? She hadn't even admitted it to herself. Rebecca pulled away. "He's my friend."

"Black man can't have no white woman friends. If some was to see him close to you, they'd be paying him a night visit with their ropes and flaming crosses."

"I don't want to get him in any trouble—"

"Sh-h-h. Willie'll be coming." Lorinda Jane put a finger to her mouth.

"But, he's in trouble. I need to see him." Rebecca said.

"Trouble?" Lorinda Jane struggled to sit up in bed. "What kind of trouble?"

"He's wanted for Stumpy Morris's murder."

Lorinda Jane gasped. "That boy didn't have nothing to do with no killing. I heard him and Willie talking, when they found that poor old Mr. Morris, God rest his soul, the man was already cold."

"I know, he told me, but if I don't bring him down the mountain, the sheriff's coming after him."

"You gonna turn him in? How's that gonna help?"

Outside the cabin, the report of a gun rattled the windowpane. Angry voices hollered urgent commands. The door burst open and Willie stumbled in, his hands in the air. "Please don't shoot, I ain't seen him all night."

Sherriff Blakely and Chester Johnson followed Willie into the room, their guns drawn. The sheriff looked at Rebecca.

"What are you doing here?"

"I happen to be tending to this woman and her newborn son, but since you don't seem to recall, I also said I'd talk George Henry into surrendering. There's no call for you bringing your guns and terror into this home."

"Where's he at?" Chester shoved Willie to the floor. "You'd best talk or I'll plug you right here and now."

Rebecca jumped in front of Chester, pushing the shotgun aside. "You leave this man be, Chester Johnson. If you so much as touch a hair on his head, I'll go straight to the State Police." She pointed at the sheriff. "Maybe he won't uphold the law, but I'll find someone who will."

"Put down that damned gun, Chester." Sheriff Blakely holstered his pistol. "There won't be any shooting today, ma'am, not unless that boy resists arrest. Where is he?"

"See for yourself." Rebecca took in the cabin with a sweep of her hand. "He's not here."

"You, Willie, or whatever your name is, where's your brother?" Sheriff Blakely asked.

"Never come home last night," Willie said. "God's honest truth."

"He's lying." Chester kicked the sole of Willie's boot. Willie pulled back and clutched his knees to his chest.

Sheriff Blakely turned to Lorinda Jane. "You, girl, is he lying?"

"He stayed away all the night long. Could be he's over to Covington. He goes up that way every now and again, selling that man's moonshine liquor." Lorinda Jane nodded toward Chester as she pulled the blanket over the infant at her breast.

Chester jerked his shotgun away from the sheriff. "She's lying too."

"Johnson," the sheriff said, "will you shut the hell up?"

"You gonna take the word of a nigra?" Chester wagged his finger at the sheriff. "Folks hear you're going soft on the darkies, they might not take kindly, come election time."

"Damn it, Chester, wait outside." Sheriff Blakely jerked a thumb toward the door.

Chester scowled and stomped out of the cabin.

"Who does he see in Covington?" Sheriff Blakely said.

"Don't know. He sells bottles in the colored part of town, ask around down there." Willie stood and brushed off his trousers.

"If he comes back, you come get me, you hear?" The sheriff pointed at Willie.

Willie nodded.

"And I'll have a deputy watching your place, Miss Marshall." He looked at Rebecca. "It's for your own good. He's already killed once. When he finds out we're after him, he'll be twice as dangerous." Sheriff Blakely tipped his hat to Rebecca and left.

Rebecca watched through the broken window as the sheriff and Chester Johnson headed down the path. He'd already been judged and found guilty. They'd hunt him like they'd hunt a rabid dog. She wiped a tear from her eye and turned to Lorinda Jane. "I didn't realize . . . they've made up their minds. They won't listen to anything you or George Henry have to say."

With a sigh, Lorinda Jane pointed to the food basket. "Willie, he'll be needing these vittles worse than us. Best get on up there and let him know they's hunting him." She turned to Rebecca. "Sorry, Miss Rebecca. You'd best be going home. There's no place in this for a white lady."

"Tell me where he is," Rebecca said, snatching the basket from Willie's hands. "I'll take him the food. You need to stay here and protect your family."

Willie glanced at Lorinda Jane, as if seeking her guidance.

"You said you wants to take him off the mountain," Lorinda Jane said. "You wants to turn him in."

"No, not now." Rebecca shook her head. "Not after this. He must escape, but he also needs to know who's after him, and he needs food. Let me do this one thing. Willie should stay here with you."

Lorinda Jane appeared to ponder the idea. She beckoned Rebecca closer. "You know the stream that brung you here?"

Rebecca nodded.

"You leave here, you go on up the mountain one and a half, two miles. Trail goes off to the right. Cross the ridge, you'll find an old cabin, ain't fixed up pretty like this'n, used to be a deer camp. Roof burnt off ten, fifteen years ago." Lorinda Jane smiled. "He took some canvas up there last year and covered it over. He goes there sometimes when the frogs ain't talking."

* * *

George Henry placed a small log on the fire. The smoke drifted up the stone chimney away from the pile of blankets on the earthen floor beside the hearth. "You shouldn't have come here, Miss Rebecca. They's after me, not you."

She trembled. Was it the cold—or her fear? "You needed food." She pulled a blanket under her and sat beside the fire.

"You's mighty kind, but foolish deeds ain't gonna help neither one of us." He settled beside her and took the sandwich she offered.

"What will you do?"

"I'll be safe enough here for now." He stared into the flames. "They won't be tracking before the storm breaks. If I can put some miles behind me, that rain'll wash away my scent."

As she poked the fire, sparks drifted up the chimney. "Where will you go?"

"Was thinking about Florida. I might hop a freight, slide on down to Miami, maybe catch a steamboat and head to South America."

She stole a look. His eyes sparkled as he studied the flames. "That's so far away. I've never been to Florida," she said. "How will I . . . how will we know if you make it there safely?"

George Henry set his sandwich down and turned toward her. "It's wrong for you to be here."

"Lorinda Jane said this is where you come when the frogs aren't talking."

"Miss Rebecca, the things I been thinking on lately, those frogs don't understand. Shoot, I don't understand."

She placed her hand on his arm. "I know what you mean."

His expression seemed to be one of curiosity.

She smiled. "The frogs are just as confused about the questions I ask."

"I gets scared just thinking on what you might be talking about," he said. He shook his head, but he didn't pull away. "It ain't right. Can't no good come of it."

"George Henry, you listen. We're God's children. His rules didn't make us separate, it was man's rules that did that."

"And them man's rules will lynch a colored man just for looking at a white woman—or drive her from town on a rail for allowing him to."

Over and over she'd played those games in her heart, not thinking of the consequences. But they weren't games. Whatever tugged at her heart right then was as real as the warmth of George Henry's whispered words . . . and as real as the men who were hunting him down. She touched his cheek and laid down on the blanket.

He settled beside her, his head resting on his hand, and curled a lock of her hair around his finger. "Come evening, I'll be gone," he said.

"When will you come back?" Rebecca asked. "Once they've given up looking, will you let me know where I can find you?"

He placed his hand over her heart. "I'm hoping you'll always find me right here."

"Is this love?" she asked.

"I don't rightly know." he said, closing his eyes. "I reckon if I ever asked them frogs, that's what they'd call it."

He reached inside his shirt and pulled a lanyard from around his neck. A wooden token the size of a matchbox hung on the rawhide cord. "This here was my granddaddy's. His father carved it for him when they was slaves. See that star carved right there?" He pointed. "That's the North Star."

"What does it mean?" Rebecca turned over the token, examining it closely.

"When his time came to go north, that's the star Granddaddy followed. He called it his freedom star." George Henry placed the rawhide cord around Rebecca's neck, then bent down and kissed her softly on the lips. "I'd be pleased if you'd hold this for me. One day, when this world ain't such an angry place, maybe then I'll have my own boy to pass it on to."

Chapter Thirty-two

Sunday 3:18 PM

I knelt beside the moss-encrusted boulder and peered into the ominous hole.

Ann glanced over my shoulder. "You're not thinking of going down there?"

"Are you kidding?" I turned toward her and scowled. "Have I ever done anything to make you believe I'd be that crazy?" A dead branch covered with dried leaves blocked the opening. I pushed it aside and gingerly leaned into the mouth of the cave. What if critters were hibernating down there?

"I can't see diddlysquat—it's too deep." I tossed a stone into the opening. Somewhere below the stone bounced and landed with a thunk.

A groan followed from deep within the cave.

"Did you hear that?" I whispered. "Something's down there. Listen."

"It better not bite." She knelt beside me and cocked her head. "I don't hear anything."

I tossed another pebble. The sound came again, louder this time, more guttural. "It's got to be an animal." I pushed away from the hole. "Let's get out of here before it blames us for waking it up."

"Wait," a weak voice called from the darkness.

"Mitch, there's somebody down there!" Ann nudged me aside and cupped her hand around her mouth. "Hello? Hello?"

"Help," the voice called, louder this time.

"Erica? Honey, is that you?" I nudged Ann aside and leaned into the opening. "Damn, it's as black as midnight down there. I can't see a blessed thing. Hold on . . ." I dug out the carabineer attached to my car keys and twisted its top. The green glow of the LED light revealed a lone figure lying on the cave floor, hands and feet bound. "Erica? You wait, honey. I'll be right there."

"No, it's . . . I'm Peter," the figure said. "Peter Douglas." He looked up. Shredded tape clung to his face. Apparently, he'd been able to work it free from his mouth.

"Peter?" I said. "Where's Erica?"

"She's not here. He has her tied up."

"What? Who has her tied up? Where?"

"I don't know."

"You're not making any sense. Where is she?" I demanded.

"Please, mister," Peter pleaded. "Get me out of here."

"I'll get you out when you tell me where my daughter is."

Ann grabbed my arm. "Back off, Mitch. Can't you see the boy's scared and hurt and God knows what else? She's not here, but he might know how to find her."

She was right, as usual. My chances of finding Erica hinged on first rescuing him. I took a deep breath. "Okay, kid, sit tight. I'll be down there in a minute." I turned to Ann. "Find a rope, a vine, anything I can use to reach down to him."

"Where?" she said, searching the bushes around the outcropping. "There's nothing here."

I scrambled up the hill and found a stout limb, almost as thick as my forearm and about three feet long. I lowered it into the hole. "Can you hold me?"

Ann leaned across the backs of my legs while I stretched as far as I could. "It's no good," I said. "It's still not long enough."

"Can't you just drop down?" she asked. "It doesn't sound very far."

"You're right. Why don't I drop you down? You'd only fall a few feet."

"Are you kidding? That's seriously a bad idea. Spiders, bugs—no way."

"Okay, then let's try this—give me your backpack."

She tossed me the bag.

I unbuckled the straps and spread them apart, placing one end over the heavy branch. "This should give me five or six feet, right? I can tie one end around here like this, jam the branch across the cave mouth and, voila!" I braced it across the opening and tugged on the backpack's strap. "Should be strong enough to hold me."

Ann shook her head. "I don't know . . ."

"Come on, we have no choice. Once I'm in there, you brace your feet against that branch so it doesn't slide." I gripped the strap and squeezed feet first through the small hole, lowering myself into the cave.

When my feet touched the ground I shined the LED around the cave. The space was larger than it had appeared from above. The ceiling sloped away from the opening toward a wet, slimy wall about eight feet away. I shivered. The air had to be ten degrees colder than outside—and dank. Five or six feet to my left, the cave ended in a low, hollowed out shelf. In the other direction, the light disappeared into what seemed to be a black, endless void. Rivulets seeping from the far wall trickled down a broad, rocky tunnel and disappeared into the darkness.

Peter lay on his side, curled against the wet wall. "Hey, kid, what do you say we get this crap off you and get the hell out of here?" I tugged at the duct tape around his wrists. Whoever had wrapped him hadn't scrimped. "Damn, this stuff's too thick and I can't find the end. Ann, you got a knife, a nail file, anything?"

"Try this."

I turned toward the daylight. She held out her hand and dropped something—a Swiss Army knife. "You do come prepared. Anything else up there? Sandwiches? Sleeping bag? You didn't happen to bring a lantern?"

"Knock off the wisecracks and get him out of there," Ann shouted.

I cut the tape on his wrists and around his mouth. "How are you doing, kid?"

He rubbed his face. "Okay, I guess. You got any food?"

"We'll take care of that once we get topside. Man, this place is creepy. How long have you been down here?" I cut the tape binding his ankles.

He stretched. "What day is it?"

"Sunday."

"We started hiking on Monday . . . hard to keep track of the days. He kept me tied up at a cabin until yesterday. That's when he dropped me down here."

"He who?" Mitch said. "And where's Erica?"

"I told you, I don't know who he was—some crazy old man. She's probably still at his cabin."

"What cabin? Can you find it again?"

Peter shook his head. "Everything's a blur . . . I don't know. I don't think so."

"He dropped you down here without food or water?" I said. "How'd you manage?"

He pressed his hand against the damp wall. "Seepage. I got the tape off my mouth and licked the wall. Lichen, minerals, plenty of water—a body could survive for a few weeks if he conserved his energy."

"Nice theory, but let's not test it. You ready to stand?" I took his hand.

"MITCH!"

I looked up as Ann fell through the hole and crashed on top of me. Together, we tumbled to the ground.

I eased her off my chest and sat up. "What the hell?" I said, rubbing my head. "Are you okay?"

"Somebody pushed me," she replied.

Daylight filled the opening. The log and Ann's backpack lay beside us.

"I'm not kidding," she said. "Somebody snuck up behind me and shoved me."

"Seriously?" I turned toward the opening and cupped my hands. "Hey, if you're still up there, drop us a rope. Get us out of here."

No response.

I clawed at the slick wall, but couldn't catch a foothold, so I tossed a rock through the opening and hollered again,

"You up there, if you can hear me, we need help. Give us a hand."

Silence.

"You sure you didn't just slip?" I helped her to her feet.

"I leaned in to see what you were doing and somebody grabbed my ankles," she said. She brushed herself off and examined her hands in the dim light. "Nothing's broken, except maybe a nail."

"It must be the same guy," Peter said, "the one who threw me down here. Watch out, he has a gun." Peter slowly rose to one knee.

"By the way," she said, "I'm Ann."

Peter nodded. "Hi."

"Sh-h-h." I placed a finger on my lips. "Cut the chatter. He might still be there."

"I don't hear anything," Ann said. "Maybe he left."

"One of you climb up on my shoulders," I said. "Maybe you'll be able to crawl out and set up that log again."

"I'll go," Ann said. She nodded toward the kid. "He's too weak from his ordeal."

I braced my back against the wall and interlocked my hands. "Take a quick look. If he's still out there, we'll sit tight until he leaves. It's probably the same guy who shot at me."

She placed her foot in my hands and stepped up. Suddenly, from somewhere above us, came the sound of rock scraping against rock. Ann jumped down just before the circle of daylight disappeared and an inky blackness filled the cave.

"Mitch, he blocked the entrance!" She grabbed my shirt and pulled me close.

I turned on the light. "It's okay, stay cool." It was easy enough to say, but my heart was pounding. "Whoever that sonofabitch is, he's going to pay . . ."

"Pay?" Ann's voice quivered. "We're the ones trapped. What about us?"

"Maybe we can push that boulder aside," Peter said. "Let me give it a shot, I think I'm strong enough."

"Okay, it's worth a try." I handed Ann the light. "Come

on, Peter, give it a go."

He stepped into my hands and climbed to my shoulders. Boots dug into my collarbone as he tried moving the rock. After a few grunts he said, "Too heavy. No way to get leverage."

"How about if both of you try? Ann, hand me the light and hop on up there." I hooked the key chain on my shirt pocket and hoisted her. Peter balanced on my right shoulder. Ann climbed onto my left. Their boots dug into my neck and shoulders. I leaned against the jagged rock. "Hurry," I said through gritted teeth.

"Nope. It won't budge." Ann said. "I'm coming down." She slid down my chest, kneeing me in the face. Peter followed.

"Damn. Now what?" I shined the light on the boulder that was blocking our escape.

"We can call for help." Ann pulled out her cell phone and flipped it open, then shook her head. "Nope. No bars."

Try anyway," I said.

She punched in a number. "No service. We didn't have coverage up there," she said, pointing toward the blocked opening. "What makes you think the phone company has better reception down here?"

"Great," I said. "What now?"

"Take inventory," Peter replied. He looked at me and nodded, as though seeking my approval. "That's what the survival manuals say."

"Okay, do it." I said.

"What's in that backpack?" Peter said as he pulled a bandana from his pocket. He wiped his forehead and smiled weakly. "Guess I'm feeling a little dizzy right now." He placed the bandana plus a box of matches and a compass on the ground. Ann and I dumped our few treasures into the pile.

"The survival manuals all say . . . say . . ." Peter swayed. His eyes rolled up and he collapsed like a rag doll.

Ann gasped. "Mitch?"

I felt his pulse and then touched his forehead. "I think he

just passed out." I wet his bandana in the thin pool of groundwater and dabbed his forehead. Ann sat beside me, resting her head on my shoulders. Trapped. If I couldn't get us out, what would happen to Erica?

* * *

Sunday 3:45 PM

Minutes passed. Finally, he blinked and stared at me. "Who . . . who are you?"

"Mitch Corsini. I'm Erica's dad."

He seemed puzzled. "Mr. Gillespie?"

Hadn't she ever told him her real name? I touched the wet cloth to his lips. "Gillespie's her step-father. I'm just the sperm donor."

Ann placed her hand on my shoulder and gave a gentle squeeze.

"What happened?" Peter asked. "Did I pass out?"

"You're weak. You've had a rough week, we're lucky you waited until you were at ground level before taking your tumble." I shined the light on our supplies. Thank God for Ann. I handed Peter one of her granola bars and a bottle of water. "Take it slow. You don't want to make yourself sick."

He eased to a sitting position and hung his head between his knees. Finally, he looked up. "Mr. Corsini?" he said. "I'm sorry, Erica never mentioned you."

Of course not. Why would she mention a deadbeat? "No sweat," I said. I rubbed his shoulder. "You going to be okay?"

He nodded and took a small bite.

"What happened to Erica?" I said.

Like a squirrel clutching a cherished treasure, he grasped the bar between his hands and chewed. "We were hiking. We came to a spot where the trail went into a ravine, then up the other side. I remember this gigantic oak with a really fat limb that came straight out and then curved toward the sky." Peter drew the limb in the air.

I'd seen that tree, or one just like it, but where?

"We rested beneath that tree to eat our lunch and this old

guy, must have been close to seventy," he said, "he came out of nowhere waving a shotgun and hollering. He kept calling her Rebecca."

"Calling who Rebecca?" I asked.

"Erica."

"You're sure?" I looked at Ann.

"Is that someone you know?" she asked.

I took a deep breath, but the sudden queasiness in my stomach wouldn't go away. "Nah, probably just coincidence. Go on, kid. What then?"

Water dribbled down his chin as he drank. He wiped his mouth with his sleeve. "He pointed the gun at us," Peter said, "and made us walk through the woods, maybe a mile. We came to a cabin. He forced us inside and he made Erica wrap me with that tape, then he tied her to a chair."

"He didn't hurt her, did he?" I tried to block images of Erica at the hands of that lunatic.

"No sir, not that I could tell, but she was plenty scared, me too. After a few days, he dragged me out of the cabin and threw me on his ATV—he's pretty strong for an old guy. We drove back to the big oak, and he tossed a rope with a hangman's noose over that fat limb. Then he did something weird. He stared at me real hard and then he said, 'You ain't him.'"

"Ain't who?" Ann asked. "What'd he mean by that?"

"Beats me, but he pulled the rope down, stuck me on the ATV again, and brought me here, then he dumped me into the cave and drove away."

"She's alive," I said, grabbing Ann's hand.

Ann smiled. "Then we need to get out of here and go find her."

"Inventory." I handed her the light. "What else do we have?"

"Another granola bar, a book of matches, a bottle of bug repellant, lip gloss, my penknife, a compass, some tissues, a compact, a bandanna, and a gaggle of used duct tape." She opened the compact, glanced quickly in the mirror, and then tossed it on the pile. "We're trapped down here." Her voice trembled. "What now?"

Hell, we were all scared, but they were depending on me. Nobody'd been crazy enough to do that in years. There had to be a way out and they were counting on me to find it. "Okay," I said, "we need a plan. You stay here with him. I'll explore."

"Whoa!" Ann said, grabbing my arm. "You are not leaving us here in the dark."

"Nothing's going to hurt you," I said.

"Wait." Peter pointed to the pile. "Let me see that bug repellant, the penknife, and the matches. Oh, and that bandanna too."

She looked at me and shrugged, then handed him the items. He tore a strip from the bandanna about an inch wide and six inches long and rolled it into a tight tube. "This should wick. We can stick it in the bug repellant and it'll be our lamp, you know, like in the olden days, like in the Bible?"

"Despite rumors to the contrary, I wasn't around then," I said, "but it sounds interesting. Show me what you got." I held the light.

He unscrewed the top of the bug repellant bottle, poked a hole in the cap with the penknife, and then threaded the cloth through the hole until only a half inch showed above the cap. Then he pushed the long end of the cloth into the bottle and screwed the cap back on. "The trick's not to let too much wick stick out or it'll burn too fast." He struck a match and touched it to the cloth. The flame flickered as it caught the cloth. When he pulled the match away, the wick continued to burn.

I turned off the LED. The glow in the cave turned from green to yellow. "How long will it burn?"

"It's hard to say. Real wicks are a lot thicker, but we don't have to keep it burning all the time now that we know it will work." Peter tucked the matches in his pocket. "We'll blow it out while you're gone, but if you call, or if there's trouble, I have the matches, and I can light it again."

Ann stood. "You're crazy if you think I'm sitting here in the dark with God knows what crawling all over me while you go off exploring." She grabbed my sleeve. "I vote for sticking together."

"But Peter's in no shape to be climbing around," I said. "What if he passes out again? What if he bangs his head on a rock? We don't know what's down there."

"Can't be any worse than what's up here," Ann said. She folded her arms. "Why not leave it to Peter, see how he feels?"

I looked at the kid.

"Meaning no disrespect, Mr. Corsini, but the lady's right. All the survival manuals say to stick together. I'll be okay, just give me a minute to finish this granola bar."

I was going to stake my life on the word of a nineteen-year-old? Hell, at least he'd read the damned manuals.

Chapter Thirty-three

George Henry rose on one elbow. Rain tapped a rhythm against the canvas stretched across what used to be the roof of the burned out cabin. Beside him, Rebecca slept, her chest rising and falling rhythmically with each breath. The corners of her mouth twitched, then turned up in a smile. Was she dreaming? Dreams was all she had and there'd be a passel of nightmares coming soon enough.

Leaning into the hearth, he blew softly on the bed of coals. A tiny red glow brightened, then burst into flame. She'd be chilled when she awoke, scared too. He added twigs, then sticks. The fire grew. She'd also be alone.

The crackle of damp wood burning filled the small enclosure. Lord, let them clouds hide that smoke rising up the chimney. If he hopped a southbound freight, he could be clear to Richmond before the rains let up.

Would it be any different when he returned to Philadelphia? That city drew boundaries, same as down south, with whites in their neighborhoods, Chinese in their own section, and blacks huddled around the manufacturing plants and warehouses down by the river. But by Clifton Forge standards, they'd had a fine home up north, and he'd earned more money making furniture than most white engineers made on the railroad. Nevertheless, money wouldn't change what he was—or the color of her skin. Was there any place they could ever go where that wouldn't matter?

It was time. One final kiss? He leaned toward her, then hesitated. If she awoke, he'd never be able to leave. He tucked the blanket around her shoulders and added another log to the fire. Silently, he stood and slipped out the door.

The steady patter of rain against the spring leaves deadened his footfalls. No noise, no scent—a bad day for tracking meant a good day for running. He'd stop by the cabin and ask Willie to come get Rebecca and walk her home, then he'd head to the rail yards. He glanced over his shoulder one last time. Would she be standing in the doorway?

No, and that was for the best.

Ducking beneath an overhanging branch, he eased down an embankment into a stand of rhododendron growing beside a small stream. Water gurgled over the rocks. He hopped to a flat stone in the middle, then on to the other bank. The rain brought a chill to the air. He shuddered. Rebecca had his slicker. Just as well, bright yellow wasn't the color for hiding.

In time, he reached the clearing around their cabin. Would the sheriff have lookouts? Who might be hiding there in the forest, waiting? He couldn't take any chances.

George Henry crouched behind a bush and tossed a pebble against the cabin. Nothing. He tossed another. A moment later, Willie emerged carrying a bucket. He walked toward the stream, stealing glances into the woods. When he turned toward George Henry, their eyes met.

Willie quickly scanned the forest, then rushed to George Henry. "Been watching all morning. Nobody's around that I can tell. Miss Rebecca find you?"

"She's at the old hunting camp. I need you to make sure she gets home safe."

Willie's eyes widened. "What's she doing up there?"

"Sleeping."

Willie flinched. "You didn't—"

George Henry put a finger to his lips. "You watch over her, keep her safe. I don't reckon I'll be back this way, but if I gets to Florida, I'll try to send you word, and you pass it on to her."

Willie turned his head. "Is there something I need to know, brother?"

George Henry smiled. "Go see if Lorinda Jane can manage without you for an hour or so. I'm heading to the yards and I need you to scout the trail ahead of me."

"Got food?"

"Just what I can carry." George Henry patted his pockets. "I'll steal a chicken when I get hungry."

Willie hurried to the cabin and ducked inside. He reemerged a few moments later. "She said for me to get you on your way, then come back for Miss Rebecca. You remember that whippoorwill call?"

George Henry nodded.

"If I sees anything bothersome, I'll give the call and you stop. If you hear it again, it's all clear, you come on down. You don't hear it again, you skedaddle, okay?"

"You take real good care of Lorinda Jane and that young'un," George Henry said, clasping his brother's shoulders. "Rebecca says he's a strong baby, has a real good chance of making it. You get Doctor West to look him over, soon as this storm lets up."

"I'll look in on Miss Rebecca from time to time, too," Willie said. He looked into George Henry's eyes and smiled. "I don't want to know what kind of mess you got yourself into, ain't none of my concern, but I won't let nothing bad happen to her."

"Good." George Henry pushed Willie away. "Now, walk normal, like you got no worries and like you ain't being followed. I'll trail behind."

Willie disappeared around a bend in the trail, then reappeared before dipping below a rise. George Henry placed his feet carefully, avoiding loose rocks that might roll down the path and give him away. A mile into their journey, he began to relax. Too wet and cold—deputies wouldn't be out and about—they'd figure on snatching him tomorrow, when the weather cleared.

Mid-afternoon? Without the sun, he could only guess. What would Rebecca think when she awoke and found him gone? She'd asked if what they shared was love. What else could lift his heart so sweetly—or break it with such pain?

He had to leave without saying good-bye, yet he'd always wonder, what if he'd stayed? What if there was a path around those troubles? He'd find a way to return, he must, but only if he could be sure she wouldn't be in danger. How long would she wait?

The call of a whippoorwill drifted up the trail. George Henry froze, then quietly ducked behind a tree. Who was out there? Sheriff Blakely? How long should he wait for Willie's next signal? Could it have been a real bird? He might never know. If that second call didn't come soon, he'd break brush, go south across the ridge and skip the yards. Easy enough to catch a train a few miles down the tracks. He crouched and waited.

A shotgun blast cut the stillness.

Willie?

George Henry circled away from the trail, creeping toward the location of the shot. Willie'd given his signal, he'd protected him, now it was George Henry's turn. He'd look out for his little brother. Could be nothing, a hunter, maybe, or kids, but he wouldn't leave Clifton Forge with that sound in his ears and that doubt in his mind. Willie'd do the same for him.

The woods gave cover, masking the trail from his view, but hiding his movements as well. He dropped to his stomach in a thicket of evergreens, crawling under the twisted branches. Ahead, voices. He crept closer and peered through a break in the undergrowth.

"You's hiding that murdering 'coon and you and me both knows it. Tell me where he is or I'll blow your balls off." Chester Johnson aimed his shotgun at Willie's crotch.

"Don't know where he is, Mr. Johnson. That's the truth. I 'spect he took off last night, like my Lorinda Jane said. You go on over by Covington, you'll find him there." Willie trembled, holding his hands in the air, then clutching his crotch, as though that would protect him.

Could he circle around behind and take Chester's gun away? Maybe bust open his skull? George Henry studied the lay of the ground. The bushes would give him cover. Once he was behind Chester, Wille'd see him and be ready to jump out of the way of any shot. He inched away from his hiding place overlooking the trail.

"That boy close by? You'd best holler for him to come save your black ass." Chester's laugh was followed by a shot.

Willie screamed.

With a yell, George Henry burst out of the bushes, plowing into Chester and folding him in half like a cheap jackknife. They landed hard, with George Henry on top. He straddled the smaller man, pummeling Chester's head with his fists.

"Please, don't hit me no more." The little man covered his bloodied head and sobbed.

"Willie, you okay?" George Henry said. He held the back of Chester's shirt in one hand, his other raised in a fist.

His brother leaned against a tree, blood oozing from his foot. He clutched his leg and grimaced, then his eyes widened as he focused somewhere behind George Henry.

George Henry turned.

Chester Johnson's brother stepped from behind a tree, his rifle pointed at George Henry. "Looks like what we got here is murder, bothering white women, and beating my brother near to death." He motioned with the rifle. "Boy, you stand up slow and careful and get over there with that other colored boy. It's time the two of you answered for your high crimes."

Chapter Thirty-four

Sunday 4:10 PM

"Stay close. We can't afford to become separated." I drew an arrow on the wall with Ann's lip gloss indicating which direction we'd come from. "Watch your head," I said as I ducked under an overhanging boulder. My world had been reduced to a keychain flashlight, a petrified woman, and some know-it-all kid who had no business getting my daughter tied up in the mess she was in.

We left the familiar section of the cave. I led Ann and Peter down a tunnel just wide enough to pass through without having to turn sideways. Solid rock—cool, wet, and slippery—formed one wall, damp shale the other. Beyond the tight cone of green light, darkness threatened with the malevolence of every childhood nightmare. Rocks and water covered the uneven ground.

"Hey, are we going downhill?" Ann asked. "That can't be good."

"We did some spelunking last year in our hiking club," Peter said. "These caverns climb and fall, wind every which way. They follow the erosion."

"What erosion?" Fear crept into Ann's voice.

"Groundwater," he said. "It seeps through from above and washes out all the soft stuff: dirt, limestone, shale. That's what makes the caves." Peter reached over Ann's shoulder and broke off a crumbly section of stone. "This turns to mud. Give it another hundred thousand years and this little space could be the size of a basketball court."

"Sorry," I said. "I forgot my ball." I placed an arrow on the hard stone on the opposite wall. "How are you doing, kid?"

"Weak, maybe a little scared, but I'm okay. I'll try not to pass out again."

"Yeah, we're all scared, but no fainting, right?" I gave him a smile. "Ann isn't real eager to carry you, or sit here in the dark while I find a way out." I braced against a rock outcropping and lowered myself over a ledge. "It drops off here. Give me your hand."

Ann sat and took my hand. Holding the LED in my mouth, I reached up and eased her off the rock. She fell against me, then regained her balance and stepped away.

"You're next, kid. Come on." I braced and offered him a hand.

"Just hold the light so I can see. I'll be fine."

Wise-ass. It'd serve him right if he broke his leg, but we had enough complications to deal with. "Okay, easy, kid. Don't fall."

Peter scooted off the boulder, landing on his feet.

"Feels colder." Ann wrapped her arms around herself. "Maybe we should go back."

"And do what, wait for whoever barricaded us in here to bring us some hot coffee and a few Philly cheesesteaks?" I marked an arrow on the wall and then shined the light into the tunnel ahead. The place was creeping me out too, but our only chance of escaping and finding Erica alive rested somewhere ahead.

"He's right, miss. There's no way out back there." Peter looked into the darkness above. "There are probably four or five places where this cave opens to the surface. We just have to find one before we lose the light."

I stopped. "Lose what light?" The LED glowed bright and green, no less than when we'd started.

Peter felt his pockets. "Wish I had my old light. It'll go forever on three double A batteries. Those things," he said, pointing to my keychain light, "are good for maybe five or six hours, not much more."

"And then what?" Ann's voice quivered.

"We'll be out of here by then," I said. "Come on." God, I hoped so. That madman still had Erica. I didn't even want

226

to think about the obscene terror she might be experiencing.

I stepped over a jagged rock and continued down the tunnel. Cold, smothering blackness magnified the scrape of boots against stone, amplified Ann's labored breathing, and highlighted the drip of water onto a rock. No echoes, no din of wind or traffic, every sound was pure, clear, and absolute. What would it be like to turn off the light and become lost in the experience? Another sound intruded on the quiet—a deep, rhythmic, pounding—was it in my chest? Best keep moving. I placed an arrow on one wall and climbed over the next rock.

"Gets narrow up here." I turned sideways. Jagged outcroppings dug into my chest and back.

"Don't get wedged," Peter said. "Maybe I should go first."

"You didn't do so well the last time you led an expedition," I said as I pushed through the gap.

"What are you talking about?" Ann said.

"Yeah, what expedition?" Peter blinked as the green light swung across his face.

Was he clueless? "Look, I'm just saying Erica wouldn't be tied up in some hillbilly's cabin if you hadn't dragged her out here for your little walk in the woods."

"Stop it, Mitch. You can't blame him for that."

"Anyway, it was her idea," Peter said. "I didn't twist her arm."

I looked at the two of them. Nothing to be gained by having it out down here. "We'll deal with that once we're topside. Stay close. Looks like we're crawling for the next fifty feet or so." I laid on my belly and inched into the narrow space.

"I can't . . ." Ann whispered.

"You have to. There's no other way," I said. I couldn't turn to see her, but I held the light over my shoulder. Maybe it would give her enough to see by.

"I'll get stuck."

"Miss, if Mr. Corsini can fit through, we sure can. And he's right. There's no other way."

Was he calling me fat?

"I . . . I'll try." Ann said. "Can you keep the light shining back here?"

I crawled a few feet and then aimed the light behind me. Ann scooted ahead, followed by the kid. I pushed forward again. Ann followed.

"You okay?" I called over my shoulder.

"Why'd I ever let you talk me into this?" she replied.

"Just a bit further. It looks like it opens up again." How long could I get away with that lie? There wasn't anything up ahead but more of that same damned terrifying darkness.

Ann tapped my foot and I edged another few feet. Water trickled off the wall onto the rock beneath me. My shirt soaked up the cold wetness. I twisted around a bend. The cave opened into a space the size of two phone booths, large enough to stand. I squeezed out of the tunnel and straightened. "We're clear." I turned the light toward Ann. A look of relief washed the panic from her face.

She dropped into the open space and sat. "I can't do that again. Give Peter the flashlight. We can light his bug spray lamp and wait for him here."

"What happened to us all sticking together?" I asked.

She covered her face with her hands. As her shoulders heaved, a sob escaped into the cavern. I pulled her into my arms and squeezed. "I'm right here. Everything will be okay, but we have to do this together."

Peter crawled out of the tunnel. "Man, that was tight. How'd you manage, Mr. Corsini?"

"Look, kid, my daughter's being held captive because of you. I'm stuck in this damned cave because of you. Do you think you can lay off the fat guy jokes, at least until we're out of here?"

Ann tugged on my sleeve and whispered, "He didn't mean anything by that."

I sucked in my stomach and adjusted my belt. "Let's take a breather before we push on."

"Hey, Mr. Corsini, maybe Ann has an idea . . ."

"We're not splitting up." I rested against the smooth

stone wall.

"No, I mean the lamp." He dug into the cargo pocket on his trousers and pulled out the wick and the bottle. He unscrewed the cap and inserted the wick. "Once I light this, turn off the flashlight." Peter held a match to the cloth and a flame spread.

I turned off the flashlight. The cave brightened in a warm, orange glow.

"That's much nicer, Peter. Thanks." Ann said.

Peter pointed at the flickering flame. "Look."

"Okay, nice flame," I said. "What's your point?"

He slowly moved the lamp in a wide circle. The flame pulled toward a narrow gap in the rocks. "Air's moving," he said. "It's going somewhere—there has to be a way out."

"Mitch, he's right." Ann jumped up. "Look at the smoke." A thin bluish thread stretched from the flame to a gap in the rocks.

"If there wasn't any place for the smoke to go," Peter said, "this cave would soon fill and we'd be choking. Somewhere ahead there's a chimney, an exit to the outside." He moved the lamp again, watching the trail of smoke disappear into the darkness.

"It goes around that boulder and up there." I pointed to a gap above, between two flat rocks. "Wait here. I'll check it out." I turned on my flashlight and climbed up a rocky ladder to the opening, then laid on my back and slid into another cavern directly above where we'd been.

"Pass me that lamp," I called to Peter.

The flame appeared below the vent I'd just climbed through. When I lifted the lamp aloft the flame stretched, bending toward a tangle of tree roots protruding from a hole no bigger around than a basketball.

"Guys, there's something here. Come on up." I wedged the lamp into a crack in the rocks and took out my flashlight. Roots hung over a massive boulder like the legs of a lazy octopus. Were we close to the surface? I followed a thick root until it disappeared beneath some rocks. Holding the light in my teeth, I grabbed a long, flat rock with both hands and tugged until it pulled loose and dropped by my feet. Using the rock as a step, I shined the light into the opening. Something as thick as my arm, black with brownish blotches, moved sluggishly no more than a foot from my face. I jumped backwards, landing on Peter.

"Snake!"

"What kind?" he said.

"Who the hell cares what kind? What's it doing up there?" I picked up the light and shined it toward the rocky shelf.

Peter grabbed my light and stood on the rock, peering into the hole. "Timber rattlers. There's a bunch of them in there. You must have uncovered their den."

"Snakes? We have to get out of here. Now." Ann tugged on my arm.

"They won't bother us," Peter said. "They're hibernating. This time of year they're usually very low energy."

"That gives me zero comfort," Ann said. She pushed me between her and the rattlers' den.

Peter climbed down and handed me the light. "The good news is they usually hibernate just below the frost line. Around here, that's not very deep. We're close to the surface."

"Well, I'm not going that way." I pointed toward the serpents. "Besides, the smoke went out over there." I reached above me and clawed at the dirt around the basketball-sized hole. Dirt and rocks fell into the cavern. The opening widened.

"Peter, come here. Climb on my shoulders and see if you can dig through that." I cupped my hands and leaned against the rocks.

Peter set his foot in my hands and pushed into the dark hole. He bounced, digging his boot into my shoulder and raining debris on my head. Then he bounced again and his weight disappeared. "Mr. Corsini, I'm out!" Six feet above, Peter stared through a rock and root lined hole. The glimmer of daylight framed his face.

"Ann. Get up here." I cupped my hands again. "Peter,

you help. You pull her through."

She hesitated. "Tell me there aren't any snakes up there."

As she spoke, something dropped onto a rock beside my foot. The rattler I'd first spotted in the den twisted itself upright, then settled and lay quietly.

I inched away from the creature. "I don't know about up there," I said, "but you see what's down here."

Ann climbed over my chest and into the opening. I put my hands under her feet and lifted. She rose and then her feet left my hands as she pulled free somewhere above.

"Mitch, grab hold. Come on." Ann lay above the opening, her hand outstretched.

"You can't pull me up. You don't have the strength." I set my boot against a ledge on the rock wall and jumped. My fingers closed around a slick, muddy root. I pulled. I had to get out for Erica's sake. Four feet more and I'd be free. What else to grab? My shoulders wedged between two rocks. I twisted and tried to pull up again. "It's no use. I'm too big. I won't fit through."

"You have to fit. I'm not leaving you there." Ann dug frantically at the sides of the hole.

"The rocks are too big to move, too tight to get around. You guys go for help. I'll be okay." I brushed the dirt from my eyes.

Peter poked his head in the hole. "Mr. Corsini, here's Ann's knife, and the matches. I'm feeling kind of weak so it's going to take awhile for us to get to town."

"Not surprised. You've been through hell. Ann?"

"Yes, Mitch."

"I'm going back to the first cave, the one where we found Peter. There's no room in here to sit and I'm not keen on sharing the space with that rattler. When you get help, can you find your way back there?"

"Wait." Ann walked away. A moment later she reappeared. "Yes, I can see it. It's right over there, maybe a hundred yards at the most." She leaned into the hole. "You sure you want to go back through all that? What if you get lost?"

"I have my light, my lamp, my penknife, and all those arrows I drew on the walls. I'll be fine."

"Watch out for those snakes," Ann called through the hole.

"And you watch out for the two legged variety up there." I blew out the lamp and turned on my flashlight.

Chapter Thirty-five

April 1936

She awoke in darkness and sat up with a start. So cold, so damp . . . George Henry? Rebecca searched the small cabin—only four empty walls. Rainwater drizzled from the canvas tarp above into a puddle beside her on the muddy floor. He said he'd be leaving, but without even a good-bye? No last words? No final kiss? Could he outrun the dogs? When would she see him again? What if he never returned? A wave of hopelessness washed over her as she buried her face in the musty blanket and surrendered to her tears.

Had it been hours, or only moments? When she rolled over, stars twinkled between patches of leaves above the opening in the cabin roof not covered by the tarp. How late was it? She'd need to get home. Rebecca stood, wobbly at first, steadying herself against the chimney. The basket of food sat by the hearth. She picked it up. Only a can of soup and a salami were missing. Everything else was as she'd left it. Did he not need the food? Had he left it for Lorinda Jane? And what of her and Willie, and their baby? Were they still in danger? She'd stop on her way to town and drop off the food basket.

She smoothed her dress as she choked back a tear, then she ran her fingers through her matted hair. She must look a mess. What would Lorinda Jane—or her father think? George Henry's rain slicker hung by the door. She put it on, thankful for the added warmth, and stepped outside. The only sound was the staccato drip, drip, drip falling from the leaves. The rain had ended, and with it, the wind. Better for her hike down to Lorinda Jane's cabin, but would it give the dogs an advantage?

Rebecca stood in front of the cabin and studied the terrain. Everything had a different appearance at night, but the stream she'd followed up from Lorinda Jane's had to be somewhere to her right. She hitched her dress and began her downhill trek.

* * *

A light shone through the broken window pane. Rebecca knocked softly, then eased the door open. If Lorinda Jane was sleeping, she'd find out from Willie what he knew of George Henry, then make her way down the mountain.

Lorinda Jane lay in bed curled protectively around her baby. "Come in, child." She placed her hand on the chair beside her bed. "Have a seat."

Rebecca shook the water from her slicker and closed the door.

"Where's George Henry?" Lorinda Jane gave her a puzzled look. "He come down here this afternoon. He and Willie went to the rail yards. Where was you?"

"I stayed at the hunting camp." Rebecca sat beside the bed.

"Then you seen him go?"

Rebecca's face grew warm. "I was asleep. I don't know when he left."

"My Willie come get you?" Lorinda Jane tilted her head and looked at the door. "He was supposed to go up the mountain and bring you down, soon as his brother was on that freight to Richmond."

"No," Rebecca said, "I haven't seen Willie since this morning, when I left here." She tucked the blanket around Lorinda Jane's neck and fluffed the pillow. "Is there anything I can get you? Have you eaten?"

"Ain't like that boy not to come home when he says he will."

"I'm certain he'll be home soon. Is it cold in here?" Rebecca walked over to the cast iron stove. "It's certainly too cold for that baby of yours. Did your fire go out?" She opened the door and poked the coals, then shoved a few pieces of kindling into the firebox and blew on the embers. In a moment, an orange glow danced on the blackened iron. She added two small logs and closed the door. "That's better."

"Do you love him?" Lorinda Jane asked. She fussed with the blanket surrounding the baby's face. "You scared of knowing?"

"Of knowing what?"

Lorinda Jane smiled and pointed to the wood stove. "Fire's nice. It were getting a mite chilly, weren't it?"

Rebecca nodded. And of course she loved him, but it wasn't allowed. How could she face the truth?

Lorinda Jane patted the chair again. "You come sit and tell Lorinda Jane what's troubling your heart. We don't need no secrets in this here house."

"How'd you know when you were in love with Willie?" Rebecca asked.

Lorinda Jane laughed. "Sometimes, love comes later. Sometimes, I hear, it don't come at all."

"What do you mean?"

"Pretty white woman like you, you got men following you all up and down this mountain. Marrying ain't a question of if, you just need to choose your right man." Lorinda Jane ran her fingers through her hair. "Me, I had slimmer pickings. Sure, there was plenty of gandy dancers would love to get on that dance floor and do a slow grind, but not so many that wanted to settle and raise a family. Willie, he was different. He brung me flowers."

"And that's why you married him?"

"No," Lorinda Jane said, "I married him because he was handsome, like his brother—that, and George Henry wouldn't have nothing to do with me."

Rebecca gasped. "You loved George Henry?"

Lorinda Jane patted her hand. "No, honey, I just loved looking at that man. You know what I mean?" She laughed.

Rebecca's face warmed.

"I married Willie and got the window dressing too. I reckon I done pretty good!"

Rebecca smiled. "So it was Willie you loved all along?"

"No, that loving part come later. First, we got married."

"How can you marry a man if you don't love him?" Rebecca said. She got up and fixed herself a sandwich.

"I learned to love him. Weren't hard to do. Other than gambling, I can't find no serious faults to speak of."

Rebecca returned to her seat. "What time is it? Shouldn't he be coming home?"

Lorinda Jane frowned. "Past midnight, best I reckon. Don't like him running these hills late at night, especially when that sheriff has men with guns out looking for George Henry."

"He'll be fine." Rebecca fought back tears. But was that true? And what of George Henry, had he caught his freedom train? How would she ever know?

"Miss Rebecca, that sheriff, is he a good man?"

Rebecca wrung her hands. "Papa says so. He voted for him last election."

"Your papa's a good man. If he says the sheriff's good too, that holds weight with me." Lorinda Jane shifted the baby into the crook of her arm. "Little feller's sleeping good. You reckon he'll be all right?"

"He's a beautiful child," Rebecca said. "He'll be as fine as fine can be, and when Willie gets home, he'll smother that baby with sugar and sweetness."

"And that's why I married the man." Lorinda Jane smiled.

"If it's as late as you say, I'll stay here the night, or at least until Willie comes home. I don't want you up here alone, and I should be here if that sheriff comes around in the morning."

Lorinda Jane pulled back the covers. "Slip out of that wet dress and slide in here. I reckon we got us enough talking yet to carry us 'til dawn."

Rebecca took off her wet clothes and slid between the covers. "He really is one handsome man, isn't he?"

Chapter Thirty-six

"Sit. Stay." I held up my outstretched hand as I backed away from the coiled serpent. So what if it was hibernating, it was still alive. My choice came down to tunnels or rattlesnakes? Talk about your no-brainer . . . . I slipped between two large boulders and dropped into the relative safety of the cavern below.

Smoke trails had led me there; my memory and lipstick arrows on the walls would have to lead me back. I allowed myself one final glance at the sliver of daylight that touched the rocks above and then twisted and wriggled into the dark tunnel, pushing Ann's day pack and my meager supplies ahead of me.

After about ten feet, my shoulders became wedged between the unforgiving walls. I pushed harder. No good. Maybe I should back out. No, even if I could, there was no way I'd shove my head up through that hole again knowing that damned rattler was waiting. But my nemesis was now a different breed of serpent. With every move, rocks, like the coils of a python, tightened their grip. I was trapped. God, I was going to rot down there—but if I did, who'd find Erica? Damn it, she'd figured me for being AWOL long enough. She deserved better. With the limestone ceiling mere inches from my face, I twisted, clawing at my stone coffin. Finally, after long, terrifying minutes, the rocks released their grip. I tumbled into an open space.

An arrow pointed to an opening above a tall boulder. I'd slid down from that rock when we were headed the other way. There'd be no help from gravity now; I'd have to figure a way to climb over it.

Other than my own labored breathing, no sound reached my ears—only a cold, absolute silence. Was that what death would be like? I turned off the light. Darkness, far beyond anything I'd ever imagined, crawled over every inch of my skin like a thousand icy spiders. Quickly, I twisted the top of the flashlight.

Nothing.

God, no, not now . . . . My stomach tightened as I turned the housing the other way. A soft green glow filled the small cavern. Slowly, I exhaled. Thank you, Lord . . . but how much time remained on that cheap LED light? Those rescuers better hurry.

The smooth surface was void of useful footholds. I tossed the pack onto the top of the boulder and proceeded to climb the opposite wall. When I reached a strategic point slightly above the top of the boulder, I turned and jumped, hitting the boulder spread-eagled. My hands clutched furiously for a grip, but found only smooth rock. I slid down the face of the boulder, crashing onto the jagged rocks below. Pain shot up my arm and through my shoulder. If I'd broken any bones I'd never get out of there alive. The pain was intense—but probably nowhere near what Erica must have been enduring. I chided myself for giving in to my self-pity and rubbed the soreness. There'd probably be one hell of a bruise, but the arm still moved. I'd best get going. I climbed and jumped again, this time catching hold of a small crack near the top with my fingertips. Ignoring my pain, I clawed my way to the summit.

From there, the journey became easier; an uphill climb through a damp tunnel ended at our original cave. The proximity to the opening, blocked though it was, offered a peculiar sense of security. I found a dry spot on the ground and settled in. Water dripping from the far wall filled the silence with a monotonous rhythm. I checked my watch—it would be getting dark soon. I laughed. How would I know?

I set up the bug repellant lamp, lit the wick, and then turned off my flashlight—no sense wasting what little power remained in the batteries. The orange flame provided a welcomed change from the eerie green electronic glow. The shadows seemed to celebrate it too, dancing in the warmth of the new light that surrounded them. I could almost relax, but for the realization that somewhere in those woods, that maniac still held my Erica hostage. Every minute in that hole was one less I'd have to find her.

What about snakes? That was the last thing I needed. I'd best check before I got too comfortable. A sweep of the flashlight beam around my immediate surroundings revealed nothing slithery. On the far side, the floor sloped away, under an overhang, into what appeared to be a space large enough to hold a bear—or whatever else might decide to hibernate. I got on my hands and knees and slowly crawled closer. I didn't want to awaken anything, but I had to know if I was alone. The green beam pierced the darkness.

"Holy—" I jumped back. What the hell? I hesitated and then cautiously peered into the crevice again. Not two feet away, the hollow eyes of a human skull stared at me. And it wasn't just the skull, there was a whole damned skeleton in there. I shuddered. Was it a lost hiker, or worse, another victim of Peter's whacked out hillbilly? Fragments of cloth clung to bones that had been long devoid of flesh. The remains of a shoe defined where a foot must have been. The skeleton locked me in an endless gaze.

"Tell me you weren't snake bit," I said, forcing a nervous laugh. It was either that or scream. How long had he been there, a year? Ten? Fifty? I lay on my side and extended to my full length, stretching until my feet were even with the empty boots. He had me by at least two inches—had to be a man, and a tall one.

Just where I wanted to spend my evening—next to some dead guy in a cave crawling with snakes. I swallowed the bile rising in my throat and turned off the flashlight. The pale glow of the bug spray flame flickered on the grinning skull. "So, what passes for fun in these parts?" I asked, taking a deep breath.

He must have been the shy type—but at least he wouldn't keep me up all night arguing. Strangely, his presence seemed to give me a degree of comfort. I had a companion, no matter that he was dead, to share my solitude. "Corsini's the name. Richmond Journal News. You mind if I ask you a few questions?"

He didn't voice an objection.

"You got a name?" I asked. "How about a favorite football team?" Why were skulls always depicted as such sinister, malevolent things? This guy was neither. What misfortune could have landed that poor fellow in this forsaken place? "Hey, buddy, tell me about your family. Did you leave a wife and kids?"

Kids—what about Erica? That nut had her stashed somewhere, probably gagged and bound. She must be terrified, and me helpless, stuck in a stinking cave. If only I'd been there sooner, been a real father, maybe she wouldn't have been in those woods . . .

"Hey, mister," I said, propping my head on my hand. "Can I tell you about my kid? She's had it rough. Her old man's a jerk. You know the type?"

* * *

I awoke with a start, engulfed in inky darkness. Where was I? My hand brushed against the rocky ground. I'd hoped it had only been a dream, some perverted nightmare, but when I pulled the flashlight from my pocket and turned it on, the green light revealed my now familiar cavernous prison. The bug spray lamp sat where I'd left it, the wick burned down to the mouth of the bottle. I turned the beam toward the darkness beside me. My friend hadn't moved, which was probably a good thing. I extended the wick from the bottle's mouth and lit it again. The cave awakened in a bright yellow glow.

I turned to my companion. "Hey, do you have any food down here? A granola bar, perhaps some spare ribs?" I laughed. "Sorry, no offense."

There was only a swallow of water left in the bottle. I polished it off, then refilled the bottle from a rivulet trickling down the wall and drank again. Cool, sweet—someone should bottle that. My watch said a few minutes past midnight—or was it noon? What was keeping those rescuers? Dampness permeated the cave. My clothing clung to me without providing warmth. A fire would be nice, but no fuel. It would have smoked me out anyway. I glanced at the skeleton.

"So, how'd you end up in this hell hole?" I imagined putting a face on those bones. Dark hair or blond? Lots of images, but nothing stuck. Horrible way to die: alone, in total darkness. Had he suffered? He might have been murdered. I resisted a sudden urge to crawl down and search the skeleton for clues. Best leave that to the cops.

Had Ann and Peter even made it out of those woods? And what about Ann—was she safe? What about the guy with the rifle—the one who threw Peter down here—he'd better not lay a hand on her or I'll . . . . Wow, where'd that come from? Ann and I were good friends and all, but could there possibly be something more? The thought was more than I expected—and much more than I could handle. I didn't even want to go there. My life was already too complicated. I turned back toward my less complicated silent companion.

"Hey, mister, should I give you a name, something I could call you, like Sam, or Leo?" I considered the possibilities. "Nah, you already have a name." I reached into the opening and rested my hand on his skull. "And if I get out of here I'll find out what it is. I promise."

Something high above scraped the rocks. Dirt fell on my face and then a flash of brilliant whiteness blinded me.

"Corsini, you down there?"

Johnson? Of all the rotten SOBs they could possibly have sent to rescue me, why'd it have to be that particular SOB? What if I just didn't answer—would he leave me alone? Nah, besides, he might have a candy bar or a packet of peanut butter crackers he could share. Oh hell, I had to get out of there anyway, I needed to find Erica. "Hey," I whispered to the skeleton. "Try not to laugh when you see this clown."

241

"Sergeant Johnson? Is that you?" I moved away from the opening. "Drop me a rope, or better yet, come on down here. There's somebody I'd like you to meet."

The beam from his headlamp darted across the cave as Johnson slid down a rope. When his foot hit the ground he stumbled forward. I caught him and propped him up.

"You okay?" I said.

He brushed himself off and then looked me up and down. "The better question is, are you?"

"Doing fine," I said. "What have you found out about Erica?"

Johnson shook his head.

"How about the boy?"

"Peter Douglas?" Johnson asked. "They've got him at the hospital overnight for observation, but looks like he'll be fine. Captain McConnell called his old man. Miss Richardson told me what happened. You get a look at the guy?"

"Nah. It all happened too quickly." I pointed to the opening. "Ann came flying in on top of me, we hit the ground, and then some joker rolled a stone over the opening."

Johnson rubbed his chin.

"You know who did it?" I asked.

"Later." He shined his headlamp around the cave. You said there was someone else down here?"

I pointed to the low cut out at the base of the wall.

Johnson flashed me a quizzical look as he knelt. "Damn," he said. "Where the hell'd he come from?"

"Treat him well," I said. "We've become rather chummy."

Johnson crawled into the crevice. "Hey, did you check this out?" He scooted forward until only the lower half of his legs protruded.

"Sorry, whatever you find down there is police business, not mine."

"So," Johnson called over his shoulder. "You missed the other one?"

"The other what?"

"Your buddy has a friend hiding behind him."

Two bodies? Damn. Had it been a cult? Perhaps a murder/suicide? "Can you tell what they died of?"

Wiggling backward, Johnson worked his way out of the fissure. He stood, brushing himself off, and turned toward me. "I ain't for certain. The state crime lab boys will need to get down here, but from the traces of rope around their necks, I'd say they'd been lynched."

Chapter Thirty-seven

Monday 3:00 AM

"Corsini, get the hell out of here. One of my deputies can run you to the hospital. You need to get checked out." Johnson waved me away as he shined his headlamp into the cave that was now filled with state police crime lab examiners.

"Later," I said, tapping him on the shoulder. "First fill me in on that crazy hillbilly that Peter described. Do you know him?"

He shook his head. "I can't discuss an on-going investigation."

I grabbed the collar of his jacket. "My kid's out there. I don't give a rat's ass about your investigation, but if that lunatic harms one hair on her head, you'll answer to me."

"Who the hell do you think you are?" Johnson swatted my arm as he pulled away. "You do that again, I'll lock you up."

"Down there, you seemed to know who he was." I pointed into the cave.

"I might have an idea," Johnson said. "It's only a hunch and none of your concern."

"My daughter is my concern."

A state police lieutenant climbed out of the cave and stepped between us, brushing himself off. "I can't believe I got called out in the middle of the night for this."

"What'd you find, Officer?" I said.

He looked me over. "Who are you?"

"Name's Corsini."

"You a reporter?"

"I spent the night down there with your two bodies. I

figure that makes me family."

The lieutenant studied me again and then looked at Johnson.

Johnson shrugged.

"Okay," the lieutenant said. "I guess it can't hurt. This crime is too old to get excited about anyway."

"What do you mean," I asked. "How old?"

"Age wise or how long they've been down there?" The lieutenant said.

"How long you think they've been there?" Johnson asked. The beam from his headlamp caught the officer square in the face.

The lieutenant covered his eyes and looked away. "You want to turn that damn thing off?"

"Sorry." Johnson flipped his headlamp up, aiming it into the trees. "So, how long?"

"Well, this is very preliminary stuff," the lieutenant said. He looked at me. "Not to be released, you got that?"

I nodded.

"I can't tell ages, but we have two bodies, both probably male. One's about six foot four, the other maybe five ten. There was tissue on some of the bones, so we might be able to extract a good DNA sample. That makes me think they haven't been there all that long, maybe twenty or thirty years?" He shrugged.

Johnson shook his head. "Nobody's been missing from these parts that I know of."

"Remember," the lieutenant said, "it's all preliminary. Hell, you could use that cave as a morgue—cool, constant temperature, limestone walls—a body would keep down there for a long, long time."

"There were traces of rope," Johnson said. "How long would hemp keep in a place like that?"

"Hold on." The lieutenant held up his hand and hollered into the cave, "Hey, Jimbo, how long will hemp keep in that environment?"

A hollow voice echoed through the opening, "They found ropes on the pharaoh's barge at Giza."

The lieutenant chuckled. "I guess that answers your question, but I doubt we're talking antiquities. From the scraps of clothing, shoes, belt buckles and such, I'd say we're looking at mid-Twentieth Century."

"Sergeant Johnson said he thought they'd been lynched," I said.

"It's too early." The lieutenant shook his head. "I'm not commenting on cause of death."

"But you did see the nooses?" Johnson asked.

"There were indications that their hands and feet might have been bound. We did find a fairly well preserved stretch of rope with what looked to be a noose tied on one end." He poked his finger in my chest. "That better not show up in the papers before I'm ready to release it officially."

I drew an X across my heart.

"Good." He turned toward the cave and cupped a hand beside his mouth. "Hey, Captain, did you know you had press up here?" The lieutenant wagged his finger at me as he walked away. "Not a word, mister. Got it?"

McConnell climbed out of the cave. He saw me and turned to Johnson. "What's he still doing here?"

Johnson jerked his thumb in my direction. "He was just leaving, Captain."

"Good," McConnell said. "Now, tell me again about Ambrose. You checked him out, right?"

"Yes sir, Captain." Johnson fidgeted. "Just like you told me to. I went to his place the very next day, right after them dogs lost that trail. He hadn't seen nor heard nothing."

"You searched his cabin?" McConnell asked.

"There's only the three rooms."

"And you looked in them?"

"Mostly."

"Mostly? Whoa." I waved my arms and stepped between them. "Time out. Who in the hell is this Ambrose guy, and what does he have to do with my daughter?"

"Probably nothing," McConnell said, "and you need to get on home, get some sleep. I'll brief you tomorrow if we find anything."

"That's not good enough," I said. "The way I see it, your men have already botched this investigation every way possible, and now your sergeant says he mostly searched that guy's cabin? What's going on?"

"Calm down, Corsini," Johnson said. "It's just this old coot; he lives a few miles from here. He's harmless, but once we get this crime scene sorted, I'll head yonder and check him out again." He pointed toward the ridge behind us.

"How soon will that be?" I asked.

Johnson studied the sky. "Nothing's going to happen before sunup."

Dawn? That was still hours away. "Okay," I said, "I need to get back to the hotel and catch some shuteye." I turned to McConnell. "I'll stop by the hospital sometime tomorrow; I'll touch base with you after."

"You want one of my men to walk you out?"

"I'm a big boy," I said. "I'll find my way."

Johnson tossed me a flashlight. "When you get lost, flash this three times."

* * *

Monday 3:37 AM

I turned on the light and headed toward the trail. The car was only a few miles away—or was it? Damn, Ann had taken it to drive Peter to the hospital. I'd been struggling with what to do, and that cinched it—I'd find that damned cabin. Erica couldn't wait for dawn or Sergeant Johnson. I switched off the flashlight and turned onto the trail of upturned leaves tracing a dark path across the ridge.

Johnson had waved in that general direction. If I got lost, it wouldn't be the first time. No big deal. The disturbed leaves showed distinctly against the forest floor. Someone had been down that path recently, and they were none too concerned about being followed. Guess I wasn't supposed to survive my cave adventure. I'd better keep that in mind—he might not be so careless next time.

Damn, the air was cold. My clothes still held the dampness from the cave and one trouser leg was soaked clear to my thigh. I walked faster. A few miles—what had Johnson meant? Two? Seven? The trail, at least, was easy to follow.

He had a gun, so I needed a plan. How could I arm myself? First things first: find the cabin and then figure out the situation. The gun would only be an issue if he saw me first.

Upturned leaves led over a ridge, down a gulley, and up another hill. By my watch, I'd walked about twenty minutes when the path intersected a narrow dirt road so overgrown that no vehicle, at least no conventional vehicle, could traverse it. Trees and brush crowded the narrow track. Weeds, ferns, and even saplings grew in the roadbed. The growth was tamped down in one direction. Something wheeled had been there. Peter had mentioned an ATV. I took a deep breath and followed the tracks.

My stomach growled. It had been almost a full day since I'd had a decent meal. How about rescuing Erica and hauling her off to the diner for some quality father/daughter time—and a few good biscuits? My plan sounded perfect—all I had to do was find her. I must have walked two, maybe three miles and then the trail forked. Which way? Both directions showed signs of traffic. Nothing distinguished one from the other, but I was exhausted. The path running downhill won out.

I went at least another half mile—I wasn't too sure about estimating distances—and then I stopped and rested. I was lost, really lost, and too exhausted to continue. Maybe, after daybreak, things might begin to look familiar.

In the distance, a low, mechanical whine started and then grew louder. I slipped off the trail and ducked behind a tree. An ATV roared up the hill from the direction I'd been walking. He passed my hiding place and the noise faded into the distance.

That had to be the guy. Erica was nearby; I sensed it. Quickly, I headed down the path again. If he returned, his machine would warn me from miles away.

After a few minutes, I froze, transfixed by the sight before me. Even in the hazy predawn darkness, I knew that tree. It would take three men, their arms outstretched, to encircle the huge trunk. The crooked limb, thick as a man's chest and ten feet off the ground, jutted at a right angle to the trunk. Johnson's deer had hung there. Peter almost had too. I rubbed my neck and recalled my companion in the cave.

Ahead, a light glowed through the trees. The cabin? Silence was critical. I planted my heel purposefully, rolling on the outside of my foot as I crept closer.

Light shone through a window. The small cabin had a covered porch, maybe a few rooms. I circled around back. A path led from the cabin into a draw where a large kettle sat on a stone platform with a copper coil resting above it. A bootlegger's still? I scanned the woods and outbuildings. No visible lookouts. I moved closer.

Crack!

Damned sticks. I froze. Would the next sound be a shot from the old guy's rifle? My heart pounded.

No one came out to investigate. I moved again, more carefully. The window was too high; I needed something to stand on. I took a log from the woodpile and propped it against the cabin. Cautiously, I stepped up.

A fire burned in the stone fireplace. An oil lamp on a table revealed the sparsely furnished room: dining table, two straight wooden chairs, a sofa with stuffing protruding from one side, and an oval braid rug. A gun leaned against the stone chimney. Another hung above the fireplace. Where was Erica?

My heart pounded as I crept onto the porch and peered into another window. A third wooden chair sat against the far wall with ropes draped across it. She'd been there, and maybe she still was. Only one way to find out.

I took a running head start and crashed through the door, sliding across the floor and ending in a crumpled heap beside the hearth. I grabbed the gun and staggered to my feet—was it loaded? No time to check. I kicked in another door. Light from the oil lamp shone on the small single bed. Pieces of rope hung from the headboard. I must have just missed her—he probably had her on that ATV that went by. I tossed the gun aside, retrieved the lamp, and returned to the bedroom. I set the lamp on a small shelf. The bed was the only piece of furniture in the room. There were no closets and no other entrances. Old photos hung on the wall—a woman in a nurse's uniform, very young, very pretty. Whoever she was, she had an admirer. There was one other photo, one I'd seen before: black railroad workers. McConnell had the same picture. I searched under the bed. Nothing. Still, she'd been there. I was close, damned close. I had to get back over to the cave and tell McConnell.

A floorboard creaked behind me.

I turned. The image of the bewhiskered, wild-eyed old coot flashed before me, almost causing me to laugh—then the butt of his rifle smashed into the side of my head.

Chapter Thirty-eight

Swirling patches of green slowly emerged from the indistinct shadows. I blinked and shook my head. Where was I? Were those trees? I must be in a forest . . . As the fog slowly lifted, the old guy seemed to materialize from nowhere, his scraggly beard encircling a tobacco stained grin. He held an old photograph next to my face. "Yup, you could be him, one and the same. I reckon I'll hang you, just to be safe."

Hang me? He couldn't be serious. I tried to raise my hand, but ropes cut into my wrists. God, the pain . . . had he broken my jaw? "Who . . . who the hell are you and what have you done with my daughter?"

The old man glanced at the photo, then stared at me and smiled. "I knows who you are, you can't fool me. She's safe; you can't never hurt that dear child again."

What the hell was he talking about, and where was Erica? She had to be close by. Through the forest, a hundred feet away at the bottom of a slope, stood that same strange old oak with its crooked limb reaching across the dirt road. Whatever the geezer had in mind, it couldn't be good, but hands tied or not, I could still kick the hell out of him. I tried to stand, but I couldn't budge. He'd propped me against a tree and had my hands tied behind it.

"Who are you?" I asked again. Every inch of my body screamed in agony. He must have beaten the hell out of me while I was unconscious.

"Name's not important." He continued wrapping duct tape around both me and the tree.

Daylight filtered through spring growth on the forest's

high branches. My head pounded. How long had I been out? Pain shot through both legs. What in the hell had he done to me? I stretched. The pain eased.

"I reckoned you'd be a mite sore." He pointed at me. "You's one big feller." His laugh was more of a cackle. "Couldn't get you up on the four-wheeler, so I throwed a few hitches around your legs and tied the rope to the bumper. I tried to go slow; hope I didn't hurt you none."

He'd dragged me through the forest? That explained the soreness. He was a nut case for sure, but he'd been strong enough to manhandle Peter, and he'd hogtied me. Despite the cool winter air, sweat trickled down my cheek.

"What's this hanging nonsense? I never did you any harm."

"You eat too much. Now I got to go into town and fetch a stronger rope." He pointed to the strange old oak. "Once I get a noose around your fat neck I'll toss the rope over that big old limb there and tie it to my four-wheeler." He smiled. "When I hit the gas, you'll do some fancy dancing—but your kind likes dancing, ain't that right?"

My kind? I strained against the ropes. "Hold on, pal. If you hang me, that's murder and Sergeant Johnson will hunt you down. We're talking a capital offense, you'll be executed. But if you let me go, I won't say anything to anyone."

"You mean Walter? He's a bad seed, that one." The old man spit. "Him and his strayed from the path years ago. I got no time for folks what don't hold with family."

"Yeah, I don't like the guy either," I said. "All the more reason to let me go."

The old man's face twisted into a scowl. "Daddy warned me. He said you might come back. I promised, right there on his deathbed, I swore you'd never hurt her again."

"Hurt who? What the devil are you talking about?" My pulse quickened.

His eyes narrowed. "You know full well what I'm talking about, nigger." The old man stretched several strips of duct tape across my mouth. "I'm talking about Miss Rebecca."

* * *

Monday 11:28 AM

Peter had been able to rub the tape from his mouth, but I had nothing to rub against. I forced my tongue between the tape and my lips. Maybe I could work the adhesive off and push the whole mess away from my mouth, but what then?

That old guy had used the name, "Rebecca." He couldn't mean my grandmother, could he? Nothing made sense anymore. The photos at the cabin—I'd never seen pictures of her and I only remembered her as an older woman—but she'd been a nurse. Was she in one of those photos, and if so, why? What fixation could that old man have with a woman who was twenty years his senior?

I moistened the skin above my lip, expanding the area where adhesive could no longer grip. My tongue rubbed a corner of the tape. I worked it with my mouth until I caught it in my teeth. Chewing through took forever, but eventually, I had a hole. Chew, twist. Lips, tongue, neck, jaws—my muscles ached by the time I finally gnawed the gag from my mouth and hollered, "HELP!"

No answer. Of course; who'd be around, other than that crazy old nut who wanted to lynch me? And what the hell made him think that was necessary? Okay, so maybe I rubbed a few people the wrong way, but lynching? That seemed a bit harsh—even Ann wouldn't go that far—and the good Lord knew that if anyone had a motive, it'd be her.

My muscles tensed at the distant whine of an engine. Whoever that SOB was, apparently, he'd returned. I'd have to fight, claw, and kick my way out if I wanted to avoid his noose. The noise grew louder, and then an ATV zipped past the hanging tree without stopping. The driver wore a leather jacket and aviator sunglasses. Johnson? Thank God. He must have been headed to the cabin in search of me.

"Johnson! Hey, Sergeant Johnson!"

At first, the motor's roar drowned my screams, but after a moment, it idled. "Help!" I yelled again. "Sergeant Johnson, over here!"

Johnson revved his engine and came back toward the big tree. He'd found the cabin empty and was heading back to town. He'd never hear me over that racket. As the ATV flew past, I filled my lungs and screamed, "WALTER!"

He stopped, then turned and drove slowly to the hanging tree. Johnson stood on the pedals, cocking his head.

"Up here," I yelled.

He removed his helmet and pulled off his sunglasses. Squinting, he seemed to look right past me. "Corsini, is that you?"

"Hell, yes. Get up here and untie me."

"What in tarnation are you doing there, Corsini?" Johnson smiled as he placed his glasses inside the helmet and set the helmet on the ATV's seat. He seemed to enjoy his leisurely stroll up the hill to the tree where I was tied.

"Just untie me before that crazy bastard gets his rope around my neck."

Johnson lorded over me, his arms folded. "So, you met Cousin Ambrose?"

"Cousin?" I spit out a sliver of tape. "That sonofabitch wants to kill me. You're a cop, cousin or not, you've got to stop him." God, had I stumbled upon some degenerate pack of inbred hillbillies?

"Justine says you tried to get in her panties."

"Whoa, don't go there, Johnson. She all but threw herself at me—but . . . but nothing happened, nothing at all."

"So, she's not good enough for the likes of you?" Johnson pulled a knife and leaned closer.

God, I wasn't being rescued—he was in on it. "I . . . she's . . . oh hell, here's the deal: I'm already involved with someone. Justine's a real beauty and all, but I had to stay true. Besides, she's too young and pretty. She doesn't have time for the likes of me." Would he buy it?

Johnson laughed. "That's pretty much what she said, except I think she mentioned something about you being old and out of shape." He cut through the tape and slit the rope binding my hands.

Old and out of shape? Yeah, that was about how I felt. I rubbed my wrists. "What's this about your cousin?"

"Old Ambrose? He's been in the back of my mind,

especially after we found those bodies. I came up here to have a look around, but I sure didn't expect to find you."

As I pulled the tape from my mouth, he cut my feet loose. "Is there a connection?" I said, stretching. After working out a few kinks, I stood.

Johnson stared at me blankly. "Connection to what?"

"The bodies, the ones in the cave. Do you think your cousin had anything to do with them?"

"Hard to say." He shook his head. "He's one crazy old coot, I'll give you that. His old man was nuts too. My side of the family's kept their distance ever since my granddaddy and Cousin Ambrose's old man had their falling out. They was brothers, you know."

My neck felt as though it had been broken in a dozen places. Slowly, I rotated my head. Vertebrae crackled. "He dragged me behind his ATV. I'm lucky that alone didn't kill me."

"Anything busted?" Johnson asked. He folded his knife and slid it in his pocket.

"Not that I can tell." I brushed myself off. "He has Erica. There were pieces of rope and signs all over that cabin that he'd had somebody tied up. He also mentioned a Rebecca. Does that name ring a bell?"

"Oh, hell," Johnson said, "not Rebecca Marshall?"

"Marshall? That was my grandmother's maiden name."

He seemed to do a double take. "Yeah . . . yeah," he said, pointing at me, "I can see it now."

"See what?"

"She ever talk to you about your people?"

"My people? I haven't talked to her in over thirty years, and she died just last week. What are you getting at?"

"This could be trouble." Johnson drew his revolver, checked the cylinder, and then returned the gun to its holster. "Let's go back and take another look at that cabin."

I climbed behind him on the ATV. He revved the engine and popped as much of a wheelie as he could with my added weight. In less than a minute, we pulled in front of the cabin.

Johnson drew his pistol and kicked open the door. He

swept the room with the barrel of his weapon before stepping inside. I followed him into the front room. He held up his hand, signaling me to wait, then threw open the bedroom door and aimed his pistol through the doorway, getting the drop on whoever might be inside. "All clear," he yelled. "Hey, Corsini, get a load of this."

The bedroom was as sparse as I remembered.

"Is this your grandma?" He held out a photo.

I studied the picture and shook my head. "I can't say. I never saw pictures of her when she was young."

A thumbtack held the photo of the railroad workers to the wall—gandy dancers, McConnell had called them. Johnson yanked the photo down, popping the thumbtack across the room. He held the picture next to my face. "Yup, it sure could be."

"That old man did the same thing when he had me tied up. What the hell's with you two?"

"Damn." The photos slipped from Johnson's grasp as he sat on edge of the bed. He buried his face in his hands and sighed. "That old bastard just couldn't leave well enough alone. All this was supposed to end seventy years ago."

"Knock off the doubletalk," I said, grabbing his sleeve. "What the hell's going on?"

He ran his fingers through his hair. "I've tried tying the pieces together a hundred times." He looked at me. "I'm a small town cop. We don't have much serious crime here about, so I've spent time trying to figure out one that supposedly took place here two generations ago."

"Your grandfather?"

Johnson nodded. "And Cousin Ambrose's old man, Chester Johnson was his name. Rumor was, Uncle Chester had it bad for this real pretty woman, a nurse, so it goes. Apparently, she was your grandma. There was also some colored fella involved."

Johnson stared out the window. "My granddaddy carried a heavy guilt to his grave. He never let on what burdened him, but Grandma used to say he'd wake up screaming in the night. Him and his brother, they'd done something awful—

that much was for sure. It ate away at Granddaddy but never seemed to bother his brother."

"Those bodies in the cave, you think they're connected?"

"You know Captain McConnell?" He leaned over and retrieved the photo of the gandy dancers. "His granddaddy and his granddaddy's brother went missing about seventy years ago, nineteen and thirty-six, or was it thirty-seven? Anyway, McConnell's grandma got left with a tiny baby and no means of support. Nobody ever knew what happened."

"Yeah, McConnell had that same picture." I pointed to the gandy dancers. "He mentioned something about a mystery surrounding his grandpa—but how does that tie in with me or Erica?"

Johnson pulled a wallet-sized photo from his pocket. "Seemed like a good idea to carry this, as long as she was missing in my territory."

The picture was of Erica.

He retrieved another photograph from the floor and held it next to Erica's school picture. "Well?" The old faded black and white was of a woman in a nurse's uniform.

"My God, they could be sisters . . ."

Johnson nodded. He handed me the photos. "My daddy once told me what he thought Grandpa and Ambrose's old man might have done, but without witnesses or evidence, hell, it's been nothing but a rumor all these years.

"But, Erica—that could be no more than coincidence—and anyway, it's a million to one shot that he sees her and makes a connection."

"Not if he's been waiting and studying old photos," Johnson said. "Not if he sees a pretty young white girl hiking in his woods with some black fella, and not if he thinks you have an uncanny resemblance to that gandy dancer his daddy lynched seventy years ago."

Johnson was insane—he'd lost his mind—just like that wacko cousin of his. They were both nuts. No way in hell that I, Mitch Corsini, could be . . . . Hell, I couldn't even bring myself to say it. Besides, everybody knew I was Italian—Sicilian, most likely.

Chapter Thirty-nine

Sunlight filtered through the cabin's dirt-smeared windows, revealing tangles of silken cobwebs in every corner. A layer of dust covered everything in the sparsely furnished cottage. Erica had been there, tied to a rickety chair in that very room, and not that long ago. What had that SOB done with her since?

Johnson slowly paced, trailing his gloved finger across the edge of the table, touching dishes and lifting utensils, as though they might offer some psychic message. Suddenly, his eyes widened and he pounded his fist. "That's it! The Marshall place."

"What are talking about?" I asked.

"Damn." He reached for the door. "Why didn't I think of that before? Come on, we have to get back to town."

I ran after him as he bounded down the steps. "Hold on, Johnson. How about filling me in on what we're doing before we go running off on a wild goose chase."

Johnson grabbed his helmet and threw his leg over the seat. "Ambrose's daddy, Chester Johnson, he bought the old Marshall place after your great granddaddy passed back in the Fifties. Owning that old house might have been Chester's way of holding onto your grandma's memory."

"Touching," I said, "but what's it got to do with Erica?"

He stared at me and shook his head. "You could be dumber, but I'm not sure how. If Cousin Ambrose has your daughter, and if she's not here, the only other place I know where he could stash her is that old house. You coming?"

* * *

Monday 2:25 PM

We abandoned the ATV at the trailhead and climbed into Johnson's pickup. He flipped a switch on the dash and the blue lights mounted above the cab flashed a pulsating warning as we pulled onto the hardtop.

"I never figured old Ambrose for something like this." He gnawed on a toothpick as he swerved through the sparse traffic. "Always knew he was a mite dim, but kidnapping? Attempted murder? Damn." He spit the toothpick out the window. "I never saw that one coming." We pulled onto a street lined with gingerbread houses desperately in need of paint and skidded to a halt in front of a faded yellow two-story on the corner.

Johnson slammed the gearshift into park and raced up the steps to the porch. I followed as quickly as I could. He kicked open the door.

"Ambrose? Ambrose Johnson. This here's Walter." He drew his pistol and ducked around a corner. "You come on out now, you hear? I don't mean to hurt you, but I will if I have to."

A beat up old sofa with clumps of stuffing hanging from gashes in the cushions and an ancient floor model radio were the only furnishings in the living room. No sign of Erica. We searched the kitchen and the pantry: bare shelves, dust, mouse droppings, and cobwebs.

"Upstairs." He pointed. "There's a couple of bedrooms." Johnson ran up the stairs.

I took a deep breath and followed.

"Dammit." Johnson leaned against the door jamb, his pistol close to his chest. Ropes dangled from the headboard of a small bed. He placed his hand on the worn, disheveled quilt. "It's still warm—we must have just missed him."

Erica had to have been terrified, spread eagled and lashed to that bed, never knowing what was going to happen next, and being ogled and manhandled by that degenerate old maniac. If I ever got my hands on him I'd kill him. "Now what?"

"I'm fresh out of ideas." Johnson shrugged. "If you

come up with something, you let me know, you hear?"

I snatched one of the ropes from the headboard, twirling it in slow circles as I studied the situation. "He had her at the cabin. We tracked him there. He brought her here. We tracked him here. How's he staying one step ahead?"

Johnson scratched his stomach. "Beats me. Maybe he's got a police scanner."

"Great," I said. "That explains how he knows what we're doing—but what's his next move?"

"You're asking me to read the mind of a madman?" Johnson kicked the footboard on the bed. "Hell, he's capable of damned near anything."

"You live in a fantasy world . . ."

"What the hell you talking about, Corsini?"

"No," I held up my hand. "Not you. Follow me on this. He lives in a fantasy world. To him, Erica is Rebecca, and he thinks I'm some black guy from seventy years ago. Even though his daddy strung me up once, he wants to lynch me again. He can't have his fantasy woman—or his father's woman—or whatever she's supposed to be, so his only recourse is . . ."

Johnson snapped his fingers and pointed at me. "Destroy what he can't have?"

"You got it. We need to get out to that hanging tree."

Johnson thumbed the button on a microphone hooked on his shirt pocket. "This here's Sergeant Johnson. Put out an APB on one Ambrose Johnson. He's suspected of kidnapping the Gillespie girl. Consider him armed and dangerous. If spotted, don't apprehend. Y'all get hold of me, you copy?"

"Walter," the radio squawked. "McConnell here. Where are you headed? Over."

Johnson keyed his handset. "Captain, I got Corsini with me. We're leaving the old Marshall place now. Ambrose had that girl here, but they're gone, probably headed back to the cabin. Can you have a unit meet me there? Over."

"I'm on my way," McConnell said. "Don't do anything before I get there. We'll need to set up a cordon. I'm calling in the state hostage negotiation team. You copy?"

"Roger. Out." Johnson sneered. "Hostage negotiators, my ass. We got a hanging to stop."

I took the stairs two at a time, beating Johnson to the truck. I hopped in on the driver's side and had the wheels burning rubber as he climbed in on the passenger's side.

"Dammit, Corsini, who taught you to drive? Don't screw up my transmission."

"Shut up and hold on," I said. "How about hitting those blue lights?"

Johnson flipped the switch on the dash.

We turned onto the interstate, then off again at the next exit and onto a winding two-lane road. I veered around a semi hauling logs and fought to hold the road as we skidded through a curve that was a whole lot tighter than it looked. Finally, Johnson's ATV came into view—right where we'd left it beside the road. Kicking up dust and gravel, the truck slid onto the shoulder as I stood on the brakes, bringing Johnson's truck to a stop moments before slamming into another pickup that was parked behind the ATV. The other truck had a steel ramp propped against its open tailgate.

"Ambrose," Johnson said, pointing to the other truck. "It has to be. He's headed to the cabin." He jumped out and clambered onto his ATV, then beat his fist against the handlebar. "Damn."

"What is it?" I asked as I climbed from the cab.

Johnson pointed to the ignition and shrugged. "He took the keys."

"You left your keys in?"

"We were in a hurry," he said. "Remember?"

I ran my hand through my hair and stared at the suddenly worthless vehicle. "You do have a spare, right?"

"Yeah, at home."

"What the hell," I said. "Give me your knife."

He gave me a puzzled look and offered his pocketknife. I grabbed the knife, shoved him off the seat, and popped open the ignition. After a bit of scraping, I touched the bare ends of two wires together. The engine coughed and then sputtered to life.

"You didn't learn that in college," Johnson said. He stepped across the saddle in front of me and revved the throttle.

"Money was tight growing up," I said. "Sometimes I borrowed stuff."

He eyed me over his shoulder. "Must be why you looked so all fired natural when I had you locked up."

"You gonna talk or drive?"

Johnson revved the engine and shifted into gear. Tires spun in the loose sand. We took off down the wooded lane.

"We sure won't sneak up on him," I shouted.

"You want fast or you want quiet?"

The dirt road curved. Johnson steered us onto the path to the cabin. "He's a passable good shot," he said. "Watch yourself."

"I have you for my shield," I shouted.

"Kiss my—" Suddenly, Johnson pitched forward, falling to one side.

I reached around him and grabbed the handlebars, squeezing the brakes.

"I'm hit!" Johnson yelled, as he clutched his shoulder. Blood seeped from between his fingers. "The sonofabitch shot me!"

I dumped the ATV on its side and pulled Johnson to safety behind it.

He frowned. "Hey, careful, that machine cost me four month's wages." He crawled beside me. "Can you see him?"

"Do you mean have I stuck my head out so he can shoot me too? Hell, no."

"Ambrose. Ambrose Johnson," he yelled. "This here's Walter. You got yourself in a real pickle this time, but I come to bail you out."

"Walter," the old man yelled. "You know I ain't turning myself in, especially when you got that nigra with you."

I wish he'd stop that nonsense. I was Italian.

"Ambrose, let the girl go. Let's talk this out like family."

"You ain't none of my kin, Walter Johnson. You and

your daddy burned that bridge years ago." He fired a shot into the tree across the road.

"What about the girl?" Johnson called out.

"Time was she might could've turned her life around, but them days are gone. She's come to taunt me with that nigra friend of hers. Now she'll hang there beside him."

"He's lost it." Johnson drew his pistol.

I grabbed his hand. "You can't shoot. Erica's up there."

He rolled his eyes. "You really are as dumb as you look, aren't you?"

I shrugged.

"Now, listen up," Johnson said. "When I fire in the air, you peek around there and tell me what you see."

That made sense, sort of. I still wasn't keen on sticking my head out, though. I swallowed. "Okay, go for it."

Johnson fired.

I ducked around the corner of the ATV and then quickly retreated. "She's there. I saw her. He's got her all tied up down by that big tree, the one he calls the hanging tree. He has a noose around her neck."

"Can you see him?"

I looked at Johnson. Unfortunately, that question also made sense. I poked my head around the corner again. A shot echoed through the trees as dirt kicked up on the road a foot from my face. "He's behind that big oak. He can cover her and keep an eye on us. You got any ideas?"

Johnson seemed to ponder my question. "You're no hunter, but how are you at sneaking up on stuff?"

I rolled onto my stomach and brushed dirt out of my eyes. Johnson was down. He'd be of little help. That was my kid up there. No time to call for backup. I had to do whatever it took. "What do you have in mind?"

"If I distract him," Johnson said, "do you suppose you can run up that hill?" He motioned with his pistol toward the rise on our right.

"Here's a better idea," I said. "You distract him and I'll run straight up that road." I pointed in the direction we came.

"Damn, Corsini. I figured you for some spine, but you're as yellow as they come."

"That's probably so, but listen. He'll see me if I go up the hill. I'm unarmed. He has that rifle. End of story—and Erica pays with her life."

"Yeah, and so . . . ?"

"He sees me run, he'll figure I'm turning tail, so he'll focus on you. Meanwhile, I'll get behind that bend, then go uphill and circle around. It's still a long shot, but I like my chances—and Erica's—if he's focusing his full attention on trying to kill you."

Johnson nodded. "Can you be quiet once you're up there?"

"I can if you can make enough racket down here."

"And then what? You want my pistol?"

"Tempting, but I'm not a hunter, remember? I'd probably shoot her." I rolled over and patted my stomach. "Look, I go close to two-thirty. Once I'm steamrolling down that hill, even if he shoots me, I'll plough through him like a runaway freight train and wrap a bear hug on his scrawny ass that's guaranteed to bring tears to his eyes."

"That's a thirty 'ought six he's shooting. It'll bring down a bear."

"Then as soon as you hear me yell, you'd better drag your butt up there and finish him off before he hurts Erica."

"Corsini," Johnson said.

"What?"

"You're one crazy brother, or Pisano, or whatever the hell you are. Anyway, good luck." He pulled the bloodied hand from his shoulder and wiped it on his shirt, then held it out.

I shook his hand. "Whenever you're ready, Sergeant."

Johnson fired three shots in quick succession.

I sprinted up the road. Had he seen me? God, what if he was drawing a bead on me right then? If nothing else, that thought probably improved my forty-yard dash time. I ran until the road turned. Two more shots rang out. Johnson— or his cousin? It sounded like the revolver. I searched the woods. If I couldn't see Cousin Ambrose, it was a safe bet that he couldn't see me. I took a few deep breaths, then trudged up the slope. Johnson was sure doing a hell of a lot of hollering. Had the ruse worked?

Johnson filled the air with all manner of incredible vulgarities, references to family heraldry, and other assorted insults and then the engine on one of the ATVs fired up. If that was Johnson, good for him, more noise. The crack of Ambrose's rifle filled the woods, followed by two smaller reports from Johnson's service revolver. I reached the crest of the ridge. Ambrose crouched behind his tree aiming at Johnson. He fired.

Johnson screamed.

Was he hit, or just keeping the old guy distracted? Only a hundred yards more, then a downhill sprint to my game-ending tackle.

I ducked behind the ridge and counted off one hundred paces in the direction that I hoped would take me directly in line with the old man. When I reached the end, I crept up to the summit again and surveyed the ground below. Perfect. I was behind him and less than thirty yards away. Maybe I could creep up on him. Nah, that would never work—I couldn't creep up on a good night's sleep. I'd better stick to the direct approach. I filled my hands with rocks, heaving one into the woods behind him. The old geezer turned toward the sound of the rock landing across the road. That was my chance. I glanced upward in a quick, wordless prayer and then let out the best blood-curdling scream I could muster. I charged down the hill, screaming and throwing rocks as I charged into what I expected would be a deadly hail of bullets.

Instead, the old man dropped his rifle and ran.

Hell, that wasn't supposed to happen, I must have been a lot more intimidating than I thought. I quickly scanned the woods. Finding no sign of the old man, I allowed my gaze to fall upon Erica. My dear, sweet child . . . finally, her terrifying ordeal was over. She sat helplessly, with her mouth taped, her hands tied, and that damned noose strung around her neck.

The rope draped loosely across the huge limb on the old tree, then snaked along the dirt road, ending in a loop around the hitch on Ambrose's ATV.

"It's okay, Honey. I'm here now." Cautiously, I moved toward her. "You'll be fine."

Without warning, the old guy sprang from the bushes and jumped on his ATV. The engine coughed and sputtered as he furiously twisted the throttle.

"God, no!" I flipped open Johnson's knife and dove for the rope, catching it just above Erica's head. Sawing furiously, I sliced through one strand and then another. Please, God don't let that machine turn over. I glanced at the old coot as I worked on the rope. His gaze met mine and he smiled. Suddenly, a deep, mechanical rumble replaced the high pitched whine of the ignition. He revved the engine. The ATV slipped into gear with a metallic "clunk" and headed away, pulling the rope across the top of the big limb. Desperately, I yanked the slack over to my side and pulled myself up, adding my weight to the rope. The ATV jerked to a halt, spinning its wheels in the loose sand, and then slowly, regained traction. Inch by inch it lifted me off the ground. The noose tightened. I locked my legs around Erica's waist, supporting her weight and lifting her with me as I desperately hacked at the rope's final strand. Pain shot through my arm as the rope pinned my hand like a giant scissors against the limb. I let out a scream and slashed at the last stubborn fibers. The rope snapped. Erica and I tumbled to the ground in a tangled pile of leaves, bodies, and duct tape.

I pulled her close and gently stroked her disheveled hair. "Thank God, you're safe, " I whispered. "I won't let anything happen to you again."

She stared past me. After all she'd been through, she couldn't even bring herself to look at her old man? Suddenly, terror filled her eyes. She screamed through her duct tape gag.

I locked her in my arms and rolled.

The axe dug into the ground where we'd been.

The old man stood with his legs apart, hefting the axe in

both hands and lining up his next swing. His face twisted in a savage sneer. "You cheated the hangman once, but no more. Today you're gonna die . . ."

"Wait, mister." I held up my hands. "We're not who you think we are."

Ambrose smiled. "Daddy told me all about you, boy. He said you'd come back, try to take her away again, but I got me an extra heavy rope this time, so's the both of you can dance from my hanging tree."

"Drop the axe, Ambrose."

A wave of relief swept over me as I turned toward the voice. "It's about damned time . . ."

McConnell stood behind me, his pistol drawn.

The old man jerked his head up in response to McConnell's voice. His surprise quickly turned to anger. "Your kind do stick together, don't you?" He swung the axe above his head.

A pistol blast shattered the stillness.

Ambrose jerked. A small, dark hole appeared above his left eye.

Chapter Forty

The door to the hospital room opened no more than a crack and a short, brassy-haired nurse peered out. "I'm sorry, Mr. Corsini, she'd rather not see you right now." Her tight smile seemed incapable of masking her distain as she closed the door.

Why wasn't I surprised? I tossed the flowers on a small end table and took a seat in the waiting area.

"She's been through a lot," Ann said. "Give her time." She took my hand. "How are you holding up?"

"You mean other than worrying about Erica?" I rubbed the back of my neck. "I feel like I spent the day in a cement mixer with two bowling balls and an angry wildcat."

"That good, huh?" She smiled. "Not everyone gets dragged through the mountains behind a four-wheeler. Think of the story you'll write."

"Yeah, once the rope burns heal enough to type again." Under the bandages, my fingers throbbed.

"At least your drug charges were dropped."

"McConnell told you?"

"He said that girl's prints were all over the bag. She stuffed it in your glove box the night you drove her home and then put the cops onto you to punish you for turning her down."

"It serves me right for trying to do her a favor," I said. "Hey, did you hear? They're getting married."

"Who?"

"Johnson and his little cowgirl." I laughed. "A match made in heaven."

"Cut it out." She gave my knee a playful slap. "They'll

probably be good for one another. By the way, did Bill mention anything about those skeletons?"

"Yeah, they're doing some DNA tests." I picked up the flowers, turning them slowly in the artificial light. Daisies might have been too ordinary. Maybe that's why she hadn't accepted them. That big basket would have worked better, but then she would have refused anything coming from her dear old dad. I dropped the small arrangement on the table. "What do you think they'll find?"

"I'm not sure," Ann said. She seemed to study my face. "What are you expecting?"

That was a good question. I shrugged. "That old man, Johnson's cousin, he sure had some crazy ideas." I forced a half-hearted laugh.

"Bill told me about it while you were getting X-rayed."

"What'd he say?" My stomach tightened. I really didn't want to go there. "Not some rubbish about me and some old gandy dancer?"

"I'm surprised you even know what they are," she said. "It was just an old Clifton Forge folk tale. Come on." She held out her hand. "Let's find a cup of coffee."

* * *

McConnell came into the coffee shop and headed straight for our table. "What have you heard?" he asked. "How's Erica doing?"

I shrugged. "She's been through hell. Sukey said there weren't any serious physical injuries, just bruises and abrasions." I glanced at Ann. "But God only knows about her emotional state."

"Won't you join us?" Ann motioned toward an empty chair. "Erica's not ready to talk yet, so we don't have a feel for what all this has done to her—I simply can't imagine."

"I just came from Walter's room," McConnell said, sliding into the chair. "He's one lucky man—both bullets missed his vitals. They're keeping him here for a week or so."

"The two of you shared quite an adventure." Ann turned to me and smiled.

I fidgeted with my coffee cup. "I don't think I'm ready yet to call him my best friend, but when he gets out of this place, I'd like to buy the guy a drink."

"You're lucky too, Mitch," she said. "I'd hate to think of what might have happened if Bill hadn't come along."

"Yeah, thanks, McConnell," I mumbled. I owed the man my life, Erica's too. Hell, it might have been worse: what if I was forever indebted to Johnson—or ended up a headless legend roaming the forests around Clifton Forge?

"No sweat," McConnell said. "It goes with the job. You would have done the same for me if the tables were turned."

"And if I knew how to shoot straight." I raised my cup in a mock toast.

McConnell laughed. "By the way, I gave the state police a DNA sample. They're running it against whatever they found from those bodies in the cave. I have to believe the smaller man was my grandfather. The bigger fellow had to be his brother, George Henry." He looked at me as though he thought that should mean something to me.

Ann smiled and patted my arm. "Mitch knows all about DNA testing."

Yeah, Italian DNA. My mouth went dry. I took a sip of coffee. "So, if one of those guys turns out to be your long lost granddaddy, what then?"

He paused, as though collecting his thoughts. "Well, nothing changes. I'm still who I am. He'd still be the same grandpa I thought he was. I guess all it does is close the final chapter on the mystery—and give us the chance to lay him to rest after all these years."

"A funeral?" I said. "Why not? Better late than never."

"His widow is still alive," McConnell replied. "She's been waiting and worrying for seventy years."

"Wow, she must be one ancient gal." I smiled.

"Ninety-four, and a woman to be reckoned with." McConnell smiled. "You should meet her."

"Maybe someday." I drained my coffee. "If you guys don't mind, these last few days have taken their toll. I think I'll head back to the hotel and get some rest."

"You want some company?" Ann gathered our cups and placed them on the tray.

Company? I didn't want to hurt her feelings, but what I needed to sort out wouldn't happen in a crowd, even a crowd of two. "Thanks," I said, "but I'm looking for some shuteye. Call me if there's any change with Erica."

* * *

Monday 9:45 PM

I stuffed a pile of shirts into the suitcase. Erica was safe, but she wasn't ready to see me. I had no reason to hang around. I'd leave a note on Ann's door. Once back in Richmond, I'd send McConnell a sympathy card, but sympathy for what? For burying a guy who'd already been dead for seventy years?

That big guy in the cave—McConnell called him George Henry—what if he had known Grandma, so what? That didn't prove anything. I studied the skin on my forearm. McConnell already knew who he was. DNA testing wouldn't change him . . . .

It was all nonsense. I tried to brush aside the disquieting thoughts. Besides, I couldn't dance a lick. I laughed at the thought. If soul brothers had an organization, I'd definitely be barred. I flipped on the radio. A song came on and I struck a pose in front of the mirror. What'd the kids call it these days? Busting a move? I tried a feeble, jerky motion like I'd seen on TV, then another. Nope, no rhythm at all—none, zero. If that wasn't white, I didn't know what was.

The telephone rang. Thank God. I shut off the radio. "Corsini."

"Hi, Ann here. We're still at the hospital. Bill just got a call from the police lab. They have a positive match, isn't that incredible?"

A match to an ancestor he'd dreamed of finding—but what if he didn't want to find that missing link? What if a guy was perfectly satisfied with who and what he was?

"Mitch?" Ann said. "Mitch, are you there?"

"Yeah, sorry. It must have been a bad connection. Look,

tell McConnell I'm heading back to Richmond tonight. Erica's mother will be at the hospital soon and there's nothing more I can do here. I'll catch up with you at the office Tuesday morning."

"You sound awful. What's wrong?"

"Nothing. I'm just tired," I said. "Things are wrapped up here; I'll sleep better at home."

"Are you sure? I could come over," she said. "How about we grab a bite to eat before you leave?"

"Thanks. It's late and I'm okay. I'll catch you in the morning." I hung up.

So, that really was McConnell's granddaddy. That meant my buddy in the cave had to have been that George fellow. Well, at least now I knew his name. I dropped on the bed and covered my eyes with my forearm. Would anything change? Hell, no. Besides, Grandma would have never crossed that line.

* * *

The telephone jarred me awake. News about Erica? I grabbed the receiver. "Corsini."

"Mitch, when I noticed your car still there last night I stopped by your room, but the lights were off, so I figured you needed your sleep."

"Ann?" What did she mean, last night? I checked the clock. "Hey, I must have dozed. Have you had dinner yet?"

"Dinner? Wake up, tiger. It's the middle of the morning. I'm heading over to Bill and Sukey's. I'm working on a piece for the Human Interest section on Bill's grandfather—unless you'd already planned on doing that?"

The newspaper? Yeah, I did do that for a living, didn't I? It must have slipped my mind. "Nah, no problem," I said. "Go for it. There's no story there for me." I rubbed my eyes. Man, when had I ever slept that hard?

"Why don't you meet me there?" she said. "You can say good-bye to Bill and Sukey before you head to Richmond."

"Sure," I said, "why not? But first I need to shower and finish packing. I'll meet you there in an hour."

"One hour," Ann said, "no more. I'll ask Sukey to put the coffee on so don't you lie back down and fall asleep again."

"I'm awake, Ann. I'm awake." I hung up the phone and sat up, rubbing the soreness in my neck. A hot shower would sure feel good, but I needed a bit more waking up first.

I splashed cold water across my face, shocking me into full consciousness. As I stepped away from the sink I caught a glimpse of myself in the mirror. That gandy dancer, George—the big guy Johnson's wacko cousin thought I looked like—he must have been one handsome dude. I smiled as I stepped into the shower.

Chapter Forty-one

Ann's car was in the driveway when I pulled in front of McConnell's house. He'd turned out to be an okay guy, but I wasn't going to hang around all day while he resurrected his entire family history. Ten minutes max, I'd say good-bye, and then it'd be time to hit the road.

"Mitch, we're so glad you could make it." McConnell met me at the door. "Come on in." He shook my hand and steered me through the foyer. Ann and Sukey glanced up from the couch in the living room and smiled.

"Good morning, Mitch." Sukey set her cup on the end table as she stood. "Coffee?"

I nodded. "Thanks."

"Black, right?" She poured from a silver pot and handed me the cup. "Did Bill tell you about his DNA match?"

"Yes, I heard." I raised my cup in a toast. "Congratulations."

A pile of old photos covered the coffee table. Sukey retrieved one depicting gandy dancers working the rails. "I wish we had more. Bill's family didn't have money back then—photography wasn't something gandy dancers could afford. We're thankful for the few we've been able to find."

"The railroad archives had some," McConnell said. "They allowed me to make copies." He pointed to a smiling man in bib overalls wearing a wide brimmed hat. "That's my granddaddy, Willie Terrell McConnell. We'd never have found him if it weren't for you."

"Glad to help," I said. "The next time you need a volunteer to drop into a cave full of dead bodies and rattlesnakes, just say the word."

Sukey laughed. "I understand you and George Henry have become close friends."

"He was good company for one night." I took the framed picture from the mantel. The skeleton had given me a sense of his height, but it couldn't begin to reflect the ready smile or the power that must have been in those arms. "I'll say this, he was a patient man. Not many would have endured my ramblings that evening without feeling the need to interrupt."

"And Erica?" McConnell asked. "How's she doing?"

I glanced at Sukey. She'd been on the case, certainly she'd already filled him in. "I talked to the hospital this morning. They'll discharge her as soon as her mother gets there."

"Had she mentioned anything more about her ordeal with old Ambrose?" McConnell swung a leg over the side of his armchair and sipped his coffee

"Not that I've heard," I said, shaking my head. "But I doubt that she's ready to come to grips with any of that. Maybe in a few weeks."

"Or months?" Ann took the photo from me and studied it, then she grasped my chin between her thumb and forefinger and turned my face toward her. "I see what you mean, Bill."

Not her too? Was everyone on the planet trying to make me out to be something I wasn't?

Sukey raised an eyebrow and looked at me. "Can you spare a minute?"

I checked my watch and shrugged. "Yeah, sure. I guess so." What'd she have up her sleeve?

"Will you excuse us?" she said, turning to Ann and McConnell. Sukey took me by the arm and led me down the hall. "There's someone I'd like you to meet."

In the family room, an old woman nodded off in a wheelchair beside the window. A blanket covered her lap.

"Grandma," Sukey said, "this is the man I was telling you about, Mitch Corsini."

Slowly, the ancient one raised her head. "He the one who found my Willie Terrell?"

There was something vaguely familiar about her. Where had I seen her before? I gave Sukey a questioning glance.

"I'm sorry," Sukey said, "allow me to finish the introductions. Mitch, this is Lorinda Jane, Bill's grandmother. That was her husband you found in the cave."

She had to be close to a hundred. I raised my voice. "Nice to meet you, ma'am."

Sukey rested her hand on my shoulder. "I'll leave the two of you to get acquainted." She winked. "If she falls asleep, don't take it personally."

"Wait—" I reached out.

Sukey placed a finger to her lips as if to hush me, then pointed to a chair and left.

"I won't bite." The old lady flashed a toothless grin.

Great. So, how long would it be 'til she dozed off? I glanced at my watch.

"I remember you from Miss Rebecca's funeral. You was in a hurry then, too."

So that's where I'd seen her, Grandma's funeral. "I'm sorry, ma'am," I said, speaking in a loud, precise voice. "I don't mean to seem edgy. Guess there's a lot going on I just don't understand."

"I'm old, not deaf."

"Sorry . . ."

"Sit." She waved a shriveled hand at the chair.

I pulled the wooden straight-backed chair beside the window. We faced one another, our knees almost touching. "Did you know my grandmother?"

"Young man, I'm ninety-four years old. Most days I don't feel so good. I can't walk, and I hate being out in the rain. Why in tarnation would I ride an hour on bumpy roads, get my rheumatism all worked up, and suffer that Tom Fool preacher you hired if I didn't know the woman?"

I hung my head. "Sorry, ma'am. I guess that sounded like a foolish question."

"Which it most certainly was." A fit of coughing nearly doubled her over. When she regained control, she cleared her throat, and then wiped her mouth with a hanky. "Young man, you have no idea who I am. You don't even know who you are. Let me ask you something."

"Okay." I nodded.

"Miss Rebecca, your grandma, she ever give you anything?"

I rubbed the back of my neck and gazed out the window, sorting through so many foggy memories. "There was a toy train . . . and an old hat. That was it; at least that I can remember."

"You don't recollect a small wooden pendant with a star carved on one side?"

"Yes . . . yes, there was something like that—on a rawhide lanyard. The nursing home sent it over after Grandma's funeral, along with some letters and such."

"So, in her own way, she did get it to you." The old woman scowled. "Her choice—not for me to question."

She was rambling and it was past time for me to hit the road. I stood. "Ma'am, I'm not sure what all this is about, but I do have a few hours driving ahead of me and I really need to be going. It was a pleasure talking with you."

"Anthony Mitchell, you sit and hear me out." She pointed a crooked finger at my chair.

How'd she know that name? I hadn't used it in years. Last time I recalled seeing it was on my college diploma. I promptly obeyed and took my seat.

"Your grandma and me, we didn't have no secrets. Time was, folks didn't hanker to her mixing with my kind, but there weren't none of her own people reaching out that hand of friendship when she needed it."

She opened a tapestry handbag that had been tucked beside her in the wheelchair and removed a packet of letters. With great effort, she worked the top letter free from the faded blue ribbon tied around the bundle. "Miss Rebecca said I'd know when the time was right to give you these. I ain't got but a short time left on this here earth, so I reckon I'd best not wait—today's as good a day as any."

"Letters from Grandma? Thanks," I said. "I'll read them when I get home."

"You read that one." She tapped her finger on the top letter. "After, if'n you feels the need, you read them others." She lowered her head to her chest. In a moment, her breathing became soft and regular.

* * *

Tuesday 1:47 PM

The vending machine at the rest stop splashed steaming coffee all over. I lifted the plastic window, retrieved my half empty cup, and returned to the Chevy. My departure from McConnell's had seemed abrupt, almost as though I'd just walked out on them—and Ann too—yet there was no reason to hang around. I'd finished my business there and I had a life in Richmond that needed putting back together. I blew into the cup and took a sip.

Damn. Why'd I always do that? I pressed a knuckle against my scalded lip and set the cup in the holder.

My hand throbbed and my neck and shoulders still ached from being dragged behind Ambrose Johnson's ATV. As I stretched, rotating my head and massaging the soreness, the letters on the seat caught my eye. Why would Grandma write those, but not mail them? And why'd she give them to that old woman? I picked up the top envelope, the one the old lady said to read first, and peeled it open. A beautiful, practiced penmanship flowed across the page in blue ink.

Dear Anthony,

I promised to watch you today while your mother worked. I don't often get to Richmond anymore, but I do so look forward to these few moments we spend together. Almost three years have passed since your papa died—and thirty or more since I felt the warmth of his father beside me. You, dear one, are now the man in my life.

How old are you as you read this? Thirty? Forty-five? I try to picture you all grown, with your wavy hair and your beautiful brown eyes. You will no doubt grow into such a handsome man, much like your father and his father before him.

I will ask my friend to hold this and other letters until she feels you are ready, but then I wonder, will you ever be ready for what I must say? What kind of a man have you grown to be, Anthony?

Anthony Mitchell Corsini—such a beautiful, proud Italian name. Do you know where "Corsini" came from? I took it from the telephone directory in Secaucus, New Jersey. I'd moved there before your father was born. Virginia wouldn't have accepted him, and I had hoped he might find an easier time of it up north—and with an Italian name. In truth, Jim Crow laws were no more hurtful than the hypocrisy we found amongst the northern liberals.

In my day, so many beautiful souls were judged harshly—and wicked ones much less so—for no reason other than the color of their skin. I too used that measure, I am ashamed to say, until I met your grandfather.

When he swung his hammer, no three men together could drive spikes faster, yet his caress was as soft as butterfly wings on a baby's face.

You may become angry as you read this, and you certainly have that right. Your mother and I have deceived you, and perhaps that was wrong. We only wanted what was best, and safest, for you. Does it change who you are when you realize the truth? I pray not. I pray you are as strong, fair, and loving as your grandpa. If so, you will forgive me—and embrace him.

I have written you many times. In each letter, I have tried to give you another glimpse of your grandpa: his humor, his wisdom, his abiding faith in God Almighty, and especially the love he would have shown for his children and his grandchildren, if only he'd been permitted to know you. But then maybe, in God's own way, He has already brought the two of you together. If that is so, I pray my George Henry enjoyed his time with his only grandson. I also pray you find it in your heart to accept your grandpa and me as you now know us to be.

You may read the other letters or put a match to them. Either way, it won't change the man you've grown to be.

With all my love,
Grandma

My hands trembled. I dropped the letter and closed my eyes, squeezing back the tears. They'd been right—Johnson, McConnell, even that crazy Ambrose—they'd all suspected what Grandma's letter confirmed. All those years . . . she'd lied, Mom had lied—hell, my whole damned life had been a lie. They had no right . . . . I pounded the dash. The pain that coursed up my arm couldn't begin to supplant the ache burning deeper within me. Who was I? Hell, what was I? My entire world, and all those damned paradigms Ann loved screwing with—all were shattered.

Why should it matter? It wasn't as though I was prejudiced or anything . . . . Yeah, right, and if Peter had had blond hair and blue eyes I wouldn't have reacted any differently to him dating my daughter.

Would people see me differently? Hell, they'd have to—I already did—but what had changed? I picked up the letter and read it again.

What kind of man had Grandma imagined me to be? No doubt very different than what I'd become. She'd be disappointed, and why not? My own daughter couldn't stand the sight of me. Black or white, African or Italian, I needed to find out who Mitch Corsini really was, and he'd better be a hell of a lot more than skin deep. Suddenly, questions swirled in my mind. Did George Henry hold the answers?

I dug into my pocket and retrieved a fistful of quarters. If I was going to sit in a parking lot poring over old letters, I'd better hit the vending machines again.

Chapter Forty-two

April 2007

A mahogany casket? He probably would have been more at home with oak, but Grandma would have insisted. Ann slipped her hand into the crook of my arm as Reverend Paterson delivered the homily. He'd nailed it at Willie's funeral at the Second AME church in Clifton Forge so I dropped a C-note in the collection plate and lured him down to Roanoke for Grandpa's service.

"You couldn't have asked for a more beautiful day," Ann whispered.

It sure beat the blizzard we'd had at Grandma's funeral— what a difference a few weeks could make. Stray clouds floated in an azure sky above the lush green mountains. I looked to Lorinda Jane, seated in her wheelchair, and smiled.

She nodded.

The small gathering joined in the final hymn with singing and clapping. As mourners filed past the grave, they sprinkled handfuls of dirt on Grandpa's coffin. McConnell pushed Lorinda Jane's wheelchair close to the grave. She opened her handbag and retrieved shards of broken pottery, which she dropped in the hole.

I must have given Ann a curious look.

"Slave tradition," she whispered. "I'll explain later."

After paying our respects, Ann and I walked up the hill toward the parking lot. We paused on the grassy lawn and greeted other mourners as they walked past. Daffodils and azaleas splashed their spring colors across the cemetery.

"Nice service," McConnell said, shaking my hand. "Old George Henry would have been pleased."

"You can thank your preacher for that," I said. "I was

only in charge of the weather." I held out my hands, taking in the splendor of the day.

"No offense, Mitch," Sukey replied. "But as to who arranged this beautiful day, I'm putting my money on Rebecca." She laughed and patted my arm. "But I do love what you did with the headstone, even if it does stretch the truth just a tad."

"George Henry McConnell and his beloved wife, Rebecca?" I waved dismissively toward their grave. "In a different time, they wouldn't have had to wait for death to bring them together. There are many truths in this old world. That seemed the right one for them."

Lorinda Jane tugged on my coattail. "Did you bring that Freedom Star?"

"As a matter of fact . . ." I pulled the small wooden token from my pocket. "I thought you might like to have it."

"No." She shook her head and gave an agitated wave. "George Henry meant to pass that on to his boy, and his boy was supposed to pass it to you. Now that you has it, you give it to your own young'uns."

"I only have the one, and there's some serious fence mending I need to do with her." I forced a smile.

"Then you'd best get to it," she said. "You got no excuse." Lorinda Jane tapped the arm of the wheelchair. "Get a move on, Billy. We'll be late for 'Oprah.'"

McConnell laughed. "See you Saturday. We'll look for you around five."

"I'm working on Erica," I said. "Peter is too. With his help, we'll all be there to meet the family."

"Great. See you then." McConnell leaned into the wheelchair and pushed Lorinda Jane up the hill.

Ann turned toward me. "You've talked to her?"

"Last night. She finally took my call."

"How'd it go?"

"Too quickly, but she didn't hang up."

"That's a start," she said. "Give her time. Maybe one day you can write the story of her ordeal. Do you think she'd let you do that?"

Her ordeal? That had begun long before her hike in the mountains. I shook my head. "She needs a daddy, not a reporter. But their story . . ." I nodded toward the grave. "Sunday, page one, above the fold—and you'd better get used to it."

"This Sunday?" she said. "Why didn't you tell me?"

"What's the matter, afraid of a little competition?" I winked.

"How can I grow as a writer without competition, someone pushing me for column space?" She leaned against my arm and smiled. "It's good to have you back."

We waited as the last of the mourners climbed the gentle slope to the parking area. Cemetery workers stood beside the grave, poised with their shovels. "I suppose they're waiting for us," I said. "Let's leave them to do their job."

Ann took my arm as we continued up the hill. "How are you doing?" She said.

I shot her a look of mock disgust. "I don't sing, I can't dunk a basketball, and I'm a lousy dancer. Do you call that fair?"

"Mitch Corsini, you're impossible." She slapped my arm. "When are you going to stop with all your disgusting stereotypes?"

"When they no longer get a rise from you?"

The playful bump of her hip knocked me off stride.

"I have a confession," I said, retrieving the wooden pendant from my pocket.

She drew away, as though afraid of what might come next.

"When those DNA paternity results proved I hadn't fathered that kid, I almost felt a twinge of remorse."

She feigned horror. "You wanted those child support payments?"

"No, I sure don't need more expenses . . . maybe it's because I screwed up with Erica, but I figured if I had another chance, I'd do better."

Ann shook her head. "Like Lorinda Jane said, first you'd best mend the fences you have. Even if that girl's all grown and ready to head out on her own, she still needs her daddy." She looked away. Her voice softened to a whisper. "A girl never outgrows that."

There was a void I could never fill for Ann, but maybe I still had time with Erica. "Do you think she'd like this?" I held up the pendant.

She seemed to force a smile. "Only if it meant something to her. First, give her back her daddy, then you can dazzle her with family heirlooms."

"Yeah, you're right," I said. "By the way, I talked to Peter. He's coming to Richmond for a weekend. We'll catch a ballgame, do some guy stuff. I think he can help me soften her up."

"Oh great," Ann replied. "Maybe I'd better call Erica and warn her!"

I laughed.

We walked on in silence for a few steps and then Ann said, "Let me guess, you began losing her when training bras took the place of catcher's mitts, right?"

"Yeah." I grinned. "Something like that. All that female stuff just sort of snuck up—and scared the hell out of me. What was I supposed to do?"

"I know what I would have wanted . . ." Ann leaned against my arm. "A daddy to tell me how pretty I looked, and who threatened to chase away the boys, a daddy who waited up if I was out too late, and who got mad if I didn't call." She smiled. "Moms can handle the training bras."

"And I suppose I could have too, if I'd thought about it. I guess I used that as an excuse. It was easier to blame her than to hold myself accountable."

"So, what if that paternity test had gone the other way?" she said. "What if that boy was yours?"

"It's not like I haven't given that a lot of thought. I'd be there this time. We'd toss the football, I'd teach him to throw a nasty split-fingered fastball, maybe we'd even do some camping—like Erica and I used to do."

"Before the training bras?"

"Exactly!" I laughed. "And who knows, maybe she

would have joined us. Grandpa missed those times with my dad, and Dad never had them with me. I blew my first chance with Erica. I'm not quitting on her this time." I studied the pendant and then slipped it around my neck. "This might sound crazy, but if that boy was mine, I'd also teach him about his family, his heritage. I'd want him and his sister to know who they were—to feel a part of something— like I never did."

"You're a part of something now."

"Yeah, and it feels pretty good," I said. "Kind of scary, though."

"Scary?"

"You know, fences to mend, new opportunities to stuff my foot in my mouth, learning how to dance."

Ann laughed. "We'll work on your foot stuffing, maybe your foot work too. Other than that, you're doing fine."

"Tell me," I said, "do you think she would have enjoyed having a little brother?"

"You mean Erica?" Ann seemed to hesitate, and then she turned, locking me in her gaze. Her lip quivered. "She still might."

I swallowed hard and took both her hands in mine. "Ann, you know there are no guarantees—we might start her off with a baby sister."

ABOUT THE AUTHOR

Jeff Andrews was born in Mt. Holly, New Jersey and grew up in neighboring Moorestown, New Jersey. He has an undergraduate degree in Business Administration from Baldwin-Wallace College and a Master of Science in Administration from George Washington University. Jeff served twenty years in the U.S. Marine Corps, including service in Vietnam and Beirut, Lebanon. After retiring from the military Jeff worked in financial services and taught college (part-time) before turning to writing. He now divides his time between writing, church, volunteer work, and family.

Jeff and his wife, Mary Lou, live in Virginia Beach, Virginia.

The Freedom Star
A novel by Jeff Andrews

This powerful saga immerses readers in the lives, dreams, and sufferings of two families, one slave and the other their masters, bound together by the tobacco fields of South Boston, Virginia at the beginning of the Civil War.

Isaac yearns for the freedom that Henry, his childhood friend and owner's son, takes for granted. After enduring false promises, failed escapes, imprisonment, and the threat of being sold, Isaac's only hope of fleeing slavery and beginning a new life with the woman he loves lies in accompanying Henry and the Confederates on their march north. When Henry is wounded and taken prisoner, Isaac finds himself behind Union lines and free, but with a choice: continue north toward his dream or return to slavery to save his friend.

The author's thoroughly researched portrayal of the Civil War era adds a rich backdrop to this poignant and suspenseful work of historical fiction. In *The Freedom Star*, the author presents vivid characters and compelling layers of story that will hold readers until the very last page.